DEEDS OF MERCY

BOOK THREE IN THE MARK TAYLOR SERIES

By

M.P. MCDONALD

This book is a work of fiction. People, places, events, and situations are the product of the author's imagination. Any resemblance to actual persons, living or dead, or historical events, is purely coincidental.

Edited by Felicia A. Sullivan

Cover Art: M.P. McDonald

THE MARK TAYLOR SERIES

MARK TAYLOR: GENESIS (PREQUEL)
NO GOOD DEED: BOOK ONE
MARCH INTO HELL: BOOK TWO
DEEDS OF MERCY: BOOK THREE
MARCH INTO MADNESS: BOOK FOUR

"Though justice be thy plea, consider this,
That, in the course of justice, none of us
Should see salvation: we do pray for mercy;
And that same prayer doth teach us all to render
The deeds of mercy."

~Portia, *The Merchant of Venice*

CHAPTER ONE

Mark Taylor swerved the van to the curb, threw it into park and bolted from the vehicle towards the bungalow on the quiet street. The house matched the one in his photo and as he raced across the postage stamp sized front lawn, he prayed he was in time.

The dream had shown a brief flash of a black wristwatch, the time 2:14 p.m., but his own watch was a few minutes past that. If only he'd left the studio sooner, but the model he'd booked for a print ad had been thirty minutes late, throwing the whole shoot off.

The intermittent pounding of a hammer broke the stillness of the street, and Mark breathed a sigh of relief. If the man was still fixing the gutter, then he wasn't too late. He followed the sound around the corner of the house and found a portly older gentleman perched on a ladder, hammer in hand. As Mark paused to size up the situation, the front leg of the ladder slipped off the narrow walkway and into the soft dirt of the flower bed.

Mark rushed forward, intending to hold the ladder, but the man's fall had progressed too far, and he toppled on top of Mark, sending them both to the ground in a heap. Grimacing, Mark clutched his elbow and glared at the paving brick jutting up at a decorative angle.

The other man groaned, and elbow forgotten, Mark scooted from beneath him, worried he might have been too late after all. Maybe he hadn't prevented the man from breaking his neck. "Sir? Are you okay?"

"Oh, hell. Yes, I'm fine, but look what I did to the eave." He pointed up and Mark followed the gesture to see the gutter hanging with the trim dangling.

Relieved the man was unhurt, Mark squatted back on his heels and shook his head. "Yeah, well, it could have been a lot worse. You could have broken your neck." He stood and held out a hand to the older man, pulling him to his feet. "You're sure you're okay?"

The man took his eyes off the damaged gutter and nodded. "I might be sore tomorrow, but I'm fine." He squinted and nodded at Mark. "What about you? Is that blood on your arm?"

Mark turned his arm to get a look at his elbow. "Just a little scrape."

* * *

Ten minutes later, Mark was back at his studio rummaging in his desk drawer for a pen to take down numbers from the messages on the studio's voicemail. His elbow throbbed and when he touched it, he found it still oozing blood. He thought about running upstairs and grabbing a Band-Aid from the medicine cabinet in his loft, but before he could, the bell above the front door jingled. He glanced up in irritation. It was after hours and he didn't have any late appointments scheduled. He knew he should have locked the door after entering. His stomach rumbled and his eyes burned with fatigue as he stood and rounded the corner from the office to the front of the studio.

"Sorry, we're clos--"

"Hello, Mark."

Hunger and exhaustion forgotten, Mark stared at the man facing him. His face was shadowed, the setting sun casting a perfect back light, but Mark didn't think he would ever forget that voice. The slight Middle Eastern accent gave it away.

"Mo?"

Mohommad looked different from the last time Mark had seen him. Of course, that had been at least four years ago. Now clean-shaven and sporting short hair that in days past would have been called a crew cut, Mo appeared nothing like the bearded guy with shoulder length hair that Mark remembered. Anger punched through Mark's initial shock. How many times had he wished for just such an opportunity? A chance to ask why?

Mo nodded. "Yes, it's me. How have you been?" He took a step closer and the overhead light caught the glint of wariness in Mo's eyes.

"*You sonofabitch*!" Mark clenched his fists and strode to within an arm's reach of the other man. "How have I *been*? After what you did to me, you have the guts to ask me how I've *been*?"

Mo's head dipped for a second as he acknowledged Mark's question. "I understand your anger, friend, but you must understand...I had no choice."

Mark quivered with rage, hanging on to control by the slimmest thread. This was the man who'd turned his life into a living hell. "I ought to rip your head off and shove it up your ass!"

Before Mark could follow through with the idea, the studio door opened a second time. The man who entered was close to Mark's height, but it was the flash of a gun tucked into the man's waistband that caught Mark's attention. He pointed towards the newcomer. "What's going on, and who the hell is this?"

Mo took a step closer to Mark. "It's a friend of mine."

"A *friend*? You don't even know the meaning of the word," Mark spat out. While looking at Mo, he gave a nod towards the friend. "Does he know your history with how you treat 'friends'?"

"I didn't come here to discuss friendships. I came to ask your help."

Mark lunged, and grabbed the front of Mo's shirt in his fist. Out of the corner of his eye, he caught a flash of movement, but his fist connected with Mo's cheekbone an instant before a burst of light and pain exploded in his own head.

CHAPTER TWO

Mark blinked his eyes, confused as to why he was lying on his stomach on the floor of the studio. Had he tripped and hit his head? The metallic taste of blood filled his mouth. He ran his tongue around the inside, finding a ragged place on his inner cheek. His right hand throbbed and it all flooded back to him.

Mohommad.

He tried to move his hands to shove up from the floor, but found his arms restrained behind his back somehow. *The goddamn bastards!*

"Mo! Untie my hands!" He rolled partially on his side, and with a push of his elbow against the floor along with a counter-push with his legs, he was able to gain a sitting position. His head spun and he had to close his eyes a moment. After the dizziness subsided, he looked around the room. No one was in the studio area, but the blinds had been closed and the door of the closet where the extra equipment was stored hung open, the door jamb broken. Quick footsteps sounded on the hardwood floor above him in his loft.

As quietly as he could, he lurched to his knees and then to his feet. He rushed to the front door, but when he caught the handle with the crook of his elbow to pull it open , it didn't budge. They'd locked it. Without the use of his hands, he couldn't turn the bolt. He leaned down and used his chin to push against it, but he just kept slipping off the rounded metal. He turned, trying to reach it with his hands, but it was just a little too high. *Shit!*

Thinking through the throbbing in his head, he remembered the footstool they used for group shots. It was kept in the closet. One look in the closet and he knew that option was out; the footstool was buried beneath piles of equipment.

Mark glanced up at a loud thump. He had to either escape or get help. He rushed to the office, but found both phone cords disconnected. There had to be something he could use to get help. The computer was in one piece, but he wouldn't be able to type anything, so even an email was out. Wait. His secure phone given to him by Jim had been in his jacket. His eyes shot to the coat tree. His jacket hung where he'd left it a few days ago.

He prayed the phone was still tucked inside the pocket. Gripping the leather jacket with his teeth, he lifted it off the hook, and let it fall onto the desktop, cringing when it hit with a thump. With a glance over his shoulder, he turned, felt for the pocket and found the slit. Desperately, he fished around inside for the phone. In his concentration, he forgot to listen for the sound of the men. His hand closed around the phone at the exact instant that footsteps sounded on the stairs. Frantic, Mark yanked the phone out and felt for the buttons.

Jim had programmed the number on speed dial. It was the only number on it, but it wasn't a direct connection. The call had to be relayed after Mark used the code word along with punching in a series of numbers. Only then would the call go through. He knew he found the speed dial button when he heard it ringing. Bending over the phone, Mark said the code word, and stretched to get a pencil out of the cup on his desk with his mouth, intending to use it to punch the numbers, but before he could make the attempt, he was shoved head first onto the desktop. Stars exploded behind his eyes and his knees buckled, but either

Mo or the other guy pressed him so hard against the desk that he didn't sag to the floor.

"What are you doing, Mark? Who did you call?" Mo grabbed the phone and leaned into Mark's field of vision, shaking it in his face.

The other guy must be the one applying the pressure.

Mark grunted, unable to get a deep enough breath to respond, but felt a small surge of satisfaction at the deep bruise on Mo's cheekbone. That explained the waves of pain in his right hand. At a gesture from Mo, the pressure on Mark's back eased. Mo repeated the question.

Glaring, Mark didn't answer, but sucked in a few deep breaths while he could. The other man grabbed Mark's left wrist and yanked it up towards the middle of Mark's back. His right arm dragged beneath it.

Mark couldn't suppress the first groan at the pain in his shoulders and elbows, and especially his right hand, but he bit his lip to keep the second groan from escaping. After a few seconds, he managed to grind out, "I was calling for a pizza."

Mo eyed him silently for a moment before laughing. "With sausage and mushrooms?"

The pressure on his arms lessened, Mo's apparent good humor at Mark's response eased the tension in the room. Memories of their past good times rushed into Mark's mind. "Yeah. And a veggie pizza for you and your buddy." He swallowed hard.

"Ah, you remembered. No pork for me." Mo shook his head and sighed, before holding up the phone. "This is encrypted. Where'd you get it? The FBI?"

Mark averted his face, unwilling to give anything away unintentionally, and winced at the renewed pressure on his arms.

"You know what, Mark? I really don't care. What I want to know is, where is it--where's the camera?"

Shock bolted through Mark. "Camera? You're doing all this for a goddamn camera? Well, look around, there must be at least a half-dozen in the studio. Take your pick. That Nikon over there on the tripod is one of my favorites."

Mo paced in front of the desk and didn't even glance at the one Mark indicated. "You know which one I want. Where's the *magic* camera? "

"Excuse me?" Mark tried to play it off as a joke. "Come on, Mo. Pick a camera and leave me alone. Hell, take them all if you want. Just tell me why you lied to the feds about me." His offer was rewarded with another tug on his arms. The left shoulder still caused him problems from his encounter with the cult three months ago, and he groaned as it grated in the socket.

"You mean the feds that you're now buddies with?" Mo held the phone up as evidence. "I did it for the same reason you told them about the camera--the one that sees the future. I wanted the agony to stop. Isn't that why *you* told them?"

A sense of betrayal ignited and smoldered in Mark. Had Jim or Bill been the ones to pass along the story to Mo? Or shared it with Mo's team of interrogators? Shame mingled with betrayal.

Mo seemed to read Mark's mind. "Oh yes. They told me all about your crazy story." He put a finger to his chin and tilted his head as though wracking his brain for the memory. "What was it they said about you? I believe they told me that you had more imagination than I did--just before they burst out laughing."

Mark struggled against his bonds as sweat popped out on his forehead. What he'd give to knock the smirk from Mo's face. "It was all a lie. I had nothing else to give them, and you knew that."

Mo made a motion to his friend and the pressure let up again. "You know, Mark, that's what I thought for a long time. Then, all this business came up in the news about you. All those things you did as though you had advance knowledge."

Dread froze Mark. No way. Mo wouldn't believe in magical cameras.

Mo shook his head. "You know I'm not a stupid man. I put the two stories together." He paused, leveling a look at Mark. "I think it's true about the camera."

Should he deny it? Or remain silent like it was too absurd to even discuss? Mark decided on the latter. He glared at Mo and glanced over his shoulder to include Mo's friend in the hostile look.

Mo shrugged. "So, here's what I want. You give me the camera, and then Hazim and I will be on our way."

"You always were gullible, Mo. How could you believe anything those bastards told you, let alone something as ridiculous as a magical camera?" Mark forced a snort of laughter. "I *wish* I had one."

Eyes narrowed, Mo reached across the desk and grabbed Mark by the collar, yanking him to within an inch of his own face. "I didn't come here to argue the existence of this camera. I *know* it exists." He tossed the encrypted phone on the desk. "That phone alone is evidence that someone in the government has recruited you, and I can't think of any other reason they'd want *you*."

Mark fought to keep from falling onto the desk, and then almost toppled backward when Mo suddenly released him. Before he could respond, Mo swept everything off the desk. Mark's jacket fell in a heap against the opposite wall.

"Hazim, secure him to the desk. I would like to practice all the ways I've learned to make men talk."

Twisting, Mark evaded Hazim's grip and lowered his shoulder, ramming it into the man's chest.

Mark scrambled away, intending to dive through the front window if he had to. At least he'd have a chance of survival. Before he could reach the window, Mo grabbed him by the back of his shirt collar. Mark gagged as his shirt threatened to strangle him and he fell backwards, his fall broken by Mo's grip on the collar. Hazim caught Mark's legs, wrapping his arms around them despite Mark's frantic kicking.

Mo held onto the shirt and Mark's left arm and the two men wrestled with him, half-carrying, half-dragging him to the desk where they tossed Mark like he was a sack of potatoes.

Mo pinned him down while Hazim found a roll of duct tape in the studio and returned to secure Mark's feet to the desk. They wound the tape around his legs and beneath the desk, doubling the tape. Mo joked about how it was a good thing the roll was so big--there was no danger of running out.

"Get off, you bastard!" Mark twisted and fought, but only succeeded in wearing himself out. His chest heaved as he struggled to no avail against the tape.

The two debated whether to release Mark's arms to stretch them over his head, but decided it was too risky to let him go, so instead, they left him with his arms trapped beneath his back, still bound at the wrist. Mo grinned when he came up with the idea to tape Mark's head to the desk.

Mark jerked his head forward, trying to head butt first Mo and then Hazim, but they stayed out of his reach. The tape caught in his hair and pulled the skin of his forehead. "Mo, why are you doing this? I never did anything to you," he panted.

"You might not have before, but with a magic camera, you might in the future. I *need* that camera, Mark. I can't have you telling your friends about something my group is planning before it happens." Mo swiped his forearm across his brow, apparently as out of breath as Mark was from the fight. "I have to prove myself, you understand. We lucked out on 9/11 when nobody believed you, but I doubt we will be so lucky in the future."

Mark tried a different tactic. "Listen, you're right. There *is* a magic camera, but I don't have it anymore. The FBI has it."

Mo looked thoughtful for a moment as though considering the possibility. "I don't think I believe you. Not about the FBI taking it." He shook his head. "I think it's hidden away somewhere. Perhaps a safe deposit box? A safe? The recent events with that cult and the newspaper article makes me sure you haven't given it over to anyone. I don't think you'd let it be far from wherever you are, otherwise, how would you be able to use it?"

Mark glared at Mo. He knew he should be pleading for Mo to believe him, but he just couldn't do it. Lying had never been his forte.

Mo met his glare, and after a long look, he sighed. "Mark, we had some great times in the past. I really wish I didn't have to do this, but it isn't just about me, you understand?" He spread a hand over his chest. "I must return with the camera."

True regret shone in Mo's eyes and a shiver of fear shook Mark. Breaking eye contact, Mo glanced into the trash can beside Lily's desk and reached into it. "This should be perfect." He held up an empty Big Gulp cup. "Hazim, fill this with water from the cooler over there."

Mark tried to raise his head to watch, but he couldn't lift it high enough to see. He discovered he didn't need to see what was going on. Hazim took the cup from Mo. The trickle of water gurgled into it. It was the only sound in the room and it went on for what seemed like a lifetime, but was probably only thirty seconds.

His mouth went dry, and he wished he could laugh at the irony. "Don't do this, Mo." The trace of pleading in his tone embarrassed him, but he couldn't help it.

Mo ignored him and rifled through the desk drawers, pulling out a soft silk cloth that Mark used to clean lenses. "I knew there would be one of these handy." He draped it over

Mark's nose and mouth. "I'm sure you remember the rules. You tell us what we want to know, and we'll stop."

Hazim poured the water over Mark's face, but he must not have water-boarded anyone before because the cup was empty after only a few seconds. Mo laughed, and Mark felt a surge of relief. They were just trying to scare him. As Mark coughed and sputtered, it crossed his mind that he needed new friends since at least two of them were familiar with the finer points of waterboarding. He tried to be thankful that he hadn't felt the familiar terror of drowning. Instead, he was just cold and wet.

Then he heard the gurgle.

"Let me show you how it's done." Mo pulled the cloth a little higher on Mark's face. He tilted the cup, allowing just a thin stream to pour out. At first, Mark was able to hold his breath, but Mo kept just enough water dripping that the cup was still half full when Mark had to breathe. He tried to turn his head, moving it a fraction, but Hazim clamped a restraining hand on his forehead.

Gasping, Mark fought, bucking so hard the desk jerked forward. Water flooded his nose and his sinuses, burning and triggering the irresistible impulse to take a deep breath and snort the water out. The breath sucked liquid down into his lungs, and he coughed, unable to stop. Each cough tore through him and pulled more water into his lungs. Mo asked him where the camera was, but Mark heard him only dimly through the roar that filled his ears. His coughs weakened. The room whirled in his vision and everything went black.

It didn't feel like he'd been out long when Mark blinked his eyes open. His head ached and his throat felt raw, his chest tight. After a fit of explosive coughing, wet at first, then finally subsiding to dry hacks, he lay limply, panting.

Mo hovered over him, Big Gulp cup tilted menacingly. "Tell us where you hid it."

A drop of water splashed on Mark's cheek and he flinched, his heart racing. "I told you before--the Feds took it."

"Liar."

Already out of breath, it didn't take long for the darkness to claim him this time.

Mark awoke to a stinging slap against his cheek. Disoriented, he stared at Mo, wondering where he'd come from. "Hey. What's going...?" The feel of wet cloth against his lips as he spoke triggered his awareness. At the sight of the cup in Mo's hand, pure panic set in. Mark twisted, turning his face away, ignoring the pain of the tape ripping at his skin and hair. Jack-knifing his legs, he almost escaped from the tape.

With Mo and his buddy right there, getting free was impossible. Mo simply put his hand on Mark's brow, forcing his head back down, and Hazim re-taped it, followed by another loud rip as Hazim tore off another long strip to re-fasten Mark's legs to the desk.

The water cooler bubbled and made a loud noise, as if belching. Mark couldn't control the trembling of his body and his heart galloped at a flat out sprint inside his chest. In prison, the sessions would always stop if he passed out. He'd never lost consciousness twice in one session. Even then, the knowledge that a physician had been present had added a small measure of security in Mark's mind. The officials wouldn't let him die if they could help it. Mo and Hazim had no such reluctance, and there was no doctor standing by.

Mo handed the cup to Hazim this time, as though bestowing a great honor upon him. "You watched, now show me how it's done. Unless..." Mo made a stop gesture with his hand, "unless Mark has decided to tell us where the camera is hidden."

His mouth dry despite the recent dousing, Mark licked his lips. He had no doubt that they'd kill him if he told, but he wasn't sure that they wouldn't kill him anyway. "Release me, and I'll get it for you."

"Ah, so now you can get it? I thought the feds had it?" Mo crossed his arms, resting one elbow in the palm of the opposite hand, and scratched his chin. "What should I believe? Just a few minutes ago, you swore the camera was no longer in your possession."

"I know, but I'm telling you the truth. Let me go, and I'll get it for you. I don't even know why I was resisting, the thing has been nothing but a curse since I bought it. You're welcome to take it off my hands."

The camera had made Mark's life hell, and the truth of that must have shown on his face because Mo nodded, waved his hand over Mark, and said to Hazim, "Get him off there, but leave his arms taped."

Mark grimaced as Hazim ripped the tape off his head none too gently, taking some of Mark's hair, and possibly some of his skin, along with it. He tried to sit up, but felt like a turtle stranded on its back until Hazim gripped his elbow and yanked him upright.

A new fit of coughing overtook him as water that had filled his sinuses drained down his throat in an overwhelming rush. His stomach convulsed and he leaned over to vomit into the wastebasket.

Shaky and drained, it was all he could do to stand. "I need my keys. They're in my pocket." He pointed his chin at his right front pocket.

Mo's eyes narrowed and he indicated for Hazim to reach in and pull out the key ring.

Mark tried to take a deep breath, but the effort only set off another coughing jag. *Damn it hurt.*

"I was out using the camera earlier and it's in my van. Look under the tarp in the back. I think that's where I put it."

Hazim started to go towards the front of the studio, but Mark shook his head and said, "It's in the alley out back."

Once Hazim was out of ear shot, Mark turned to Mo, finding the other man watching him.

"It was not my intention to drag you into any of this, Mark."

"So why did you? Why lie and get me to go to Afghanistan?" Mark shook his head and gave a snort of bitter laughter. "I was so damn proud to go help you on that book. I felt like I had a chance to make a difference to those poor women, but instead it was all just some sick, twisted ruse."

He stepped closer to Mo, straining against his bonds. If only he could wrap his fingers around the other man and choke the truth out of him. He had to settle for crowding him and getting in his face. "Can I ask why me? You had lots of friends who were photographers. Why did you choose to ruin *my* life?"

Mo retreated a step. "That book wasn't a ruse. I wrote it and even sent it out to a few publishers, but while we were in Afghanistan, my uncles and cousins welcomed me. For the first time, I was amongst people like me. Or like I should have been. I'd strayed and lost my way. I became American." He spat the last word like it was a vulgarity.

Mark felt a cough building, but suppressed it, unwilling to interrupt Mo's explanation. He heard the door to the van slam, and knew it would only be a matter of seconds before his own fate was decided.

Mo glanced towards the back door, but resumed speaking. "I dated American women, I watched American television, and I..." He paused, his face flushing as he glanced away. "I even took photos of nude women." The red flush turned deeper as anger replaced the embarrassment on Mo's face. "I broke the laws of Islam."

"What does that have to do with what you did to me? Or more importantly, what you wanted to do to innocent men, women and children? How could killing them atone for *your* sins?"

His face now ruddy with anger, Mohommad closed the distance between them. Mark fought the urge to flinch when the other man lifted his hand, but Mo only prodded him in the chest with his finger as he said, "You wouldn't understand. None of you Americans understand."

Mark and Mo glared at each other. Every muscle in Mark's body quivered in rage. How could he have ever been friends with this man?

The sound of footsteps broke the tension as Hazim returned, holding the camera aloft in triumph.

Mo gave Mark one more hard look before crossing to Hazim and grabbing the camera from the other man's hands "Ah, this must be it. It's the one you bought in my country." He glanced at Mark as he turned the camera over in his hands, examining it. "I remember you showed it to me. It is only right that I should return it to Afghanistan."

Hazim nodded and said something to Mo that Mark couldn't understand. Mo shrugged, still focused on the camera. Hazim pulled the gun from his waistband and crossed to Mark, putting the gun to Mark's head.

"Mo...don't do this." The cold barrel pressed hard against his temple.

With a sigh, Mo said something to Hazim, who grunted and glared at Mark as he lowered the gun.

Mohommad stepped close to Mark. "Do not try to get this back. I've been keeping track of you. Of course, that wasn't difficult. All I had to do was turn on the news." He smiled, the humor not reaching his eyes. "I also heard that you had something going with that pretty detective. Too bad that ended. However, your business partner is very easy on the eyes, and I would hate for anything to happen to her."

Seething, Mark dipped his shoulder and rammed it into Mo's chest. "Don't you dare touch her, you mother--" Before he could finish, he saw a blur of movement and an instant later, nothing.

CHAPTER THREE

Jim Sheridan saved the file he'd been working on and clicked the off button. Another week over. He stretched while the computer whirred as it closed programs and shut down. The weekend loomed before him with nothing on his agenda. He chuckled at the thought of how just a few months ago, that was the norm, but lately the weekends had been crammed with activities.

Lily was a whirlwind, with lots of friends, and most accepted Jim, despite some initial awkwardness. As a CIA officer who headed the Chicago FBI field office, he didn't quite fit in with her free-spirited crowd, but she didn't seem to mind. She never forced him to be one of the gang, but made sure to include him in conversations.

Since they'd started dating, he had met dozens of new people. A chuckle rumbled out of his chest. He felt like an old dog trying to learn new tricks, but he was loving every minute of it. It surprised him how much he enjoyed the shows and concerts she invited him to. They had gone to see some of the improv. He couldn't remember the last time he'd laughed so hard tears had come to his eyes.

He sighed and rolled his sleeves down, buttoning the cuffs. Lily had been gone only a few days on the trip she'd planned with a friend months ago, but he missed her already and wasn't quite sure what to do with his time for the two weeks.

The computer screen darkened, and he stood, grabbing his suit jacket off the back of his chair. As he shrugged into it, his desk phone rang. For a half-second, he thought about ignoring it. It was Friday, and he'd put in twelve hours today. Duty won out, and on the fourth ring, he answered.

"Officer Sheridan." He tucked the phone against his shoulder and ear as he buttoned the jacket.

"Sir, I'm sorry to bother you, and I'm not sure if this is important or not, but Washington called, relaying a message that there was attempted activity on your phone."

Jim stilled. He only had one encrypted phone registered to him and Mark normally just called him via his cellphone. "What time?"

"About an hour ago."

"An hour ago? And I'm only just now hearing about it?"

"I'm sorry, sir. The main offices there have closed for the weekend, and the switchboard only just now called about it."

"Never mind. Just give me the message."

"That's the thing. The call never went all the way through. I wasn't even sure if I should bother you with this."

Jim took a deep breath and let it out slowly. "It's probably nothing, but I'll call the phone back and see what's up. Thank you for telling me."

After hanging up, he pulled his phone out of his pocket and dialed Mark. After several clicks, it disconnected. It could be broken, so Jim set the phone on his desk and used the land-line to call Mark's regular cell. It rang four times before going to voicemail. Jim left a short message for Mark to return the call. Then he called the studio and got a busy signal. That was strange. Between the cellphones, voicemail and call-waiting, he couldn't remember the last time he'd gotten a busy signal on a phone.

Twenty minutes later, he pulled up in front of the studio. It was probably overkill, but he grabbed his weapon from his glove box and put it in his suit coat pocket. He tried the front door, but it was locked. He rounded the building to the back alley. Dusk put the alley in shadows, but he sighed in relief when he saw Mark's van parked by the back door. He knocked on the door and waited.

After a second knock, he tried the doorknob, surprised when it turned in his hand, but rationalized that Mark was probably in his darkroom and unable to come to the door. He stuck his head in. "Hello? Mark?"

The light above the darkroom wasn't lit, so that was ruled out.

He blinked, his eyes taking a moment to adjust to the dim interior. Mark's desk was completely clear. He smiled. It was about time the guy cleaned it up. Jim turned to go up the steps to the loft when he heard a groan.

Reaching into his jacket pocket with one hand, he bent into a defensive crouch and took a closer look at the office. He noted a mug on the floor against the back wall, a handful of pens, pencils and paper clips scattered around it. It looked like the desk hadn't been tidied up so much as swept clean--except for a puddle of water at one end. A strip of duct tape dangled raggedly from the back of the desk. He wasn't sure what to make of that. Half beneath the desk, he spotted the phone he'd given Mark. Not a good sign.

Another groan, louder this time, came from behind Lily's desk. His heart skipped a beat, but he reminded himself that she was lounging on the deck of a cruise ship about now.

Glancing over his shoulder to make sure nobody was coming down the steps, he hurried to the desk.

Mark lay on his side, his arms bound behind his back with duct tape. Blood trickled from a swollen cut just above his temple. Jim's stomach churned. Now what had Taylor gotten mixed up in? He bent and gave Mark's shoulder a gentle shake. "Mark?"

Mark blinked, his eyes unfocused. As Jim reached out to shake him again, Mark flinched away and mumbled, "No."

"Hey, whoa. Take it easy." At least Mark was somewhat awake. "I'll be right back. Just sit tight." Jim wanted to make sure the site was secure before he let down his guard. A quick check of the studio and closets revealed nobody, and as much as Jim hated to leave Mark, he had to check the loft too. As he passed the back door, he shut and locked it.

Jim crept up the stairs, noting the wide open door. Gun ready, he slipped inside. A survey of the room revealed closets with contents tossed about, dresser drawers open with clothing draped over the edges. Whoever was responsible for the disarray was gone. It was possible Mark had interrupted a burglary in progress, but he recalled the expensive camera equipment still in the studio. It didn't make sense that they'd left it all, especially since Mark had been bound and beaten unconscious.

No longer worried about making noise, Jim hurried down the steps and found Mark trying to sit up but failing miserably without the use of his hands.

Jim wasn't sure Mark should be sitting, but assisted him with a steady pull on his elbow. The collar of Mark's shirt and the whole back was soaked. He glanced at the puddle on Mark's desk and a large plastic cup that lay on its side beneath it. In the scuffle, the drink must have spilled.

Mark swayed and Jim steadied him before moving behind him to tear at the binding. The tape was triple wrapped, and he couldn't rip it. Mark's hands felt cold and lack of circulation caused them to turn a dark red. The tape had been on awhile. He reached over Mark's shoulder and opened Lily's center desk drawer. Rising up on one knee, he spotted the scissors and cut through the tape.

"There you go." Jim tossed the scissors back in the drawer as he moved around in front of Mark.

Mark closed his eyes and grunted as he eased his arms in front of him. He rubbed his wrists while gingerly rotating his shoulders. "*Shit!* My shoulders hurt like a sonofabitch."

Jim sat back on one heel and gave a relieved chuckle. At least Mark sounded okay. He pulled out his cellphone.

Mark opened his eyes at the sound of the buttons. "What are you doing?"

Jim paused before hitting the second '1'. "Calling the police and the rescue squad."

With a grimace, Mark shook his head, wincing at the motion. He put a hand to the goose egg topped by the cut. "No. *Don't*."

"Why the hell not?"

Mark stood, leaning on the edge of the desk for support, his knuckles white. "Because I know who did it." He straightened and took a deep breath. "And he stole the camera."

Jim spotted Lily's desk chair lying on its side in the corner. He grabbed it, rolling it behind Mark. "Sit down and tell me what happened."

Blood still trickled down the side of Mark's face and Jim found a roll of paper towels, folded several into a pad, and wet them with water from the cooler. He handed it to Mark, who pressed it to his head. "Thanks."

Mark's desk chair was shoved into the far corner, and Jim pulled it to the other side of Lily's desk and sat waiting until Mark had mopped up the cut and was ready to talk.

The desk started rattling, and at first the sound puzzled Jim until he realized it was Mark's leg bouncing. He'd forgotten that nervous habit.

"Mo did it."

"Mo?" Jim tried to remember why he knew that name.

"Mohommad Aziz."

Of course. "How did he get in?"

"I hadn't locked the front door yet." Mark folded the pad and winced as he pressed it back to the injury.

Jim shook his head. "Not a good move, but I meant how did he get in the country? He shouldn't have been allowed back. I'm sure that was a stipulation of his release. Did he say anything about it?"

Mark shrugged, his eyes downcast, but his voice dripped with sarcasm as he said, "He didn't tell me, and I didn't have a chance to ask him. Maybe next time he beats the hell out of me, I'll try to remember to ask the pertinent details before he gets to the waterboarding part."

Surprised at Mark's tone, Jim glanced over to the puddle on Mark's desk, not wanting to believe it could be evidence of what Mark was telling him. "Waterboarding? What do you mean?"

"I could refresh your memory on that interrogation tactic, because it's fresh in my mind." Mark lifted his gaze, his face a mask of anger and pain. "But I'd rather not."

Confused, Jim asked, "Why would he do something like that to you?"

His voice had a hard edge when he answered, "Because you guys told him about my dreams and the camera."

Heat climbed Jim's face, but he pushed down the guilt. "Yes, we told him, but only to try and get him to confess to making up the story about you."

Mark stared at him for a moment, his eyes searching, finally he looked away with a slight nod. "Well, whatever. Bottom line, he knew, and he didn't believe any of it until the shit hit the fan with the cult and all that hero crap, so I guess it's just my luck staying par for the course."

"So, now we have an extremist in possession of the camera. All the more reason to call the police and get the ball rolling on this." He reached into his pocket for his phone again.

"You don't understand. They know all about me. About my life. About my *friends*."

Jim's hand tightened on the phone. "Did he make threats?"

Mark swallowed and nodded. "Against Lily. And no doubt they won't be too happy with me either."

Blind rage shot through Jim. "That *bastard!"* He exhaled slowly, checking his anger. Now wasn't the time to let emotions rule his thinking. "Don't worry. We'll find him."

"I'm so sorry. I should have held out. Now I've put Lily at risk."

"He beat it out of you. It's not like you volunteered the information."

"The other guy was the muscle. Mo just gave the orders."

"Other guy?"

"Yeah. Mo called him Hazim. He's the one who had a gun. I think that's what he hit me with." Mark tossed the bloody pad onto the desk and scrubbed his hands through his hair, leaving pieces sticking up.

"Well, that's even more understandable. Two against one, a gun, and they were using you for a punching bag."

"They didn't hit me until after I told them. Well, except when they first came in. The other guy hit me, I think. I never saw it coming. When I woke up, my hands were behind my back and I could hear them upstairs. I tried to get out, but I couldn't open any doors, and the phones were broken. I tried to call you, but I couldn't get past that code with my damn hands behind my back." Mark glared at Jim as though he'd programmed the phone himself.

"Hey, that's the tech guys who do that, but at least you got partially through. That's why I'm here. I got a call that someone tried to access the phone."

"Yeah, well better late than never, I guess." Mark sighed and closed his eyes, his head cradled in his hands. He remained that way, his voice slurring as he said, "You could take lessons from him on waterboarding. He put your guys to shame."

"Yes, well, I'll be sure to ask him for lessons when we find the bastard," Jim replied as he studied Mark, not liking what he saw. The guy looked like hell, and when several minutes passed without a return comment from him, Jim started to wonder if Mark had fallen asleep. A streak of red marred his forehead, and suddenly the dangling tape made sense.

With a groan, Mark folded his arms and put his head down. "I've got a killer headache."

"Another reason to call the paramedics, but whether they come here or I have to drag you to the ER, you will get checked out."

Mark mumbled something that sounded like a profanity, but Jim wasn't positive.

While Mark rested, Jim examined the office, finding clues to what had happened. Clues he'd overlooked before, but now fit into the framework that Mark had constructed. As he rounded Mark's desk, he spotted a large plastic cup beneath the desk and he bent to retrieve it, finding a wad of duct tape beside it. Suddenly, he stopped. What the hell was he thinking? This was evidence and before he ruined it, he had to get some technicians over here. It was a risk they had to take. They needed every scrap they could get to find out where the men had gone. It was a matter of national security now.

He pulled out his cell for the third time. "I'm sorry, Mark, but I have to make this call."

Mark lifted his head, his eyes dull with pain and fatigue, but still narrowed in anger as he said, "You're as big a bastard as Mo is, do you know that?"

Jim clamped his mouth shut. He was inclined to agree with Mark, but despite the risk, he had to make the call.

CHAPTER FOUR

Mohommad chose a seat in the far corner of the train car and set the book bag containing the precious camera on the seat beside him. The camera could be the key to the success of the plan, and so he was diligent in keeping the straps of the bag looped over his arm. He hadn't yet told anyone besides Hazim about the power he suspected lay within the device, and he hoped that he could impress his uncles with his coup.

His face still burned with shame every time he remembered their disappointment at his capture, and while they had welcomed him back, Mohommad felt the cloud of suspicion that hung over his head. His uncles suspected he had been brainwashed into being a spy for the CIA. No matter how many times he'd professed his loyalty to them and the cause, doubt lingered in their eyes. The warm feeling of belonging he'd felt when he'd first gone to Afghanistan had turned to a cool indifference.

He unzipped the bag and peered inside. Soon they would once again sing his praises. This mission would stamp him as a hero. Even if he didn't make it back alive, his uncles and cousins would keep his memory burning. If becoming a martyr was the price he would have to pay, then so be it.

The train lurched into motion, and he sighed with relief as he relaxed against the seatback. No one had chased him after leaving Mark's studio, but he was still on guard. Mark had certainly been in no shape to give pursuit, but to be on the safe side, Mohommad and Hazim had gone separate ways--Hazim via a train to Naperville where he had family and would be able to blend in without attracting undue attention, and Mohommad on a different train to the northern suburbs. Mohommad wished he had a welcoming family in the US, but he hadn't spoken to those relatives in years.

The train conductor entered the car, punching tickets at each seat. Mohommad fished in his pocket for his ticket and slipped it into the clip on top of the seat in front of him. He'd been watching passengers as they boarded, checking for threats. Nobody paid any attention to him. It helped that he now had short hair and was clean-shaven. He rubbed his chin, unused to the smooth feel. His idea to shave had been a good one even if Hazim had fought him on it. Mohommad grimaced as he recalled their heated discussion. Hazim felt it disrespectful of Mohommad to go beardless, but Mohommad had finally convinced him that the mission's success depended upon him being able to move freely around Chicago. Hazim already enjoyed that freedom because as a sleeper cell, he'd never been called upon until now. He'd been just living the American dream, working and raising a family. Mohommad envied him. Not for his lifestyle, but because the other man didn't have to watch over his shoulder every moment, wondering if the FBI was spying on him and ready to whisk him away to prison.

At least Mohommad had a few things going for him; his coloring, features, and his fluent Spanish allowed him to be mistaken for Hispanic, which had come in handy on his journey from Mexico north to Chicago.

Downtown Chicago passed in a blur, giving way to brick two-flats with tiny backyards. Some passengers exited while new ones boarded. Mohommad gave each new occupant a cursory glance to be on the safe side, but he wasn't expecting any problems.

His thoughts returned to his family. It wasn't like he could have stayed with them anyway. Not now. They had made it known via a few letters he'd received while being held as an enemy combatant that he was no longer welcome in their homes. Not that he cared. He didn't belong here anymore, and he had his father's family in Afghanistan. They never spoke of the shame of the family still in the States, and his uncle had even gone so far as to forbid mention of Mohommad's mother. It had been difficult to set aside his feelings, but it was for the best and while in Afghanistan, it had been easier for him to forget about the cousins, and even his two nieces. However, his mother's face still haunted his dreams. The last time she'd spoken to him, she'd begged him to come back and be the son she'd raised. It saddened him that she couldn't embrace his new beliefs.

Mohommad leaned an elbow on the window ledge, and propped his head on his palm. If he had taken a westbound train, like Hazim had, he could have dropped by his sister's house. But if the children were home, he knew he would never be allowed to see them. It had been so long now, he doubted they would even remember him. Aisha had been about seven the last time he'd seen her, so he supposed there was a chance she would know him, but the other one, Cala, had been only three when he'd left. It would be a miracle if she remembered her 'Unca Mo'. A brief smile creased his face as he recalled the last time he'd held her. Her little arms had squeezed him so tightly he'd thought he'd never get away. If only he could have convinced them all to move back to Afghanistan with him.

They had refused, citing the opportunities they had in the U.S. and how their children would grow up with freedom, especially their daughters. Mohommad conceded that the girls would have fewer restrictions in the U.S., but was that really a good thing? He sighed and eyed a young man who boarded the car. Heavy gold chains and baggy pants that hung off lean hips marked him as gangbanger or at least someone who admired the look. Mohommad wanted to hold the young man's challenging stare, but instead, he backed off, lowering his eyes and turning towards the window. It wouldn't do to draw attention to himself--it could ruin everything.

Two teenage girls took the seats in front of him, and just reaffirmed his thoughts. Did they have no shame? Their tight clothes and bold looks at a couple of young men across the aisle would never have been tolerated in Afghanistan. The girls should have been home, or at the very least, should have had a brother escorting them to keep them safe. But here in America, they were allowed to roam about freely and be targets for the lustful thoughts of men.

He just hoped his sister took care to protect his nieces' reputations. Mohommad scowled. There was nothing he could do about it. Not immediately, anyway, but soon. Very soon. Things would be different if their plan worked.

Mohommad conceded it was likely that the plan wouldn't bring the U.S. to its knees, but it would deal a crippling blow. Not all of the aftermath of September 11th had been foreseen. The staggering blow to the U.S. economy had only been suspected. It was like finding huge hidden weak spots in Goliath. They just needed to keep hacking away at that spot until the giant staggered to his knees.

The train took him through swanky towns: Kenilworth, Highland Park, Lake Forest. The people exiting the train in those places wore suits and carried briefcases. They were the ones who would be hurt most when Mo carried out his instructions. Some of the riders remaining on the train were Navy recruits whose excited chatter told Mohommad that they were returning to base from their first leave after basic training. He hoped they realized how fortunate they had it now. When he was through, he was sure any leave would be canceled for a long time.

The sailors left the train and after that it was just Mohommad, the young man, and a Hispanic family in the car. The family chattered and he listened, fighting back a smile when the mother scolded her little boy for bossing his sister around.

His stop approached and he made his way to the stairs, holding onto a rail to keep his balance as the train swayed. He swung the bag's strap over his shoulder, his excitement about acquiring the camera muted slightly by the methods he'd been forced to undertake to achieve his goal. At least it hadn't been necessary to kill Mark. He would have truly regretted that outcome. Not only would it have pained him personally, after all, he and Mark had once been very good friends, but if he couldn't get the camera to work properly, he might need Mark's assistance.

Mohommad couldn't suppress a chuckle. How would Mark react if he called him and asked for some pointers in using it? He rubbed his jaw, working it back and forth. It was going to be sore tomorrow, that was for sure, and Hazim hadn't escaped without a few bruises either. He couldn't help a little rush of pride that his former friend had fought so hard. Hazim had scoffed when Mohommad had suggested that obtaining the camera wouldn't be an easy task. The other man was sure all it would take was for them to show up and brandish the gun, so Mark's resistance would have made Mohommad smile in triumph at winning that argument if Mark hadn't hit him so hard.

The doors opened and Mohommad stepped onto the platform and headed for the cabs idling in the parking lot south of the train station. He'd committed the address to memory, and rattled it off for the cabbie.

CHAPTER FIVE

Mark sat on the gurney and held a cold pack to his head while the ER doctor jotted some notes.

"And you said this happened over three hours ago? Why did you wait so long to come to the emergency room?"

"I climbed back on the pier and I was freezing, so I drove home and changed out of my wet clothes. It wasn't until I looked in the mirror that I saw the cut, but I thought it would stop bleeding on its own."

He and Jim had concocted a story about falling off a pier and bumping his head. It explained both the cut and the difficulty breathing.

The doctor shrugged. "You should have come in right away, but we'll get some x-rays of your head and chest. I'll also order a breathing treatment. After that, I'll stitch up the cut."

As soon as the physician left, Mark tossed the ice pack on the tiny metal side table. He drew the blanket tighter across his shoulders. Jim had returned to his office to dig up any recent intelligence he could find on Mohommad.

While in prison, he had alternated between hating Mo, and wondering if he had only been coerced into implicating Mark because he had nothing else to give and he wanted the questioning to stop. On more than one occasion, Mark had wished he had something to give the interrogators, and if he'd have had a scrap of information, he'd have gladly given it.

A cough rattled up, bending Mark in half with its intensity. In his charitable moments in his cell, he'd try to come up with excuses for Mo, forgetting that no matter what, he wouldn't have sent anyone to face what he was facing just so he could get out of it.

Had their friendship meant nothing? It had gone beyond their shared interest in photography. They had both liked biking and often rode together on the paths in the various lakefront parks. Never had the man ever hinted at extremist views. The Mo he'd known was as American as Mark was. They watched baseball, talked about women, and even went to bars on occasion. There had been the one time Mo's girlfriend had broken it off and he'd come to Mark's studio looking like a beaten hound dog. That night, Mark had paid for the drinks and Mo's cab fare home.

As Mark pulled the blanket tighter, he wondered where that guy had gone? The man who had shown up tonight bore only a passing resemblance. His thoughts were interrupted by the arrival of the X-ray tech, followed shortly by the breathing treatment.

The treatment helped a little, and he took a deep breath, grateful for the ability to do so. At least every breath wasn't a stark reminder of what had happened to him tonight. The mental image of the cup tipping its contents on his face jumped to the front of his mind. The heart monitor sped up, sounding an alarm. Mark cast a baleful eye at it and closed his eyes, willing his fear to subside. It was over, he was fine and there was no need to think of it again. It wasn't like he hadn't ever been through this before.

The nurse returned and checked the leads on his chest, wondering aloud if the treatment had caused his increase in heart rate. Mark didn't try to dissuade her from that conclusion.

In an attempt to get his mind on other things, he thought of the activity in the studio after Jim had called the attack into his office. Mark was grateful that Jim had called only a few of his FBI team and hadn't involved the Chicago PD. Only agents had gone through the studio, no police. They had arrived in plain cars without lights and were quiet and efficient.

Of course, it wasn't like the CPD would make a big deal about the theft of a fifty-year old camera. They would have made a report about the assault, but it would have been one of many and probably just end up in a dusty file somewhere. Mark's biggest fear was that Lily or his parents would be at risk. Mo knew where they lived.

He could only hope that Mo was long gone and hadn't stuck around long enough to see any of the action, because even as low key as the investigation was, it would be easy to spot if someone was paying attention.

Jim had tried to send him to the ER immediately, but Mark insisted on waiting until everyone left the studio, then he locked the door and allowed Jim to take him. His head throbbed with every beat of his heart, and he was finding it harder to suppress the coughing as his chest tightened.

An hour later, the doctor reluctantly released him. He'd suggested an overnight stay for some I.V. antibiotics and observation, but Mark was adamant about leaving. In the end, Mark agreed to a couple of shots of antibiotics.

Mark was signing the discharge papers just as Jim returned.

"What's the verdict?"

"I'll live."

"Well, I deduced that already, but are they sending you home?"

"Yep."

Jim glanced at his watch. "It's almost ten p.m. Did they feed you? Because I'm starving. What do you say we pick up a pizza and you can sleep in my spare room tonight?"

Mark thanked the nurse, then exited the cubicle, Jim only a step behind. "I'd planned on going back home."

Jim shook his head. "Not tonight. I don't have the manpower to watch you and do the investigation."

"Watch me? What for? Mo got what he wanted. I doubt he'll be back." Mark shivered as the cool nighttime breeze hit him.

"You're probably right, but I can't take a chance just yet. Plus, I have more questions for you."

Mark sighed as he eased into the passenger seat of Jim's car. His head throbbed. The painkiller he'd been given was wearing off and every muscle ached. His bed called to him, but he was too tired to argue and a pizza sounded good. "Fine."

An hour later, they polished off the last slice. Mark washed his down with some orange juice, wishing he could have a beer, but they'd stopped by a pharmacy while waiting for the pizza to be ready and picked up Mark's prescription pain meds and he knew he shouldn't drink. He pulled the bottle out of the bag, ready to take one and head to bed, but Jim held up a hand.

"Hold it. I have a few more questions before you get all fuzzy-headed."

"Ask quick. With or without the pills, I'm going to be 'fuzzy-headed' soon," Mark said as he squinted at the label. It stated he could take two the first time and he hoped it would knock him out for the night. His mind was going at a hundred miles an hour, and he had the unsettling sensation of being exhausted but too wound up to sleep.

Jim opened a briefcase and pulled out a legal pad and a pen. "I know, sorry. I just want to get as many details as I can while everything is still fresh in your mind." He sat back at the table and flipped through what he had already, apparently reading the notes. Occasionally, he'd jot down a word or two.

Mark waited, glancing into the living room from the kitchen area. He'd been to Jim's townhouse only a few times. It didn't fit the image he had of Jim. It was actually...nice. A dark brown leather sofa and matching chair faced a large screen television. A bookcase filled the far wall, and he idly wondered what kind of books it held.

It had been over a year since Mark had gone to him about the Wrigley Field plot, and six months since the encounter with the cult. Oddly enough, he and Jim were friends now…sort of. Every few weeks, they would catch a Cubs game at a bar. A few times, they'd gone golfing and once, they'd gone to see Second City. Despite this, Mark felt as if Jim was still more stranger than friend. The man never spoke of his personal life or his past.

A few months ago, Lily had off-handedly mentioned that Jim was coming to pick her up to take her for dinner, and Mark had almost fallen off his chair.

Since then, Jim hadn't mentioned her when they'd go watch a game, and if it hadn't been for Lily's occasional comments about places they had gone, Mark would have never suspected Jim was seeing her. Not that he minded or anything, it just felt odd.

At the clink of the beer bottle, Mark returned his attention to Jim.

"While you were getting patched up, we combed through every file we had on Mohommad Aziz. According to the records, he was sent back to Afghanistan in December of 2002."

Mark couldn't stifle the wave of resentment that rose within him. "He was released *before* I was?"

Jim's eyes were unreadable as he tapped his pen against the pad twice before nodding. "Yes. He held dual citizenship, and so his American citizenship was revoked and he was sent back under the condition that he never return. His last known residence was with his uncle in Afghanistan." He glanced at his notes and continued, "The uncle holds office in Kundunz province and has some political connections, apparently."

"You've got to be kidding me." It was ludicrous. Mark had been released only after he had nearly been broken. He'd returned home to nothing. No home, no business, and his personal life in shambles, while Mohommad had no doubt returned to a hero's welcome from his extended family in Afghanistan. Anger heated a path from his chest to his head, and his face burned. "I guess I didn't have enough connections to get released sooner."

Jim bowed his head in acknowledgement. "I'm sorry. I tried."

Mark pushed out of the chair and paced a few steps. His instinct was to leave--to get away before he exploded with rage. It was as if everything he'd tried to forget, the anger, frustration and resentment that he'd quashed and locked into a vault in his brain, had suddenly sprung free to run amok. It was barreling around inside his head, crashing into the barriers he'd carefully constructed.

He stalked halfway to the couch, halted and faced Jim. "You've known this for how long?"

"Since shortly after Mohommad was released. I received a memo." He tossed the pen on the pad of paper and spread his hands. "What difference does it make? It's not like I personally set him free. I only questioned the man one time before he was sent to another facility."

Mark gave his head a little shake, trying to comprehend the last bit of information. "*You* interrogated him? Were you the one who told him about the camera? For some reason, I thought it was another team. I mean, it wasn't like he was held in the same brig as I was...or was he?" Mark had to know.

Jim stood and approached Mark. "I can't discuss this with you, Mark. You know that."

"Like *hell* you can't! It's not like there's some kind of interrogator/interrogatee confidentiality clause, is there?" Mark knew he wasn't being rational, but he couldn't stop. "Do you all take classes on interrogation ethics?" He flung his arm toward the bookcase, pointing. "In fact, it wouldn't surprise me if you have Torture Methods for Dummies as some of your lighter reading."

Jim flinched almost imperceptibly. "Settle down." He put his hand on Mark's shoulder in a manner meant to calm him.

Mark shrugged the hand off, ready to do more if Jim tried to resist. "Don't tell me to settle down. I'm pissed off and I think I have a right to be. You kept me locked up for over a year. I can't get that time back. I came to terms with it, but only because I thought justice had finally won out, but it didn't, did it? Because if it had, Mo would still be locked up and everyone would be safer."

"You're right. It's not an exact science."

Still fuming, Mark stared at Jim, trying to find the words that would describe his feeling of betrayal, but Jim wasn't feeding the anger anymore and his head throbbed something fierce. He turned and plodded to the couch and sat with a groan. Leaning forward, he cradled his head then moved to rub circles on his temples, carefully avoiding the goose egg. He wondered if he had enough cash to take a cab back home. It would be awkward to have to ask Jim for a ride.

He heard Jim moving around the townhome as doors and cabinets opened and shut, but other than sliding back to rest his aching head on the couch, he remained where he was.

"I put a t-shirt and some sweatpants on the bed in the spare room. You're welcome to stay up, but I'm hitting the sack. Good night."

Mark opened his eyes in surprise. "You aren't kicking me out after my rant?"

Jim shrugged. "It's been a stressful day for everyone. Get some rest."

Mark nodded but couldn't force out a return good night. He remained where he was until Jim's door clicked shut. It took almost a super human effort to drag himself off the sofa, but he stumbled to his feet and shuffled down the hall, finding the room with no problem. After a quick pit-stop in the bathroom, he changed into the clothes Jim had left and sat on the edge of the bed.

Mark wondered why Jim even had a spare bedroom. Or rather why he used the space as one when he probably could have made it into a nice office. There was a small desk, no computer. A bookcase sat beside the desk. Mark stood and stepped to it, squinting at the books. He expected to find titles on politics and such, so he was surprised at finding four Harry Potter books. Others looked like they came straight off a high school reading list: *The Grapes of Wrath, To Kill a Mockingbird, Lord of the Flies* and more.

Curious, Mark glanced around and noticed several picture frames on the dresser. The first one was of a younger Jim with a small boy of about seven or eight years old. The boy wore a baseball uniform and was missing two front teeth. Jim was kneeling beside him with his arm around the boy's shoulders. Jim's relaxed expression was one Mark had never seen on the man's face before. Was it a favorite nephew or something? He moved on to the next picture. It showed the same boy, only now he was a handsome young man in a blue cap and gown. He showed off his diploma to the camera. Mark could just make out the name on the diploma. Andrew James Sheridan. His eyes shot back to the young man, noticing the same intense look in the eyes, the same jaw. The name, coupled with the resemblance meant it had to be Jim's son. Only, Mark didn't ever recall him mentioning a son. Not that he ever brought up anything about his personal life.

Mark set the frame down, returned to the bed and climbed under the covers. After switching off the light, he laced his hands behind his head and stared up into the darkness. He realized he knew next to nothing about Jim. His own life had been deconstructed and examined from every angle by Jim and his team., leaving him not a single secret. Meanwhile, Jim had divulged nothing more private than his love of baseball.

For the last few months, Mark had thought of Jim more as a friend than as his contact at the agency. Jim held the dual role of CIA officer and head of the Chicago FBI on counterterrorism unit. The FBI agents he directed didn't feel comfortable enough under a CIA officer to socialize with him, and so, like Mark, he'd been alone in the city. They both loved baseball and even with their rocky history, they'd formed a friendship. Or at least, Mark had thought of it that way. Now, he wondered. A friend would mention their son. A friend would, at some point, let their guard down and talk about something personal, but Jim never had.

The pain meds were kicking in big time, but Mark fought them off long enough to doubt his own instincts on how to judge friendships. First, Mo, then Jim. Hell, he could even throw Jessie in there for good measure. They'd started out as friends, of sorts, before it turned into something more. Since the events with Kern, they only saw each other occasionally, and he missed her company. He couldn't blame her though. At least she had never lied to him, or about him, like Mo had done. Or probed every corner of his life and never revealed any of her own, like Jim had done. Still, she was gone. He'd let her slip away.

* * *

Mark couldn't move. He lay on his back, limbs immobile while Mohommad smiled down, extending a slice of pizza towards him. The pizza looked great at first. Steam rose from the piping hot slice and melted cheese oozed over the edges, dripping in a long string. He could feel the heat and cringed as the burning hot cheese came within a millimeter of touching his cheek.

"Stop, Mo! What are you doing?" Twisting, but paralyzed, he couldn't escape and could only try to flatten his body to avoid the blistering goo. The strand became a thin stream of liquid cheese, and cascaded over his face in an unending stream, filling his nose and mouth. He couldn't speak. As the weight of it settled like a mold over him, he couldn't breathe. His efforts to get away increased, but the cheese cemented him to the desk. Suffocating him.

"Ahh!" Mark sat up, gasping as he clawed at his face, his chest heaving. Nothing. He rubbed his fingers together, sure he would find a handful of hot, sticky cheese, but other than a sheen of sweat, there was nothing clinging to him.

A dream. He flopped back, regretting the move as his head protested. It felt like a pinball was ricocheting around inside his skull. Sunlight slanted across his face, and he draped his forearm over his eyes.

There came a knock at the door followed by, "Mark?'

"Yeah?" He left his arm in place, peering beneath it as the doorknob turned.

Jim stuck his head in. "I thought I heard you awake. I'm heading into the office. When you feel--" He broke off, his brow furrowed. "What's wrong?"

Mark started to shake his head, but winced. "Nothing. I just had a crazy dream." It was no use fighting the pain. Might as well face it head on. He sat up and swung his legs over the side of the bed, gritting his teeth as the pinball hit a bonus spot and pinged repeatedly against his brain. "What were you going to say?" He massaged his temples.

"Just that when you feel up to it, I wanted to know if you could come down to my office and look at photos. See if we can find out who Hazim is."

Mark tried to concentrate. He had a shoot this afternoon, but he could reschedule it. It was a print ad for laundry detergent and involved a bunch of little kids playing baseball. No way could he deal with that today. "Um, yeah. I'm going to head on over to my place--that's okay, right?"

Jim nodded. "Yes. That's fine but take your phone with you. I've changed it so all you have to do is dial 119 for the call to go through directly to me. It's only for an emergency though, as it bypasses the system."

"Got it. 119." Mark stood, one hand on the corner of the desk as he waited for the room to stop its slow spin. "I don't think I'll need it though. Without the camera, I won't have photos, and Mo has no reason to return. In fact, I'm pretty certain I won't be causing any more problems for you." The smile he pasted on to temper the statement felt heavy and false, but Jim merely nodded.

CHAPTER SIX

Mark's ordeal had thrown Jim's whole schedule for a loop. Jim tossed his pen onto his desk and rubbed his eyes. His meeting with one of his teams who had been investigating a report of repeated purchases of fertilizer had been canceled. The suspicion that the fertilizer was going to be made into a bomb had been unfounded and he'd planned on halting the investigation and re-assigning the group. At least he had plenty of people to put on this new investigation, but they had very little to go on.

Jim straightened in his chair and perused his notes again. What he couldn't understand was how the hell Aziz had entered the country again. Obviously, he must have a fake passport, and to have one that would pass customs required some very high level connections. Or he had somehow been smuggled in.

A snippet of information scratched at the back of his mind. Something he'd read recently, if only he could remember exactly what it was and why it was important. He scanned through files of memos. After thirty minutes, he found it. A memo concerning the likelihood of terrorists infiltrating the country via the Mexican border.

It was a good possibility, and as Jim read through Mohommad's file, he realized that it was highly probable. Aziz spoke Spanish. According to his file, he'd taken four years in high school, and had grown up in a largely Hispanic neighborhood, and at one time had a relationship with a Hispanic woman. Another photographer had independently confirmed the finding.

George Ortiz, also a buddy of Mark's, had stated that Aziz had assisted him on photo shoots with Hispanic clients because of his fluency in Spanish.

Jim tore off a fresh sheet of paper and jotted down the notes. Okay, so if Aziz had been smuggled inside, he'd have no need of a passport, but he would require some kind of identification just to establish any kind of residency--unless he lived with someone else. The Chicago area had a large Muslim population. He could have been absorbed into it, or he could even be hiding out with old friends. They all needed to be questioned. Jim sighed and started digging through the files for names.

His phone rang and, annoyed at breaking his train of thought, he answered it with a clipped, "Yes?" It took only a second for the annoyance to dissolve. "Send him in."

Mark stuck his head in the door a few seconds later. Under the harsh fluorescent lighting, the dark bruises along his cheek and temple stood out in sharp relief. He looked like hell. Jim questioned whether he should have had him come down, but at least he didn't have the haunted expression he'd worn this morning. Jim waved him in.

"Feeling any better?"

Mark entered carrying two large cups of coffee and set one on Jim's desk. "Yeah, and I'll feel a lot better once I have some caffeine in me. I brought you a dose too." He sat in the chair on the other side of Jim's desk, wincing and rubbing his shoulder.

A peace offering. At least, Jim hoped that's what it was. It had bothered him more than he cared to admit when Mark had pointed out the bitter truth about how everyone would be safer if the right man had been kept in prison.

Sometimes he wondered how Mark could be so forgiving of what had been done to him. What if it wasn't forgiveness at all, but something like Stockholm Syndrome? Jim hated to think that their friendship was only based on a deep-seated fear and willingness to please. Taking a sip of the hot brew, he remembered Mark's attitude as he'd told Jim about the Wrigley Field plan. There hadn't been a hint of fear or willingness to please, just barely suppressed loathing and fury. Those were definitely not signs of the syndrome, but whatever had driven him to use the camera's prophetic power in the first place seemed to allow him to put aside personal grudges. For that, Jim was grateful. Mark's drive had saved hundreds of innocent lives in the Wrigley Field case.

Every once in awhile, Jim would see a hint of the resentment, but nothing like last night's explosion. Not that he could blame the guy. After a second sip, he could almost feel the caffeine seeping its way into his bloodstream as the cloud of fatigue dissipated. He lifted the cup. "Thanks for the coffee. I needed it."

Mark nodded. "So, what's the plan?"

Jim thought for moment. "I've pulled up some photographs I'd like you to look through. Take your time, and if you see Hazim, just note the number of the photograph."

"Sounds easy enough." Mark took a drink from his coffee and stood. "Am I looking on the same computer I was on during the Wrigley Field thing?"

Jim shook his head and closed and locked all his applications except the one to view photos. "No, you can use mine. I have a meeting to go to. If you see Hazim's photo before I get back, just note the number on this pad of paper. Or you can wait for me. I'd like to see if you remember anything more." He pulled out a legal pad and snatched a pen from his desk drawer. "Here you go."

***

Mark moved to the other side of Jim's desk and sat. Two years ago, he'd sat chained to a chair in front of Jim waiting to be interrogated, and now he was sitting at the man's desk voluntarily. With an ironic chuckle, he glanced around Jim's office, noting a few photos that hadn't been there last year when he'd been in the office. One was a more recent picture of Jim's son, and the other was of Lily. Squinting, Mark leaned forward, and then grinned. It was a photo he'd taken a few months ago on her birthday.

His smile faded as he recalled that day. He'd picked up a small cake for her and brought it to the office intending to present it to her at the end of the day. Just before they closed, Jim had dropped by and saw Mark coming down from the loft with the cake. He asked Mark if he was bringing the cake to the bar.

Confused, Mark had asked what bar Jim meant.

"Some of your photographer friends are having a small party for Lily over at O'Leary's. It's a surprise. Aren't you going?"

"I didn't know anything about it."

Jim had stammered about how Mark must have missed the call, but Mark knew that hadn't been the case. Jim insisted that Mark come along with them, so he had, but he'd sensed nobody was comfortable speaking to him.

Too much had happened. He couldn't fault the others, and had tried to break the ice, but eventually, a topic of conversation would move onto a subject, or reference something that had happened during the time Mark had been imprisoned. It didn't bother Mark as much as it seemed to bother them. One guy had wondered if Mark lived under a rock when he hadn't known about some pop culture trivia, but a hard elbow from the man's girlfriend had cut the man off mid-sentence.

After several conversations had come to abrupt halts, Mark had decided to spare everyone the awkwardness and had volunteered to photograph the festivities. No longer needing to include him in the conversation, the partygoers had become boisterous. Even Jim had kicked back in the corner of a booth and debated baseball with George Ortiz. After waiting for the official happy birthday song and cake distribution, Mark had left early.

Brushing the memory aside, Mark turned to the computer. This was no time to wallow in self-pity.

Two hours later, Jim returned just as Mark clicked through the final images.

"Sorry, Jim, but none of these guys are Hazim."

"Are you sure?"

"I've gone through them twice." Mark spread his hands in a helpless gesture. He moved to rise from the chair but Jim waved him down and sat in the chair on the other side of the desk.

"Okay, well we can have you work with a sketch artist so we at least have something. Also, we'll need a sketch of how Mohommad appears now."

It was late afternoon before Mark finished with the sketch artist and he entered his studio feeling completely wrung out. He plopped onto his desk chair and contemplated the flashing message light on his phone. No doubt there were calls from clients and he really should answer them, but he sat for another ten minutes staring at the red flashing light while attempting to block out the events that had transpired in this very room the evening before.

He'd almost forgiven Mo for pointing a finger at him back in the fall of 2001. Mark rationalized that Mohommad had been coerced into blaming him. Under the duress of an intense interrogation, it would be understandable. Especially if the interrogators had goaded him with details about Mark's story about the camera.

Maybe he should have been friendlier when Mo had walked in the door yesterday. Would it have changed the outcome? He felt in his gut that Mo had come only for the camera, not to renew an old friendship, but it was possible his bluff about the camera being a wild story would have carried more weight if he hadn't gone ballistic towards Mo and his accomplice the second they walked through the door.

At least the camera wouldn't give Mo much of an advantage. Mark doubted it would even be a factor in whatever Mo and his organization had planned--if there even was anything. At best, Mo would get a twenty-four hour notice of something, but it could be anything. The only advantage is that Mark wouldn't get to see it a day ahead. Plus, there was no guarantee he'd see the outcome of whatever they were planning anyway. It wasn't like he could control what the camera showed him. The fact that the only other large scale attack that would have occurred in the U.S. since September 11th had been shown to him was still not proof in his mind. Besides, he consoled himself, he wasn't the only one responsible for preventing terrorist acts. There were a half-dozen agencies which had a greater chance of preventing something than he did.

Even after running the arguments through his mind several times, he still couldn't shake the guilt that something would happen and it would be his fault if people died. He should have withstood the waterboarding. He was practically a pro at it now.

The phone rang, shattering the silence, and he nearly rolled the chair through the wall behind him when he started at the sound. On the third ring, he answered it, hoping he didn't sound as shaky as he felt.

"Martin and Taylor Photography. Mark speaking." He glanced at the caller ID and frowned when he saw “blocked number”.

"You called in the FBI. Why did you do that?"

"Mo?" Mark fumbled in his pocket for the phone Jim had given back to him.

"I let you live last night, and this is the thanks I get? I thought we were buddies. Others weren't happy with my decision to spare you."

"Listen, Mo, I didn't call anyone. Someone came by the studio and found me where you'd left me. I was in no shape to call *anyone*." He had to buy time. If he kept Mo on the phone, maybe Jim could trace the call. He set Jim's phone on the desk and pushed the keys to get through, cringing at every beep as he pressed the buttons.

"Hazim barely tapped you. He wanted to kill you but I wouldn't let him."

Mark closed his eyes and with all the sincerity he could muster, he said, "I know. I guess I'm supposed to thank you."

There was a pause and Mo sighed. "I wanted to let you know that none of this is personal, Mark. You were a good friend, but you must understand that some things are more important than friendship. I have obligations I must fulfill. We've both paid a bitter price for our countries, have we not?"

A lump pushed up into Mark's throat as a wave of sorrow washed over him. Mo's tone of voice was so familiar it caused the past to come slamming back. All the good times they'd experienced over the years before everything went to hell flashed through his mind's eye.

"What happened, Mo? I don't understand how it came to this. What happened to shooting pictures then going out and playing a few games of pool?"

The connection on the special phone clicked, interrupting Mark's train of thought. He covered the mouthpiece to the office phone and prayed Mo wouldn't hear him as he relayed the information as quickly and quietly as he could to a woman who answered. She sounded vaguely familiar and he placed her voice as the one he'd heard coming from the phone the last night just before Mo had cut it off.

"Sorry, Mark, but as much as I'd like to discuss our past good times, I can't. Only because of our past friendship, and because I realize I do owe you after what I told the CIA, I felt the need to warn you that your act of calling the FBI has been noticed. You must realize that all threats to our plans will have to be eliminated. Please don't be a threat."

The dial tone sounded in Mark's ear and he set the phone down and spoke into the special phone. "Hello? Ma'am? Were you able to trace the call?"

Jim came on the line, surprising Mark. "We're working on it, but it appears that the call was relayed through the internet and proxy servers before reaching you. Basically, he could be anywhere in the world."

"So we're back to square one." Mark sagged onto the desk chair.

"That depends. What did he tell you?"

Mark closed his eyes as he pulled up the details of the call and relayed them to Jim. "Why do you suppose he called to warn me?"

Jim's sigh sounded loud in his ear. "Hell if I know. A sense of guilt? A lingering sense of loyalty?"

"Yeah. I guess." It made no sense to Mark because Mo must have realized that any calls to him would be investigated, hence his use of proxy servers. It was still taking a chance though. And for what? "Jim...do you think there's a chance of getting Mo back on our side?"

"You mean like being a double-agent? I don't think that would work. I wouldn't trust anything the guy said."

"You're probably right. It's just that I heard something in his voice. Like maybe he wasn't happy."

"Look, Mark, I know it's still hard for you to come to terms with what Mo did to you, but you have to face the fact that the man is proving himself to be the terrorist we had accused him of being. You never really knew him."

Mark wasn't sure he agreed with Jim but he let it go for the time being "Right. Well, whatever. I'm probably just too tired to make sense of anything right now."

"How's your head feel?"

"Like a drum corps has taken up residence inside my skull." Mark massaged the back of his neck.

Jim chuckled. "Sorry to hear that." His voice sobered as he said, "Back to business. In light of Mohommad's warning to you, I'm alerting the Chicago P.D. In addition, I'll have one of my agents parked outside your studio until we decide if the threat is real or not."

Mark groaned. "Not this again."

"Whatever you do, keep the phone nearby and just try to get some rest."

CHAPTER SEVEN

After eating a bowl of cereal for dinner, Mark flopped onto the sofa and switched on the television. He didn't really care what was on, he just wanted some noise and something mindless to take his thoughts off everything that had gone on. Just as he was nodding off, his cellphone rang. It took a moment for him to get his bearings and locate it on his breakfast bar. He glanced at the caller ID and a warmth spread through him. Jessie.

"Hello?"

"Hey, Mark. It's Jessie."

He grinned and sauntered back to the sofa and sat on the edge. "Yeah. I know."

"How are you doing?" Her voice washed over him like a warm summer rain.

Mark eased back, unsure how much he could tell her. In the past, he could tell her everything, but now? "Uh...I'm good. You?"

"I'm great. I just got some fantastic news."

The excitement in her voice was contagious and he smiled in response. "Oh yeah? What is it?"

"I'd rather tell you in person. Maybe go out and have a drink, if you feel up to it."

Wariness crept into his voice. "Up to it?" Why would she ask that?

The excitement dimmed as she said, "Jim called me and told me a little bit about what happened. I'm sorry about what you had to go through...again." She paused and he was about to speak and tell her it was no big deal when she continued, "I feel like a complete idiot for not thinking about it before calling and disturbing you."

"Hold on. First, you aren't disturbing me, and I would love nothing more than to go have a drink with you. You don't know how much I *need* to hear some great news for once." He swallowed hard after he spoke, hoping like hell she wasn't going to tell him she was getting married. A few months ago, he'd run into her at a restaurant with another man. Awkward didn't even begin to describe the encounter.

"Wonderful. Can I swing by and pick you up, or do you want to meet somewhere?" The excitement was back in her voice and it warmed him.

"It'll probably be quicker if you swing by, or I could come and get you..."

"Your place is right on my way to where I have in mind. I'll be there in about twenty minutes."

Mark took a quick shower. He told himself it was just to wake up, but he couldn't rationalize the splash of cologne and mouthwash. He glanced in the mirror, wincing at the ugly bruise on his temple, but there was nothing he could do about it. Oh well. Jessie had seen him in worse condition.

Eighteen minutes after he'd hung up, he grabbed the special phone and his regular one and shrugged into his jacket, stuffing the phones into the pocket. True to her word, Jessie's car pulled up right on time.

It felt like old times as he climbed into her little sports car and he had to remind himself that he no longer had the right to lean over for a kiss. "Hey. So what's got you all fired up?" He rubbed his hands on his thighs.

Jessie threw him a grin and shook her head. "Oh no you don't. Not until we get to the restaurant.."

"O'Leary's?"

"Nope. Not this time. Thought we'd go somewhere different. Somewhere a little more upscale. Have you eaten dinner yet?"

"Does a bowl of Cheerios count?"

She laughed. "Not hardly."

Mark grinned and wasn't even sure why. "Then I guess not."

A few minutes later, she pulled in front of a well-known chop house. Mark whistled. "This must be amazing news."

"Come on. I'm dying to tell you."

Although her good mood had rubbed off on him, he couldn't help the trace of apprehension that slowed his steps as they followed the hostess to their table. After ordering drinks--a Scotch for him and a glass of wine for Jessie--they made small talk and perused the menu until their drinks arrived.

Finally, Jessie raised her glass of wine and took a deep breath, her eyes reflecting the soft light from the sconces along the walls and touched the edge of her glass against Mark's. "You are looking at Chicago's newest FBI agent!"

She clinked his glass, but he was so shocked, he forgot to drink his for a moment. Relief that she wasn't announcing her marriage warred with his mixed feelings about her working for Jim. He covered his feelings with a laugh. "Wow! Not what I expected, but congrats." He took a sip of his Scotch. A long sip.

Tilting her head, her eyes took on a thoughtful glint. "You don't sound too happy for me."

Mark shook his head. "No, it's not that. I just didn't know you wanted to be an FBI agent. I thought you liked being a detective. Also, I'm in shock because I thought you were going to tell me something else."

"I did like being a detective, but I wanted to have a bigger scope. A broader picture of law enforcement."

"Makes sense. Well, I'm very happy for you. You deserve it." He smiled and raised his glass again in a toast. Jessie did deserve it. Mark knew it first hand and despite his misgivings, he was happy for her.

After she took a swallow, she set her glass down, her finger tracing the rim as she asked, "What did you *think* my news was?"

Heat climbed his face as he stammered, "I...I thought you were going to tell me you were getting married." Sure she'd see exactly how much the idea bothered him, he studied his menu.

When his admission was met with silence, he risked a glance at her. Just as he'd thought, she regarded him, but not with the amusement he'd expected, but with a soft half-smile.

"Mark, after all we've been through, do you really think I'd do that to you? Take you out to eat to announce I was marrying someone else?" As she spoke, she reached across the table and took his hand, giving it a gentle squeeze. "There is no one else. Fact is, you're a pretty hard act to follow."

Shame that he hadn't considered her decency and how she would never be so cruel as to announce news like that so blithely mingled with a spark of hope. "I'm sorry. I should have realized." Her hand, warm and smooth, rested on top of his, forging a current between them. "So, tell me about it. When do you start?"

With a final squeeze, she released his hand, but he felt the heat even after it was gone. Before she could begin, the waitress arrived and took their order.

When she'd left, Jessie folded one arm over the other and rested them on the table. "I'm starting right away because I had already scheduled a two week vacation, so I decided to go ahead and use that as my notice." Her eye's danced as she added, "I can't wait."

"I bet." He had to ask, "Are you going to be working directly with Jim?"

She nodded and took a roll from the breadbasket the waitress dropped off. "Yes." As she tore the roll in half and reached for the butter, she paused, eyebrow quirked. "Will that bother you?"

Truthfully, he wasn't sure if it did or not. It just seemed like suddenly the few people he'd been close to were now in Jim's camp, so to speak. First Lily, and now Jessie. He shrugged. "I guess not. Jim's a good guy."

"That has to be hard for you to admit."

"Kind of. I mean, I hated his guts because he was a big part of the whole enemy combatant thing, but a lot has happened since then."

CHAPTER EIGHT

"Yes, sir. I understand, but--" Jim clenched the phone to his ear, and felt the muscles in his jaw tense as his superior cut him off. Damn bureaucrats. "Right, but if we get the camera back, we'll still need Taylor to--" He loosened his tie, all the while wishing he could use it to strangle the man on the other end of the phone.

Another two minutes passed, during which his boss stated that Mark Taylor was an expense they didn't need anymore, that only Jim had ever believed he was anyway, so Jim was to cut Taylor loose as an asset.

"What about the Wrigley Field incident? Several agents saw the photos and they were the key pieces of intelligence that prevented loss of life."

In the end, Jim's arguments fell on deaf ears. Even though his boss agreed that Mark had tipped them off to the plot, it didn't prove that he had a magical camera. A chill crept down Jim's spine when it was hinted that perhaps Mark had insider information because he had been part of the group all along as previously suspected.

In an attempt to cut off that line of thinking before it fully developed, Jim agreed to rescind Mark Taylor's status as his asset. At least, officially. That meant no special phone. In most cases, an asset received some kind of stipend to keep them returning with information, but Mark had only requested that his own funds, still mired in red tape six months after his release from prison, be once again made available to him. Jim had also wrangled a small sum so Mark could start up a new business. He'd argued that Mark needed it for a cover.

Jim set the phone down and pinched the bridge of his nose in an attempt to stave off the headache building behind his eyes. It already ranked in the three ibuprofen territory and bordered on four. He reached into his desk for the pain reliever. He swore when he opened the bottle to find only two pills rattling around in the bottom. They'd have to do.

After washing them down with the last dregs of his coffee, he reached for the phone again to call Mark to give him the news, but changed his mind. This was something he needed to do in person.

* * *

Jim rang the recently installed bell at the front of the studio, noting and approving the new security measure. Mark shouted for him to hold on a second. Hands in his pockets, Jim eyed the windows of apartments above neighboring businesses. Even now, Mohommad or his associates could be watching.

Mark opened the door, his eyebrows rising in surprise when he saw Jim. "Hey, Jim. Come on in."

Jim nodded towards the doorbell. "Glad to see you're using that."

A grimace flashed across Mark's face as he turned and led the way to the studio. "Yeah. It's a pain in the ass though. Like just now, I had to stop what I was doing to answer it--not that I'm not glad to see you--it's just that I'm finishing up a shoot."

"You may not be so glad to see me when you hear what I came to tell you, but it can wait a few moments. I'll just sit in the back until you're done."

After casting him a quizzical look, Mark returned to his customer, and Jim wandered to the back of the studio to a few chairs arranged around a coffee table spread with magazines. A water cooler that matched the one in the office area gurgled in the corner. He took a paper cup from the dispenser and filled it before sitting. Breaking the news wasn't going to be easy. Especially not after what Mark had said the other day about not being of any use now that he no longer had the camera. Jim had scoffed at the time, but here he was about to confirm Mark's suspicions.

He leaned back in the chair, sipping the water as he listened to Mark explain his pricing and timeline for the photographs. He sounded upbeat and friendly. Exactly the kind of guy anyone would want to buy photos from, and not at all like a man who'd been through what he had endured in the last three years. Jim had to hand it to the guy; he was as tough as they came.

Mark passed by the waiting area as he escorted the customer, a woman with a little girl, to the back door. He waved at the child and grinned, telling her what a great job she'd done. He turned the smile on the mother. "Thanks again. I'll be in touch."

As soon as the door shut, the smile dropped off Mark's face and he turned towards Jim. "So, what's it this time?"

Jim motioned to one of the chairs. "Why don't you have a seat?"

Eyes narrowed, Mark sat on the coffee table instead. "Just tell me what this is all about." He glanced at his watch. "I have another client arriving in about twenty minutes."

Jim gave a short nod and crumpled the paper cup, dropping it into a wastebasket beside his seat. "Okay. I had a call today from Langley. I was informed that I have to let you go as an asset."

Mark tilted his head as though waiting for more. "And? That's *it*? Hell, I could have predicted that even without the aid of the camera." Hands braced on his knees, his head dropped as he gave it a shake. After a moment, he slapped his palms on his thighs and stood. "Well, I guess that's that. Do you need me to sign something to make this official?"

"No, I just need you to return the phone. Basically, it just means I can no longer put together teams to investigate your 'leads' without approval, whereas when you were my asset, I could do it at my discretion."

Mark strode to his desk and returned with the phone in hand, and thrust it towards Jim. "Here you go."

Jim took it, and stared at it blankly for a few seconds as awkwardness built.

"What about the camera? Are you guys going to try to find Mo and get it back?"

"Mohommad will be placed on the watch-list as having been sighted in the area, but as far as the camera goes, I can't promise anything. It's not a priority."

"I suppose not, since it's just an old camera to your people."

"You know that's not what I think. I know it has powers and I'll do what I can, but I can't make promises."

"Hell, Jim. It doesn't matter anyway." Mark shrugged and moved to the back door, slamming the dead bolt home. "I have a feeling I'll never see the damn camera again. Once your guys get a hold of it, it'll be gone forever, but at least that's better than the bad guys having it. I think." Mark turned his head, his eyes fixed on the window, but his gaze was far away.

Jim tapped the phone against his palm twice, and finally stuck his hand out. "It's been an honor, Mark. I mean that."

Mark's hand remained at his side as he shook off whatever it was he was seeing in his mind and lifted an eyebrow. "An honor? I doubt that." He gestured toward Jim's outstretched hand. "Besides, I thought we were friends, sort of." Crossing his arms across his chest, his mouth set in a hard line for a moment before he nodded. "So, I take it the ball games, the friendly games of pool-- those things are all just a part of the job? Keep the informant happy and all that?"

Caught off guard, Jim let his hand drop to his side while he formed a reply. "You know none of that had anything to do with the job."

Mark stared at Jim coldly, and abruptly turned away, striding into the studio area. Jim heard backdrops retracting and walked around the corner to find Mark pulling a new backdrop down from a frame.

"Listen, Mark, I had no choice in the matter. I tried to convince them, but they didn't listen."

With a sarcastic laugh, Mark shook his head. "Why does that not surprise me?" He tightened the backdrop then turned to Jim. "Look, I understand that it was all a part of the job for you. It always has been, hasn't it? Whatever it takes." He rubbed the back of his neck before sighing and spreading his hands. "Crazy as it seems, I kind of admire that tenacity and dedication." Mark stepped forward, hand out. "It's been...an experience."

Jim clasped his hand in a firm grip. "I'll be seeing you, Mark."

CHAPTER NINE

Soon after Jim left, Mark's next customer arrived. For the next couple of hours, he tried to forget about Jim's news and concentrate on business, but if anyone had asked him details about shooting the aspiring actor's head-shot, he couldn't have given any. He just hoped the customer was happy with the results. They had looked okay on the LCD screen on the back of his camera, but he knew the image shown there wasn't completely accurate. There could be some blurring, imperfections, shadows or any number of other things that could mar the photographs. If they were crap, he'd offer a re-shoot at no charge, but he hoped it wouldn't come to that.

For once, he had no pressing business to attend to. He'd even paid all the bills and balanced the checkbook, a chore he hated. It was only six p.m. and he couldn't remember the last time he'd had too much time on his hands. At least, not since he'd been released from prison.

Mark made a sandwich and took it to the sofa to eat while watching T.V. He lifted the top slice of bread from his sandwich to tuck a stray leaf of lettuce back on top of the turkey. As he took his first bite, a story about a freak accident involving a gust of wind that toppled a tree onto a car and killed the occupant was playing on the news. The sandwich turned into sawdust in his mouth and a chill raised the hairs on his arms. The face of the victim flashed on the screen, holding Mark captive. He couldn't look away. He knew he'd never seen the woman before, and yet she looked familiar. He couldn't grasp how he knew her; just that he did. Somehow.

Closing his eyes, the image of the woman parking a car played in his head. Her blonde hair formed a curtain as she turned off the ignition and he heard the click of the door latch as she started to open the door. At the last second, she seemed to forget something and let the door hang partially open as she reached into the backseat and retrieved a large purse.

Mark's throat worked as he tried to call to her, but no sound came out. Instead of exiting the vehicle, she sat and dug in her purse for something. A sudden blast of wind sent dead grass, leaves and dirt into his face, and he raised his arm, blocking the debris. An instant later, a huge tree crushed the car--a red Mustang.

A jolt passed through him and he blinked, almost surprised to find himself still sitting on the couch. He didn't think he'd fallen asleep, the sandwich was still clutched in his hand, the bread a little worse for the wear although the lettuce had escaped again. It hadn't been a dream because it didn't have the details he was used to seeing. It had been more like seeing a random video clip. In fact, he wondered if that's what had happened. Had he zoned out while the news played a clip of the tragedy and he only thought it was a vision?

He tossed the sandwich onto his plate and ground his fists against his eyes. Even as he tried to rationalize what he'd experienced, he suspected the cause of the vision. It was the camera. Mo had used it but something had gone wrong. Maybe he'd developed the film just moments ago. Mark never had the dreams until he'd developed the film. Or someone else did.

While in prison, he'd had a few dreams after Jessie had used the camera. He hadn't known it then, and hadn't learned about it for months, but she had developed the film right away, the first time to get photos of her niece's dance recital, the second time as proof to show Jim about the camera's magical qualities.

Since then, he'd been the only one to use the camera and so he expected the dreams, but this--it had blindsided him. Would it happen every time Mo or someone else used the camera? Would he randomly get slammed with a vision he was helpless to change? Shaken, he stood and paced the loft. He picked up the phone, needing to talk to someone about this new development. It wasn't that he expected anyone else to know the answers to his questions, but a friendly voice would be nice. Someone to tell him it would all be fine.

He pressed the on button, but clicked it off after a moment. There was no one to call. Jim was no longer an option, and Jessie now worked for Jim, and he didn't want to put her in an awkward position.

Lily was still on her cruise and even if she hadn't been, she was now in Jim's camp. It wasn't fair to think of Jim as being on the other side, like an enemy, but at the moment, a cold sense of abandonment washed over him.

He looked at his speed-dial. That left the pizza or Chinese food restaurants as almost the only other numbers on his list. He shook his head with a wry smile. Although he was on a first name basis with the delivery people at both restaurants, they weren't quite what he needed right then.

There was one more number. His parents.

Mark plopped onto the edge of his bed. He had been home for Christmas, plus a few other times. Twice, his parents had come to Chicago, but the camera had loomed, straining their relationship. They never quite understood it, and after Mark had become front page news, they worried about the danger it posed for him.

If he called them now, his mother would ask a hundred questions, and his dad would want to know what he'd done wrong, but, in the end, they'd be on his side. Mark took a deep breath and dialed their number.

A few seconds later, his mother answered the phone. He could hear the smile in her voice and the corners of his mouth turned up. He made small talk for a few minutes and listened while she updated him up on happenings around his old hometown.

It caught him off-guard when she cut off her recital of Aunt Faye's hip replacement surgery with an abrupt, "What's wrong, Mark?"

He'd been about to make up an excuse that he was just calling to say hello, and not mention anything about the camera, but unprepared, he simply blurted out, "The camera's gone, Mom."

"*Gone?* Gone where?"

He poured out the story, but spared some of the details of how Mo had persuaded him to reveal the camera's whereabouts. "So, that's it. Mo has the camera and that's the end of the story."

"What about that FBI guy? Jim?"

"Officially, he can't do anything. Now that I don't have the camera, I'm of no use to them."

"You mean they'll just let Mohommad gallivant all around the country with your camera?"

The mental image of Mohommad 'gallivanting' forced a reluctant smile. "Oh, they want to catch him because he's not supposed to be in the U.S., but theft of an old camera isn't going to make him number one on the FBI's most wanted list."

There was a pause, and she asked, her voice hesitant, but with a hint of hope, "So, does this mean you're all done with...with the dreams and photos? You can get back to a normal life?"

"Yeah, I guess so." Head bent, he squished the lettuce against the table with his index finger. He'd been about to tell her about the waking dream he'd just had, but he didn't have the heart to kill the hope. He just couldn't. It was obvious what she wanted for him, and it wasn't to be some kind of modern day Lone Ranger. "Anyway, I just thought I'd let you and Dad know, so if you could just tell him about it, that would be great. I'm sure he'll be happy too. No more chance of embarrassing him by making headlines"

"He's proud of what you've done; he just has a hard time expressing it."

Mark massaged his forehead and reined in the bitter tone that ached to run loose. "Right. After that mess with the cult, his pride shone so bright, it blinded me every time I came to visit."

"That was different. You were all over the news, like...like you were some kind of freak. Your father was angry at the news media, not you, Mark. He felt helpless and was worried sick about you."

Not enough to make the trip down to Chicago though, Mark thought but didn't voice. "I know. Well, I have to get going. I'll talk to you soon."

"Wait. Now that you don't have to deal with the camera, maybe you could come home for a little vacation?"

"I'll think about it, Mom."

After he hung up, he tossed the phone on the bed and leaned his elbows on his knees, cradling his head. The vision or whatever it was, could be a one-time thing, or it might not have anything to do with the camera. Maybe he'd just conjured the whole vision while the news report gave the details. When he was a kid, he'd often been accused of having a wild imagination, so that's all it was--his imagination working overtime to make up for the loss of the camera.

* * *

The next night, Mark awoke in the early morning from a dream about a man who was electrocuted when he had the misfortune to lean against a fence connected to a light pole at a baseball diamond. The dream was too murky for him to make out details, but he tried to find the correct field. He checked the Chicago Park District's map of ball fields, and drove to more than half of them before he ran out of time. None had matched the dream.

The ten o'clock news had run the story and as difficult as it was, Mark had to watch. He had to know the name of the man he'd been unable to save. A ball of fury ignited in his belly as he leaned in to hear the story. The victim had been the father of one of the players. For the rest of his life, the son would have to live with the fact that his father had died watching his game.

He aimed the remote at the TV and jammed the off button. His anger un-sated, he whipped the remote against the opposite wall, his breath blasting out in ragged gasps as the remote exploded in a shower of plastic.

It was a completely senseless death. One which Mark could have easily prevented if only he'd had more details. He'd bet that if he had viewed the photos, like he normally would have, somewhere in them would be a sign with the name of the field, or the baseball uniforms would have the names of the teams. He would have just found out the schedule, and been at the right field at the right time.

It was late, but he needed to expend his pent up rage, so he changed into his running gear and took off.

An hour later, drenched in sweat and exhausted, he returned home and headed straight for the shower. As the water sluiced over him, he wondered if he was going to be hit with another dream that night.

Just in case, he put a pad of paper and a pencil beside the bed so he could write down as much as he could while the details were fresh upon waking.

CHAPTER TEN

Images of a train exploding as passengers boarded and exited an 'L' car filled his early morning dream. The second his eyes snapped open, he grabbed the paper and sat on the edge of the bed while he wrote down everything he could recall. He filled an entire page and was even able to remember what line and track. The time of the disaster was more of a guess, but he knew which way the tracks faced, and the sunlight suggested late afternoon. It was the closest he could approximate.

After recording it all, he scrubbed his hands down his face, the rasp of his morning shadow loud in the loft. Now what? It wasn't like he could defuse a bomb or call a halt to a train schedule. He had to tell someone, but whom? Jim would be the natural choice, but would he be able to muster an investigation based on merely a dream? He didn't doubt that Jim would believe him, but there was no proof, and without it, Jim's hands would be tied. The FBI wasn't the same as the local police where you could call in a suspicious person and they would check it out. It would probably be better to go through proper channels with the Chicago police being the logical place to start. If they felt it was a terrorist plot, they'd call in the FBI.

Mark stood and retrieved his cell phone from the coffee table. A glance out the window revealed gray skies and whirling brown leaves. He shivered as a blast of wind rattled the windows. He sat on the edge of the couch, pulled the afghan off the back, draping it one- handed over his shoulders.

Why couldn't the dream have shown him more? The face of the culprit, for starters, but also the exact time of the explosion would have been helpful. The only information he had was a location, 'L' platform, and a rush-hour time frame.

After taking a deep breath, he pressed the emergency numbers.

"911. What's your emergency?"

Mark cleared his throat. "I want to report an impending problem on the Brown line—well, actually at the Merchandise Mart station."

"Impending problem? I'm sorry, sir, could you be more specific?"

"I overheard someone talking about an explo--" This was all wrong. How could he be more specific? "Uh...never mind. Everything is fine now. The train was running late, is all." He jammed the off button and hoped they didn't call back to follow up.

Jessie. Even if she no longer worked as a Chicago detective, she'd at least be able to advise him whom to contact.

Despite the nature of the call, he couldn't help the current of anticipation that hummed through his veins as he waited for her to answer.

"Hey, Mark.'

He smiled, flattered to realize that she must still have him programmed into her phone. "Hi, Jess. I'm sorry to bother you, but I'm hoping you can help me." Mark leaned forward, elbows braced on his knees, staring at his balled up dirty socks on the floor. He felt like he should make small talk, but he didn't have time and doubted she did either. "I, uh, I had a dream last night. It was a bad one--way beyond my ability to fix it."

"What do you mean you had a dream? Did you get the camera back somehow?"

"No, but Mo must be using it because I've been getting the dreams even without having it in my possession."

"Are you *sure* they're camera related dreams? How's that possible?"

There was skepticism in her tone. He was used to it, but not from her. Not for a long time, anyway. "I have no idea how it's possible. You might as well ask how the camera gives the damn future photos to begin with." He kicked the socks over to the pile of dirty clothes in the corner. "Remember when I was in prison, and *you* used the camera? Well, same thing. I just know that I dreamed of an explosion on the platform this afternoon. At the Merchandise Mart stop. The only other detail I can give you is there were a helluva lot of dead and injured folks lying on the platform when it was over."

"Hold on. Just calm down, okay? I believe you." There was a pause and he heard her rummaging around for something. "I'm still in orientation, you know. I don't even have a desk yet so I need to find something to write on."

"I'm sorry, Jess." He straightened, took a deep breath and let it ease out before continuing, "I'm just keyed up. Without a photo to scan for more clues, I feel like I'm reading a book with half the pages torn out."

"Okay. I have a pen so give me what you have."

Mark relayed what he remembered of the dream, but the details were still too sketchy. He wished he could transfer the image in his head to a visual for her.

"That's not much to go on, Mark. I have no idea who I could convince to investigate this."

"What about Jim?'

"He had to fly out to D.C. and I barely know the guy covering for him. Besides, I'm way down on the totem pole here, Mark. Just let me think a minute."

Mark gnawed at a ragged cuticle. She had to know somebody after all her years of experience.

After a pause, she said, "I guess I could call Dan, my old partner on the force."

Relief washed over him. "That would be great."

"He may call you for details though."

"What do I tell him? After all that cult stuff, he must think I'm a crackpot."

"No, he has an inkling that something is up with you. Way back, before I believed your story, I told him what you told me in the prison cell."

"You *told* him? Jessie...*damn*." He could just imagine how that conversation went.

"It was a long time ago and it's a good thing I did because he's the only one I can think of who might be able to carry off preventing the explosion without casting suspicion on you. Good thing you called me first."

Heat raced up Mark's face. "Uh...well, you're actually the second person. I called 911 first."

"You *what?"*

"I didn't know who to call, okay? My first impulse was to call 911 because I wanted someone to do something immediately. What was I supposed to do? It's not like the dreams come with a manual! With you off the police force, I didn't know where to turn."

Her breath sounded loud in his ear, and he pictured her sighing and possibly rolling her eyes at him--not that he could blame her.

"I'll give Dan a quick call and fill him in, but I have to get to a meeting in a few minutes, so I won't be able to follow up with you for a couple of hours."

"Thanks, Jessie."

"No problem. I just hope everything works out."

Mark had the same thought as he hung up.

* * *

Mark dressed and ran downstairs to the studio to reschedule his appointments while he waited for Dan to call. Luckily, there were only two clients booked, and both were okay with the rescheduling. One even expressed relief because her son was sick and she'd planned on canceling anyway. Cramming the last bit of a granola bar in his mouth, he almost choked on it when someone pounded on the front door. What the hell?

He hurried to the door as the pounding came again. A man had his hands cupped on the front window, peering in. With the distortion of the glass, it took a second for Mark to recognize Jessie's former partner. He unlocked the door and opened it.

"How's it going, Mark?" Dan extended his hand and Mark shook it.

"Okay. Good to see you, Dan." He motioned towards the back to the office. "Why don't we have a seat?"

"Thanks. Glad to hear things are going well with you finally. It's been...what? Six months since that cult nut job tried to kill you?" He grinned. "I knew the peace was too good to last."

Mark nodded, feeling awkward in the detective's presence now that he knew the other man had seen photos of him from an interrogation session. It wasn't his best moment, and Dan, at six-foot four inches, and a good 250 pounds, was intimidating enough. "Yeah. I've been trying to fly under the radar, but today, I need some help. Did Jessie fill you in?"

Dan pulled out a notebook and flipped it open. "Yes, but I have to admit, I didn't know what the hell she was talking about. You had a dream that a train on the Brown Line blew up?"

"I'm not sure how much you know about my...ability, for lack of a better word." Mark braced his elbows on the desk and massaged circles on his temples as he tried to clarify what he wanted to say. Would it really matter if the knowledge got out? The cat was already out of the bag anyway, so to speak. The camera had been stolen, the damage already done.

"I had a camera that gave me future photos." He searched for skepticism in the other man's expression, expecting to find at least a trace, but instead, Dan merely nodded. Encouraged, Mark said, "I take it you've heard of it."

"More than that, I saw pictures of you from when you were in prison. Of course, that doesn't prove anything, but combined with your sudden release, and Jim Sheridan hanging out with you, I figured there must be something you have that's important. Something that the government had a special interest in. I might not be the smartest rat in the maze, but I can usually find the cheese."

Mark almost smiled at the phrasing but sobered as he said, "A few times, the camera gave me warning of terrorist acts."

"September 11th?"

"Yeah. I couldn't...I mean I tried, but, obviously, I wasn't able to prevent it." His failure still caused a stab of pain in his gut. It festered like a wound that wouldn't heal, a deep, raw pain that lingered. He mentally slapped another Band-Aid over it and added, "I helped stop another terrorist attack though. Remember the Wrigley Field incident last year?"

"Sure, but it wasn't much of an incident, that I recall."

"You're right, it wasn't, but that's because we *prevented* it. Hundreds would have died, and I had pictures to prove it." Mark stared at the smooth surface of the desk, his gaze focused inward as he recalled the proof of the carnage that thankfully never materialized. Superimposed upon the images were the new scenes that had played out in his dream last night. If only he had the photos to prove his story. *This* story--it would make it so much easier. *Damn Mohommad to hell.* He struggled to tamp down his anger to a manageable level so he would sound sane and calm when he told Dan about the dream.

He looked Dan in the eye. "There's a bomb planted on an 'L' train. I don't know exactly which one or when it goes off, only that it happens at the Merchandise Mart station sometime this afternoon."

"Okay, I got that from Jessie, but here's the thing." He flipped his note-pad shut. "A dream isn't something I can take to my lieutenant. Do you have some of those pictures?"

"No. I wish I did, but the camera was stolen a few weeks ago."

Dan leaned back in his chair, tapping his pencil against the pad of paper as he scrutinized Mark. After a long moment, he shook his head and tossed the pad on the desk. "What the hell am I supposed to do with that information? Jeez, Mark. Throw me a bone here. Don't you have *anything?* A name? Time? Train number?" He slapped his hand on top of the pad with a loud thump. "I need something I can take to my boss and say, 'Look, we have to act before it's too late.' Even a photo of something that hasn't taken place yet, as crazy as it sounds, is *something*."

Mark shoved out of the chair, arms spread. "Damn it! What do you want me to do? Manufacture evidence?" He gestured toward his computer. “Create some images with my graphics program? Or should I just say *I* planted the bomb so that somebody will go investigate?" He turned away in disgust and vented his anger by slamming shut an open drawer of the filing cabinet.

"Did you?"

Mark glared over his shoulder. "Forget it. Just get the hell out."

Dan stood and shrugged. "Look at it from my angle. I can't go to the transit authority with some half-assed claim that a guy dreamed a train would blow up this afternoon. Naturally they're going to want details. What train? What time? How do you know? How credible is the informant? And to tell the truth, Mark, your history is going to come back to bite you in the ass when someone looks it up."

"Yeah. I get it. I have no credibility. Sorry I wasted your time." The apology tasted bitter on his tongue.

Dan sighed. "Call me when you get some evidence." He tossed his card onto the desk and left the studio.

Mark sagged against the cabinet as he admitted to himself that Dan had raised valid points. With a sigh, he returned to the desk and slouched onto his chair. If only he had the photos. His gaze roamed the studio, landing on one of his cameras. The dream played in his mind like it was on a loop. *Loop.* An idea sprouted. He jumped up, sending the chair crashing against the back wall. If they wanted pictures, he'd give them pictures. He glanced at the clock. It was only eleven a.m. There was still time.

CHAPTER ELEVEN

Mark purchased a transit card from a machine at the Brown Line station on Wells Street and rode the train through the Loop, half hoping he'd spot Mohommad or his buddy, Hazim. If they were the people responsible, in all probability they'd planted the bomb already, but maybe he'd get lucky. If Jim was correct about Mohommad's connections, he'd have been well-trained. Mark scanned the platform as the train slowed to stop, his thumb tapping on the lens of the camera draped around his neck.

Last night's dream that had plagued his thoughts all day now played hide and seek as he sought to pull it forward to glean the details. He closed his eyes for a moment, picturing the dream and the train as it pulled away from the platform. There was a flash. Concentrating, he pinpointed the location. It seemed to start at the rear of the first car in the train.

He opened his eyes as the train rolled to a stop. There just weren't enough details. Photos would usually show him different angles and that's what he needed now, a different point of view. Standing, he moved through the car and into the next one. Every person who carried a bag was suspect. It didn't matter if it was a little old lady with a shopping bag or a mother juggling a toddler and a diaper bag. Mark couldn't let down his guard for any of them. Hanging onto the overhead bar, he continued to move through the car, but he wasn't even sure what to look for. This was completely out of his league. What did he know about bombs? Only what he saw on the news or on a police procedural.

A few people threw him dirty looks, and he realized he was openly scrutinizing the other passengers. Averting his gaze, he took the closest available seat. What the hell had he expected to accomplish? Had he expected to find the bomb all by himself? Hundreds of people had already come and gone on the train, and there were several other trains on the same line, not to mention the Purple Line also used this station. For some reason--maybe he'd had a glimpse, he couldn't be sure--but he was certain it was a Brown Line train that suffered the explosion and blew off the tracks.

So far, he'd accomplished nothing and time was running out. He fought the urge to pace the car, but his knee jerked up and down a few times.

He wished he had proof, but if wishes came true, he'd call one of the detectives on *Law and Order*. Any version. They always solved their cases. Right now, even a fictional character would have a better chance of stopping this than he did.

The train clattered along the track and swayed as it hit full speed. It was a wonder trains didn't fall off the rails with all the side to side movement. Mark bolted upright in his seat. The bomb could be hidden beneath the track.

The train had completed a full circuit of its route, and he hadn't seen anything suspicious in the cars. As soon as the doors opened, he hit the platform, dodging commuters attempting to board, and raced down the steps to street level.

Wells Street had almost a tunnel-like appearance, with buildings shoulder to shoulder on both sides. The tracks ran overhead, casting the street in permanent shadow. Mark stopped to get his bearings, lining up the platform and the approximate spot where it seemed the bomb had exploded.

If only he knew what it was he needed to look for. He guessed he should be looking for anything that wouldn't normally be found on street girders. Pigeons flew back and forth, their wings flashing light gray as they landed on the street or sidewalks to pick at bits of trash. Mark was so intent on studying the underside of the track overhead that he wandered into the northbound lane and had to dodge a speeding taxi.

For thirty minutes, he walked a grid pattern, or as close to one as he could manage with the traffic. The tail of a bird protruded from a nest and he walked beneath it, eyeing it to make sure he didn't get hit by pigeon droppings.

Trains rumbled overhead, but Mark barely heard them as he plotted in his mind where the explosion would have to originate, lining up his mental image from the dream with visible landmarks he remembered.

He'd made about ten passes from one end of the platform to the other when it occurred to him that the bird had never moved. Maybe the pigeon was so used to the racket, it didn't bother him, but he noted other pigeons had taken flight, even if it was just to hop down to the ground. He raised the camera and zoomed in.

It wasn't a pigeon's tail. The color was wrong. It was a pale creamy color with a light yellow tint didn't match any pigeon that Mark had ever seen. He clicked off a few shots, changing position and angles for several different views. It could be anything.

After another thirty minutes of combing the underside of the track for anything out of the ordinary, Mark headed back to the studio to upload the photos to his computer.

* * *

It only took a few minutes to upload the files, and as he clicked through them, nothing stood out except for the photos of what looked vaguely like a pigeon's tail. Did bombs look like that? Mark had no clue. He opened his Internet browser and did a search for images of bombs. The search called up photos of atomic bombs detonating, torpedo shaped bombs dropping from planes, and cartoon images of round black bombs with fuses sticking out of the top.

Frustrated, he poised the cursor over the search box trying to think of another name for a bomb. Explosives. This brought up photos of dynamite, more mushroom cloud pictures, and lots of clip art. He scanned through it anyway. It was all he could do. On the second page, a cream colored object in one of the thumbnails caught his eye. He leaned forward and viewed a full-size image. It was the exact color of the object he'd seen under the bridge. C4. Plastic explosives. He had it. *Proof.*

Mark pulled out Dan's card and called him. Voice-mail picked up and he groaned. Would nothing go right today? He left a brief message and said he'd be bringing in the evidence that Dan had asked for earlier.

* * *

Mark spread the photos on Dan's desk and pointed to the plastic explosives. "See? There it is, right there."

Dan lifted a picture and examined it for a minute and did the same with the others. He studied the last one and shrugged, letting the photo spin from his fingers to land atop the others. "It could be explosives, but it could also be any number of other things."

"But it's not." Mark stabbed a finger at the photo. "I searched the whole underside of the track there. Everything is gray or brown--nothing is this color."

"It could also be a compound or resin to repair a weak spot."

Mark straightened. He hadn't thought of that, but still, in his gut, he knew what he'd seen were the explosives. "Look, all you have to do is go check it out. That's all I'm asking. Get an expert over there, someone who does construction or an engineer--hell, I don't know--just someone who knows more than we do." He paused and looking between Dan and the photos. "If I'm wrong, you've wasted a few hours, and I swear I'll never bother you again, but if I'm right, you could save a hundred people. Maybe more."

Dan didn't speak as his gaze alternated between Mark and the photos. Doubt clouded his expression.

The muscles in Mark's jaw clenched and he tapped the edges of the photos into a neat pile and slid them back into the envelope. He turned to leave. *Screw it.* If Dan wasn't going to act, he'd find someone who would. Somewhere.

"Okay."

Mark whipped back to face him. "*Okay?* You'll investigate it?"

"I'll probably be a laughing stock, but yeah, I'll take a look. I have a buddy on the bomb squad. I'll give him a call--unofficially--and see if he can spare a few minutes to take a look." Dan shrugged. "It's not very far from here."

Tension drained out of Mark like water from a tub. "Thank you."

* * *

Mark sat in Dan's office while the other man phoned his friend. He tried not to look at his watch every few minutes, but he could almost feel the beat of the seconds ticking away against his wrist. Fingers tapping out a matching rhythm, Mark practically catapulted out of the chair when Dan hung up and motioned for Mark to follow him.

"We're going to meet Thomas there. He's off today but is willing to take a look."

Mark drove his own vehicle and parked a half block away from the platform, remembering to grab the envelope of photos just before he got out. Dan edged his car in a few spaces in front of Mark's and climbed out, his expression confused.

"I thought you said it was under the platform?"

Mark jogged a couple of steps to meet him, slowing to a walk as he neared. "It is, but I thought it would be safer to park here."

Dan slanted him a look. "Right." He pulled his overcoat closed and turned his collar up against the cutting gusts of wind.

The sarcasm wasn't lost on Mark, but he ignored it. It was already after three p.m. and he was sure they'd entered the window of time when the bomb might blow. The sun had eased out from behind the clouds, offering little warmth, but the added light matched more closely the angle he'd seen in his dream.

His heart galloped in his chest, and when a cab driver honked at them, Mark jumped. Hoping to cover the movement, he thwacked Dan's arm with the envelope. "Come on, I'll show you." Mark led the detective to the spot beneath the girder affording the best angle. Nothing had changed. He pointed up. "There it is."

Dan squinted. "The photos gave a better view." He turned in place, regarding the businesses and foot traffic, and waved his hand to indicate the area. "This is all going to have to be evacuated."

"So you think it's a bomb, too?" While relieved to have someone in authority believe him finally, his pulse quickened. There was nothing like standing below a bomb to make the heart race.

"I don't know, but if it is, better to be prepared, right?" He paused in his assessment to level a look at Mark. "What time frame are we looking at here?"

Mark gave a non-committal shrug. "Anytime now, but--."

Dan cut in, "For someone who could be blown up any second, you sure seem awfully calm."

Mark glared. "I was *going* to say, that in the dream, the sun was a little lower and more people were around. If I had to guess, I'd say the explosion goes off around five p.m. The height of rush hour." His nerves were beyond frayed after spending the day trying to find the bomb himself.

Dan didn't look convinced, but his focus shifted to something over Mark's shoulder. "My buddy's here."

Mark faced the approaching man. He appeared to be in his early forties, but his wiry build and the bounce in his step revealed an energy that gave a younger impression.

His dark eyes assessed Mark for a moment before he stuck out his hand. "Thomas Oakes."

Clasping with a firm grip, he said, "Mark Taylor. Thank you for taking the time, Thomas. I appreciate it." Oakes exuded an aura of no-nonsense confidence.

Acknowledging Mark with a short nod, his gaze moved to Dan. "If this is for real, time is of the essence." He shot a look around. "Where is the suspicious substance?"

Mark withdrew the photos from the envelope and handed them over. "Here's a photo. I zoomed in on it to give a better view." He pointed to the nest above them. "And there's the nest."

Thomas craned his neck and circled beneath the tracks, his mouth set in a firm line. He shuffled through the images and squinted at the girder, tossing a glance at Dan. "I can't say for sure what it is. It could be just a piece of debris caught in an old nest, but the color is right for plastic explosives and something about that nest is wrong. It looks too new. Too perfect, especially for this time of year." He pointed and said, "See how the sticks are all smoothly intertwined? This late in the season, the nest would have been up for months. It should be ragged." He paused, still studying the nest. Finally, he nodded. "I've got a gut-feeling. I say we get some more of my people down here to investigate."

Mark was too relieved to feel smug at the surprised expression on Dan's face.

Things moved quickly after that. No longer needed, but not sure if he should just leave, Mark moved his car a few blocks away per Dan's instruction to get it the hell out from under the track. By the time he walked the few blocks back, a barrier had already been placed on the street preventing traffic from entering the area. Police swarmed the site, doing their best to deal with irate commuters who found themselves with no way home from work. Although there was a lot of grumbling, most people were more curious than angry or scared, but that caused problems for the cops trying to clear the street.

Soon, news vans swarmed and helicopters circled. Too far back to spot Dan or Thomas, and unable to get through the blockade, Mark called Dan's cell number. There was no answer. Mark swore under his breath while waiting for the greeting to finish so he could leave a brief message for Dan to return his call. Hopefully, he was just too busy to answer right now and he would call back when he got a chance.

A cop approached the crowd loitering around the barrier, ordering them to leave the area. For a second, Mark contemplated bolting past the officer to find Dan and Thomas, but he decided against it. Dan would update him soon. Besides, the local news would probably have the information Mark needed. He returned to his car and headed for home.

Traffic was snarled with detours around the evacuated streets. He dialed in a news-radio station, his fingers drumming the steering wheel as he waited for traffic to move. He repeatedly checked the view out of his passenger window, expecting to see a plume of black smoke any second. The radio announcer reported that the bomb-squad was at the site, but that an unnamed source was worried about their ability to defuse the bomb. Wedged as it was high in the girders, they were having a hard time getting a good look at it. Mark breathed deeply, picturing Thomas Oakes being blown to bits and shuddered. Logically, he knew if something happened, it wasn't his fault, but if one of those bomb squad people died, he'd always know that they would have lived if he hadn't interfered. Others would have died instead. He mentally clutched at that rationale. Thomas Oakes had chosen his line of work knowing the danger it entailed.

Mark slammed his hand on the wheel. It sucked. So many things could go wrong, and he could drive himself crazy thinking of all the possibilities. He had to get his mind off the doomsday track. His stomach growled, and he almost ignored it in favor of getting home but decided getting something to eat would serve two purposes; filling his stomach and diverting his thoughts. A sandwich shop was just ahead, and he knew his kitchen cupboards were down to slim pickings. He swung the car into the parking spot in front of the shop and ran in. A line had formed and as he read the menu board, he couldn't help overhearing the chatter of other customers. Some thought the bomb threat was a hoax perpetrated by someone in city government. Mark tried not to roll his eyes and instead, selected a sandwich.

Holding the bag of food, Mark stepped out of his van and craned his neck to the sky. No smoke. A spark of hope ignited in his chest. If the bomb was going to blow, it should done so by now. He unlocked the studio and rushed up the steps from his office to his loft.

Grabbing the clicker, he turned the TV on as he passed, tossing the remote on the couch as he passed through to the kitchen. Beer or Coke? He hesitated. He was sure Dan or someone would show up to ask more questions, but he shrugged. After the day he'd had, the beer won out. The channel was on commercial, a good sign. If there had been an explosion, commercials would have been skipped by the network. The beer made a satisfying pop when he opened it, a curl of vapor escaping as he tilted the bottle and took a long swig. Mark sighed and wiped his mouth with the back of his hand.

A slice of turkey fell from his sandwich onto the paper, and he scooped it back onto the bread, almost missing when the news came back on and speculated on how the bomb was discovered. Shaking his head at their faulty theories, he chewed, amused, as they interviewed people in the crowd who said they'd seen a suspicious man lurking around the area. The descriptions varied, although he recognized a few as possibly being himself. Good thing he'd gone to Dan about this or it might have been hard to explain.

Mark choked down a bite of his sandwich when one woman gave a description of a man who could have been Mohommad.

He tossed the remains of his sandwich onto the paper and rubbed his hands on his thighs as he searched for a pen. Spotting one on the end table, he snatched it and jotted down the woman's name, Linda Mercer, as it appeared on the screen.

By the time he was done, the reporter on the street was talking once again to the newscaster at the studio.

His cell phone rang and he answered without taking his eyes off the screen, worried he'd miss something. " Hello?"

"Sorry I didn't get back to you sooner, Mark."

Jessie. He'd been so busy, he'd forgotten about her promise to call. "Are you watching the news?"

"Not yet, but I heard about it at work. I'm on my way to the site now. I wasn't sure I'd get to go, being so new and all, so I'm psyched."

Mark smiled at the energy in her voice even if it felt wrong that an event like this would be considered an exciting day of work. "What have you heard? Have they positively identified it?"

Jessie hesitated, "I'm not supposed to give out information."

Mark felt his jaw drop, but he couldn't seem to snap it shut. "Seriously?" He thumped his chest. "*I'm* the one who found it. I think I'm entitled to a little information."

"I know. I'm sorry, Mark. I can't talk yet. If my superiors found out, I could lose my security clearances."

"Just a few weeks ago, I was able to call and speak directly to Jim, head honcho of the Chicago field office. Now, I can't even get confirmation from anyone that what I found was an actual explosive."

After an awkward pause, Mark almost hung up, but at the last second, Jessie said, "It was. I'll tell you that much."

He blew out a big breath. "Thank you, Jess."

The rest of the evening, more news trickled out. Mark stretched out on the couch, flipping between the five local news channels, and occasionally turning to a national station. The incident had received only brief coverage at the national level. If the bomb hadn't been safely defused, he was sure it would have been the leading story. Instead, the talking heads debated who was responsible with the top candidates being al-Qaeda or any number of U.S. based groups who had grudges.

Mark suspected Mo but had no proof. If Mark still had the camera, would he have had the same dream? Did the user of the camera influence the photos? He'd always suspected some kind of connection, determining that he'd had some kind of association with at least one person who had ever been in the resulting photos. For the most part, they were vague connections, mere acquaintances, but Jim had shown up in the Wrigley Field incident.

Mark tuned out the newscasters' babble as he tried to piece together the magic that was the camera. When Jessie had used it while Mark had been in the prison, she'd developed photos of him undergoing interrogation.

If his theory was correct, the people who had appeared in his recent dreams would have some kind of connection to whoever was using the camera.

CHAPTER TWELVE

All Mohommad had to do was have the whole device ready to go. Yesterday, he had scouted the site and used Mark's camera to take pictures. The resulting images of a destroyed track and a train smashed onto the road below gave him a moment of relief, but he wasn't going to trust it completely. Not with something this important.

The test shots had shown accidents that had later shown up on the news to have actually occurred. Mohommad was reasonably sure the camera was showing the future.

He knew he shouldn't feel pride, but it had been his idea to use a bird's nest to hide the explosives. Instead of pride, he should be giving thanks for receiving the idea. Mohommad bowed his head in remorse at his sin. His idea hadn't come without problems. A real bird's nest wasn't strong or stable enough to use, but fake ones were easily had at craft stores and were designed to last longer than a season.

The hardest part had been attaching it to the girders, but he had once again felt pride at how well he had designed it. The explosives, with the timer embedded, had been packed into the nest. One side of the nest had been cut away to leave it flat, and he'd cut a portion of a net from a fishing net to hold the nest and form a cradle. He even put some old leaves and grass inside the net, letting it hang out to give a raggedy appearance of an old nest and to camouflage the netting. Then, he fed the fishing line through the netting at the top and spooled out about twenty feet of line before cutting it. The cut end he tied to large weighted washers.

The only thing left to do was find the girder and toss the washers over a girder, use double-sided clear tape against the flat edge of the nest to keep it from moving, and hoist it up to the girder. The hard part was pushing it securely against the wall, but he'd come prepared with a telescoping flagpole, the end wrapped so it wouldn't puncture the nest, and used it to push the nest firmly against the girder.

Between the tape, he tossed the washer around the beam several more times before using gray duct tape to secure it to the base of the girder. He disguised the tape with dirt and black grease.

He'd accomplished the whole feat in less than five minutes, and at three in the morning, traffic was non-existent. That had been his biggest worry.

This morning, he'd strolled under the track to see how it looked in daylight and even snapped a couple of quick pictures as proof of his accomplishment.

* * *

Nobody paid Mohommad the slightest attention as he crossed at the four-way stop. The neighborhood was older with lots of trees and large homes that if rehabbed, would have been beautiful, but instead, paint peeled and weeds jutted from cracks in the driveways. It wasn't a slum, but a majority of the houses were sub-divided into apartments. He'd chosen the area because it was a great place to hide. Nobody knew their neighbors.

He carried the pizza across the street and up to his second floor apartment over a laundromat. The tantalizing scent of pizza escaped the paper wrapper and his mouth watered. He'd missed good pizza, among other dishes, and while he was back in the States, he was indulging in his favorites.

He set his dinner on the rickety kitchen table, peeling back the now greasy paper and taking a slice. It had just come from the oven, and cheese stretched a foot before snapping to curl around his hand. The heat stung for a moment, but Mo didn't care. Pulling the cheese off, he popped it in his mouth, then blew on the square in his hand. The aroma was killing him, but he resolutely set the slice on a paper plate, added a couple more slices, and snagged a bottle of water from the fridge, carrying it all to the couch.

Balancing the plate on his lap while he ate, he wedged the water bottle between the cushion and the side of the couch. He didn't want to chance getting grease or water on the photos from Mark's camera. The envelope containing them lay on the coffee table. He had gone through them over a dozen times already, still marveling at the magic of seeing a print of a scene that hadn't yet occurred.

He polished off the slices and washed them down with several gulps of water. It was the first meal he'd eaten all day because he'd been too keyed up waiting for the news of the explosion to eat anything.

After developing the film last night, he had slept well. Better than he had in months and better than he'd expected. The camera had afforded him a measure of assurance that his plan worked. Or *would* work. He grinned and took a bite of pizza. The whole timeline still confused him, but one thing he was sure of, there had been no train lying on the street when he'd taken the photos.

Mohommad grasped the edges of the envelope and let the photos slide out, careful not to smudge any with his greasy fingers. His heart jolted. The photos had changed. Hands shaking, unmindful of smears, he spread them across the table.

Last night, the photos had shown a train car lying on its side, a second car dangling off the destroyed tracks. Smoke and debris had hidden the bodies from the camera lens, but they had been there. He was sure of it. He sifted through all six photos, then shoved the coffee table on its side. Slumped on the edge of the sofa, he propped his elbows on his knees and rested his head on his hands. What had happened? He had already proclaimed the mission a success based on the photos. Why wouldn't he? He'd had proof. The test shots had shown accidents that had occurred, and he'd confirmed them with news reports.

Mohommad shook his head, already hearing the scorn in his uncle's voice. His uncle expected victims. Lots of them. For him, every death was a blow against the U.S., but Mohommad preferred to count the terror as the true victory. One person or a thousand, it was all the same as far as Americans were concerned. It was the fact that terrorists could succeed that frightened them. It was the not knowing the when or where. If Uncle's associates only knew how Americans thought, they would spend more time disrupting their daily routines with small hits, rather than large, showy ones. The photos showed the tracks and the street beneath swarming with law enforcement personnel instead of littered with bodies. Obviously, the bomb had been discovered, but how? And by whom?

Mohommad tried to convince himself it was still a victory of sorts. He'd disrupted the daily routine of thousands of people, and no doubt, instilled some fear. He'd been Americanized by the time he was ten and remained so for twenty years. The best way to terrorize Americans was to keep them off-balance, to keep them always wondering if *this* would be the day, or *that* would be the train.

His uncle and his group back in Afghanistan wouldn't see it that way though. No deaths equaled failure.

The pizza churned in his stomach. How could he explain his failure? This morning, the photos had still shown the carnage his bomb had wrought.

He'd been so sure of success, he'd already begun working on phase two of his plan--a quick second hit. While security would be increased in the days after the train bombing, it would be unorganized. It had been Mohommad's idea, and he remembered the pride that had swelled within him at the praise he'd received at the suggestion. A second hit so quickly would have Americans on edge. No one would be able to sleep at night.

Plans for the second phase were well underway, and Mohommad hoped he'd be able to pull it off now. Would his uncle even trust him to continue? A year of planning had gone into this two-phase operation. Just finding enough material to make a bomb had been challenging. The main ingredients were common, but the amount needed couldn't be bought all at once without raising red flags. It had taken months to create a network of suppliers, and every time he had to contact someone about a shipment, it created another weak link in the plan. One shipment had been disrupted, and it was only a matter of time before the feds untangled the web of connections and trace it back to him. He couldn't let all that time and money go to waste. For the first time, he had played a major role in an operation. It would have been his success, but now, it was his colossal failure.

Standing, he hunted for the remote that had been flung across the room when he'd overturned the table. Aiming it at the TV, he stabbed the power button and found a news channel.

It was the story of the day, and the news anchors displayed appropriate concern, but there was no fear and no hysteria, only that a bomb had been found and safely disarmed.

The scene being shown had a reporter in front of a barrier at least a block from the L station. Police swarmed the area behind her, but the video offered no clues as to what had happened.

How had the bomb been found? He'd been sure the fake nest would be the perfect camouflage. His main concern had been that it might go off at the wrong time or that the detonator would fail. If he watched long enough, details would emerge, but he wanted them now. He clicked over to another channel. The one thing he could count on with American news was the fierce competition to break an exclusive story. If there was a hero out there, one of them would find him or her.

The bomb had to have been discovered this morning sometime after he had looked at the photos. At least, he thought that was how it worked. He should have pressed Mark for more information on the camera.

A bitter laugh bubbled up as he wondered how Mark would react if he called him and asked for pointers. Mohommad tried to recall everything the interrogator had said a few years ago when he'd ridiculed Mark and his 'magical' camera.

In his head, he saw it all clearly. He'd been chained to a chair and the man, his interrogator, had strolled around the chair, forcing Mohommad to crane his neck to keep an eye on him. The officer had casually recounted Mark's claims. He had even chuckled at some point, trying to draw Mohommad in as though they shared an amusing secret. It stood out because the interrogator had been so stern during the whole session, it had come as a shock when he had cracked a smile. The amusement stemmed from a mention of dreams. Something about Mark claiming to dream about the images and how he'd then try to change them if bad things happened to the subjects of the dreams.

Mohommad remembered that part because only a prophet would dream of future events and Mark was not a prophet. He was an infidel and incapable of prophetic dreams.

Flicking through more channels, all he could discern was that a pedestrian had spotted something not quite right about a bird's nest and had contacted authorities. The police detective investigating had immediately seen the risk and called in the bomb squad resulting in a block radius being evacuated.

Mohommad scoffed at the self-congratulatory attitude displayed by the Chicago chief of police when he gave the reporter a few sound bites about how his officers had been so observant and vigilant. Yeah, right. He shook his head. It had been pure luck. That's all. Pure. Dumb. Luck.

He sank onto the edge of the couch as the reporter shoved a microphone into a tall man's face.

"Detective, we understand that you made the first call. How did you discover the bomb?"

At first the detective tried to evade the reporter but finally, he gave a sly smile at the camera and said, "I dreamed it. While I was sleeping a little birdie came and showed me the bomb."

The reporter laughed, but Mohommad could tell she wasn't happy with the flip response. Like a flashbulb in his head, it hit him. Dreams. The detective hadn't dreamed it--Mark had. Mohommad, if he were a betting man, would have staked his life on it. It fit in with everything he recalled. It didn't make Mark a prophet, it meant that Satan had sent the dream to him in an attempt to thwart Allah's plan.

He grabbed the camera, ready to smash it to smithereens, but stopped. Instead, he glanced at his watch. There was still one more train into the city if he hurried. He dug into the back of his closet for his handgun, checked to make sure it was loaded, and slipped it into his coat pocket. *Let's see if the camera can provide a future photo of its former owner.*

CHAPTER THIRTEEN

The second beer and the profound relief that the disaster had been averted, combined with his exhaustion, left Mark dozing on the couch by eight p.m. He awoke suddenly. Disoriented and unsure what had awakened him, he glanced at his watch. He'd been sleeping at least an hour but it felt like longer. Dragging his hand down his face, he rubbed his eyes and tried to smother a yawn. The phone rang, and he dimly realized that it was what had woken him up in the first place.

Standing, he stumbled over one of his shoes, cursing under his breath as he ambled to the kitchen counter where he had dumped his keys and phone. The thought that it might be Jessie perked him up. She'd probably be off work about now, especially since the bomb had been defused. He didn't recognize the number but flipped the phone open.

"Hello?"

"What's up, Mark?"

Mark stilled. "Mo?" The way Mo had addressed him sounded exactly as he would have four years ago when they had still been friends--as if he was calling to see if Mark wanted to go have a beer. He shook off the nostalgia. This was a different man now. "How the hell did you get my cell phone number?"

"It was easy. You left your cell phone bill on your kitchen counter. I saw it when Hazim and I took a little tour of your loft. By the way, your girlfriend is stunning. At least, I assume she's your girlfriend, from the pose and all. Anyway, I simply wrote it down. I knew it could come in handy someday."

"You're real clever, Mo." A car horn blasted outside, creating a stereo effect when it sounded through the phone a millisecond later. Mark rushed to the window. Orange hued street-lights cast garish shadows on the street below, but if Mo was down there, he wasn't in plain sight. "Where are you?"

Mo chuckled. "I expect you heard that. Blasted driver. I imagine you've guessed I'm just outside your studio, but I won't be for long, so don't bother calling the police. All I want is to return the camera to you. It's no good to me. Not if you're going to dream what happens and change it anyway."

Mark took a deep breath and tried to play it cool, ignoring the comment about the dreams. "Yeah? You had a stab of conscience or something?" He cupped a hand against the window. *Shit.* Nothing. If he had the encrypted phone, he could have called Jim while keeping Mo on the line. Even if Jim was out of town, he'd have notified someone. Mark had accepted that he wasn't important, but Mohommad was a different story. He was a wanted man, and if they caught him, chances are they'd be able to connect him to the attempted bombing of the 'L' track.

"In a way, you're right. I do feel guilty and I'm not here to harm you, but only to make things right. To do that, I need to return this directly to your hands."

Mark let out a bitter laugh. "Well forgive me if I don't believe you." He turned, leaning a shoulder against the window as he attempted to see the area right beneath his windows. "Where's your buddy? Is he hiding along the wall?"

"I'm alone. I'm truly sorry for what happened before, Mark. Please, just allow me to return this. It is what I must do."

"You must think I'm crazy. I'll tell you what I'm going to do. I'm gonna hang up and call the police. How's that sound? If you want to leave the camera, fine, but I sure as hell am not coming down there to get it." Mark snapped the phone shut. His first instinct was to rush down to the street, find Mo and beat the living hell out of him, but his rational side took command and he followed through with his threat to call the police.

Two minutes later, he hung up, but anger and frustration built inside of him like fizz inside a dropped can of beer. The dispatcher had assured him they'd send a car to look around, but she was sorry. With no threat and no actual sighting of Mohommad, there wasn't much they could do. He'd tried explaining how Mo was wanted by the FBI, but she didn't seem to get it.

Next, he called the FBI, because Mark figured he was still a concerned citizen even if he wasn't an asset to anyone. After all, Mo had to be pretty high on the wanted list. He'd been an enemy combatant, after all, and banned from ever returning to the U.S. The fact that he was here should be cause enough to suspect him for the attempted bombing. He sat on the arm of the sofa, feet braced on the floor, drumming the leather as he waited to be connected to an agent. After a maze of re-directs, his call was finally answered by an agent who took Mark's information down and thanked him for the tip.

Afterward, Mark stared at his phone in disbelief. Where was the urgency? Didn't anyone care? Sure, he knew they were probably swamped trying to track down leads from the train thing, but didn't they realize there could be a connection? He shoved his phone in his pocket and strode to the windows again. The street was all but deserted. The brief nap had served to take the edge off his weariness, and Mohommad's call had left him too keyed up to sleep.

Mark noticed a police car cruising down the street towards his building. At least the cops were taking his call seriously. He shoved his feet into his shoes and grabbed a jacket, shrugging into it as he raced down the steps, hoping the cop hadn't passed already. He flung open the front door of the studio and raised his hand to flag down the officer. A sudden blast of light flashed in his face. Raising his hands, he stepped back, blinking. The sound of a camera being wound to the next frame came to him an instant before a second burst of light scorched his eyes.

"Hey!" Even as he squinted and rubbed his eyes, he knew what had happened. Mohommad had taken his picture with the camera. It had been an old fashioned flashbulb. He recognized the distinctive pop and hot scent of burning plastic. His camera had a place to screw in flashbulbs, but he'd rarely used it.

Footsteps sounded on the pavement racing around the corner of the building. Mark turned to give chase when the whoop of a police siren followed by blue flashers made him hesitate. Running from a police car was never a good idea, even if it was to give chase to the bad guy. Swallowing down his impatience, he approached the car, now parked against the curb and facing the wrong direction.

Mark motioned down the alley. "Officer, I'm the one who called about the man wanted by the FBI. He just ran around the back."

The cop rolled his window down a crack. "Step away from the vehicle, please."

"Oh, sure." Mark retreated as the officer climbed out of the car. He shot a glance to the mouth of the alley and sidled a few steps in that direction. "He's getting away. Aren't you going to go after him?"

The police officer glanced towards the alley, but made no move towards it. "Are you trying to tell me how to do my job?"

Mark bit back a sigh. "No, sir. I'm just concerned because the man I reported was just here."

"Did he threaten you in any way?"

"Not this time, but he's in the country illegally."

The cop chuckled and shook his head. "I'm not immigration, buddy."

"You don't understand--he's not an illegal alien--he's a...a..." Mark paused, unsure of the term to use. "Listen, he's a dangerous man. He was affiliated with al-Qaeda, and was *banned* from this country."

The cop cocked his head, a smirk twisting his mouth. "Really?"

It was on the tip of Mark's tongue to mention Mo's previous attack the week before, but the incident hadn't been reported. Even if he did tell them, there was no proof except what Jim had collected, and Jim had to be the one to offer that to the police.

His first fear was for his parents. Mo had threatened them, and Mark had no doubt he'd follow through. He should have never called the cops. It would only make things worse.

Mark spread his hands. "You know what? It's all a mistake. A friend and I had a disagreement, and in the heat of the moment, I called the police." He let his head dip, feigning chagrin. "We laughed it off before you pulled up, and I felt stupid for having called you so, I made up the terrorist thing. I'm sorry for taking up your time." He forced a smile.

The cop rolled his eyes in disgust and said something into his shoulder mic. "I could cite you for this, but I'll let you by with a warning because I have another call." He shook his finger in Mark's face. "Remember--emergencies only."

That night, Mark dreamed. He was the star this time. Unlike his usual dreams that showed the future, this one felt more like a nightmare. His encounter with Mo the week before and the police officer from the evening merged into a nightmare. Before he could process it, the nightmare morphed into a future dream. The edges sharpened, becoming a film playing on his personal mental screen.

Mark watched the dream aware that he was sleeping, but seeming to exist on another plane, as though in two places at once. He felt the bite of the handcuffs on his wrists and the ache in his bad shoulder when a Chicago police officer brought him to his feet by jerking up on his restrained arms. Fear, cold and heavy, grew in the pit of his stomach when the cop read the charges against him. Possession of a destructive device. Intent to use an explosive device. Transporting an explosive device. Each charge was a like bomb going off in his mind.

The worst part was seeing Jessie. She hadn't been the one to cuff him, thank God, but she was there, watching from the hallway. As he was led past her, she mouthed what looked like, 'Don't worry,' but it gave him little comfort because her gaze shifted when he tried to make eye contact.

Hot shame flooded his face, burning his cheeks. She didn't want to let on that she even knew him, let alone that they had been in love. Hell, Mark was *still* in love with her. Would they let him explain? Would he ever get out this time?

CHAPTER FOURTEEN

Mark bolted awake, his heart pounding like the surf before a hurricane. They were coming for him today. His eyes darted to the clock. Five a.m. He rubbed his temples as he tried to recall the important details. They had burst in while he was doing a shoot. An engaged couple. The appointment book would tell him when that was scheduled. He shot out of bed and tore down the steps to the office.

He traced his finger down the page of the book. Eleven a.m. He blew out a breath and raked his hand through his hair. There was still time. He needed a plan.

First, he had to get away from here before they came for him. Would they have someone watching the building? Between living with Jessie, and hanging out with Jim, he'd learned a little over the last year or so, and he decided they'd be keeping an eye on him, but probably only one agent. Jim had complained once about not having enough agents to keep track of Chicago's virtual cornucopia of criminals, from terrorists and organized crime, to the random kidnapers and the occasional bank robber.

If he left soon, he could probably slip by undetected if he walked the opposite way down the alley, and onto the next street. By traveling back alleys for several blocks, he could hop on a bus and disappear in the city and take public transportation to a far flung suburb. Which one, he wasn't sure.

His goal wasn't just to escape capture, but he needed to find Mo and find the camera. With the camera back in his possession, he could prove its magical capabilities again. He could even have an agent take a photo and Mark could give him a description of what the resulting pictures would reveal. They'd have to believe him then when he told them that is how he knew about the train bombing attempt.

Jim would back him up and Jessie, well, he didn't know where she fit into it all. She'd been there in his dream, and he knew she wouldn't have had any role in his arrest other than just being assigned to assist, but his feelings were too complicated and he didn't have time to dissect them. If he didn't hurry, he'd have the rest of his life to pick his feelings apart nerve cell by nerve cell as he rotted away in the brig.

He stripped and jumped in the shower. It was tempting to skip it and flee but the stale stench of fear clung to him from his dream. As he soaped up, his mind raced, darting off in different directions. Settle down. *Think.*

Money. He'd need money. After being arrested as an enemy combatant and returning to find all his accounts frozen, he'd taken to keeping cash in several stashes throughout his loft and studio. Never again would they take him unprepared. He even kept a box in the woodshed behind his parents' house.

It was cold enough to dress in layers without attracting too much attention. He could change his look by simply removing the sweater or button-down. Mark wished he could pack a bag, but was worried it would slow him down. He grabbed a baseball cap out of his closet. It wasn't much but it would offer at least a little concealment. Next, he retrieved the money. Three stashes of five hundred each. Another thousand was at his parents. Well, he'd have to go there anyway to warn them about Mohommad. He didn't dare use his phone as he was positive they would have put a tap on it.

He stuffed the cash in various pockets. His dad had given him a Leatherman for Christmas, probably hoping Mark would go hunting with him again soon, but it had sat untouched in his nightstand drawer. The gadget was practically a whole tool box loaded into a pocketknife and could come in handy. If nothing else, he wouldn't be totally defenseless.

Standing in the middle of the loft, he patted his pockets as he took inventory. Money. Leatherman. Wallet. Keys. His eye fell on a bowl of fruit on his kitchen counter. Food. He'd need to eat and might have to do it on the go. There were always convenience stores or fast food, but those places all had security cameras. The fewer he had to frequent, the better off he'd be. He scrounged around his cupboard and found a couple of granola bars, and a handful of snack packs of crackers and cheese. Not much, but along with the two bananas he ate as he prepared, they'd hold him until he could find something more substantial.

Mark gave a last look around his home. Would this be the final time he'd see it? Would he ever sleep in his own bed again? A lump rose in his throat but he forced it down. Time was wasting. As ready as he'd ever be, he crept down the stairs to the studio. A sliver of lighter sky could be seen out the east window. His cover slid over the horizon with every tick of the clock.

He eased the back door open and scanned the alley. It appeared clear. As quietly as possible, he crept along the side, keeping close to the shadows of the buildings. His toe connected with a beer bottle, sending it skittering under a dumpster with a dull clink. Mark flattened against the wall, his pulse thundering in his ears as the blood rushed through him. When no cry of alarm sounded, he let out a deep breath and continued to the far end. So far, so good.

The cross street had little traffic at this time of morning, and he dashed across without incident to where the alley continued on the other side. He was less concerned with sound now, and increased his pace. After five blocks, he deemed it safe to walk on the street and hailed a cab to take him to the bus station.

Mark rubbed his hands on his thighs as the cab sped through the streets. Only a few pedestrians dotted the sidewalks and he was glad he had decided on the cab. Not only was it faster, but there was less chance of being spotted. He wished he'd had time to check the bus schedules. The only time he'd taken a bus to his parents was right after his release from prison. There had been no need to hurry then, but he thought he remembered there had been an earlier one scheduled as well as the mid-morning one he had taken. If he was right, he could make it to his folks' house before anyone even knew he was gone. If not, he'd have to take one somewhere else and backtrack, but by then, the FBI would probably already have his parents' house under surveillance.

Mark tried to keep his head down as much as possible as he crossed the bus station and bought a ticket. Eventually someone would check to see if he'd taken a bus, and they'd spot him on a security tape, but he wanted to make it as difficult as possible for them to identify him. He almost sagged in relief when he found out the next bus left in just fifteen minutes and was a direct route.

The other travelers paid no attention to him, most settling in to nap for the duration. After a half hour, he reclined in his seat and closed his eyes, but sleep wouldn't come. Adrenaline still rushed through his veins, and so he used the time to plan his course of action.

Finding Mohommad was the objective; the only problem was he had no idea where to look. Mark searched his memories. Mo had a sister and Mark had even been to her house one time. She lived somewhere out by O'Hare. Park Ridge? Or was it Schaumburg? He concentrated, trying to remember. The towns all ran one into the other, and he got them mixed up all the time, but was almost certain it was Schaumburg.

In his mind's eye, he saw an invitation she'd sent him for a surprise 30th birthday party for Mo. He recalled getting lost and turned around, but had eventually found the house. When he'd left, he'd found an easier route to the expressway. It had been at least five years, but he was sure he could find her house again unless she'd moved.

He must have dozed because the next thing he knew, the bus stopped and he shot up in the seat and looked around in blind panic. It took him a moment to realize the other passengers were gathering their belongings together or making their way to the front of the bus. Mark glanced out the window.

They were here already. He stood and twisted his neck, working out a kink while he waited his turn to disembark. Outside the bus, he debated hitchhiking or taking a cab to his parents. It would cost a bit and the cabbie would likely remember him but hitchhiking wasn't a guaranteed ride, and walking ten miles would eat up a lot of time. He opted for a cab and hurried to the cab stand before they were all taken by other passengers.

His luck held and twenty minutes later, the cab dropped him off in front of his parents' house. He glanced at his watch. Any minute, the FBI would be arriving at his studio and find him gone. His head start had vanished.

* * *

The last flowers of the season lined the flower beds and it looked like his dad had put a fresh coat of paint on the porch railings since he'd last been up to the house. That had been around early June. Mark had just recovered from the attack by Kern and his followers and his visit had been unsettling. His mother had doted on him, but he could see the hurt in her eyes that he hadn't called them. The fact that they were away on a cruise during the worst of it wasn't a good reason. He'd tried to explain his mixed up feelings, his shame and how he'd just wanted to forget it all, but eventually, he'd apologized.

Surprisingly, his father had been on Mark's side, understanding his need to work things out in his head, and other than asking him to call home if something like that ever happened again, so his mom wouldn't get the news from the papers, he'd not said anymore about it, which was fine with Mark. They had worked in the wood shop in the basement with Mark helping his dad build a new bench.

The scent of burning leaves on the crisp air triggered memories of apple picking and trick or treating. All were simple pleasures which seemed foreign now. He climbed the steps, and smiled to see the bench now painted white and sporting a bright yellow cushion. Crossing to it, he skimmed a hand over the wood. It felt smooth and solid under his fingers. Solid and clean. It would last a long time.

The screen door creaked. "Mark! You about scared me half to death!"

Mark turned as his mom moved towards him, her arms outstretched. He moved into her embrace and kissed her cheek. "Hi, Mom. Sorry I didn't call first. It was last minute, and I didn't have time." He closed his eyes as he gave her an extra squeeze. The scent of cinnamon and coffee clung to her. That meant one thing. Fresh cinnamon rolls.

"Goodness, Mark." She smiled and skimmed her hand down his cheek. "It's always good to see you, whether you call or not. I was just on my way out to the shed to get your father."

"I'll get him if you save me the biggest cinnamon roll."

"Cinnamon roll?" She tilted her head, hands on her hips. "How did you know?"

Mark grinned and sniffed.

She laughed and ran her hand down his arm, hanging onto his hand for a moment. "For a second there, I thought maybe one of my cinnamon rolls ended up as a picture from your camera."

The corners of her mouth turned down. "Oh, hon. I forgot. Have you heard anything from that Mohommad guy?"

He ducked his head, scuffing his toe against a small bit of dried mud stuck to the porch. "No. Not yet." Now wasn't the time to tell her. It would be better to tell both his parents at once.

"Go on. I'll save you the pick of the litter. Your dad shouldn't be eating them anyway." She returned to the house, the screen door slamming closed behind her, but not before letting more of the tantalizing aroma escape.

If only he could freeze time and stay in this moment right here on his parents' front porch forever. If only he could pretend that this was a normal visit. If only.

Hands shoved in his jacket pockets, he trudged down the steps and around the corner to the shed. Already he could smell the sharp tang of fresh cut wood. He picked up a small branch that had fallen from the maple tree and threw it boomerang style at the trunk of the tree. It hit with a satisfying *thwack.*

His steps slowed from a trudge to a shuffle as he approached the woodshed. He searched his mind for a good excuse to send his dad into the house first so he could retrieve the box and get the cash. All he needed was a couple of minutes to work the container from behind the loose board beneath the workbench. The whine of a circular saw interrupted his thoughts and he entered the shed just as half of a two-by-four hit the floor with a thump.

His dad was examining the end left in his hand, picking off a sharp edge that remained. He lifted protective goggles, shoving them up on top of his head as he squinted at the board. Apparently satisfied, he blew the sawdust off it, his gaze rising to meet Mark's. If he was surprised, he hid it well.

"Hi, Dad." His hands once again found his coat pockets.

"Hello, Mark." He gave the board one final scrutiny before tossing it in a pile of similar sized pieces of wood.

Mark looked from the pile to his dad. "What are you making?"

"A planter for your mother."

"Sounds nice. I bet she'll like it."

His dad shrugged. "Probably." He pulled the goggles off and set them on top of the workbench. "What brings you out here?"

Tipping his head towards the house, Mark said, "Cinnamon rolls. Mom said they were ready."

His dad broke into a grin. "Well, what are we waiting for?"

A few new projects occupied the back of the shed. A large chunk of wood cut in a single naturally-shaped slab rested against the wall. "Go ahead, Dad. I'll be right in. I just want to look at your new masterpieces."

He had tried to make it sound lighthearted, but knew he'd failed miserably when his dad made no move to leave. Instead, he simply brushed some sawdust off the front of his flannel shirt, not taking too much care as several shavings remained, standing out against the dark blue of the flannel.

"What's going on?"

Mark closed his eyes, letting his chin drop as he gathered his thoughts. It was no use putting it off. "You know my camera was stolen a few weeks ago, right?"

His dad leaned against the bench, his arms folded across his chest, and nodded.

"Well, I'm still getting the dreams, even without the camera, and I dreamed about an 'L' track bombing," Mark said.

"I wondered if you had a hand in stopping that."

A warm glow suffused Mark at the pride he heard in his dad's voice. Embarrassed, he shrugged and said, "I figured out where it might be and found it in time to warn the police. They did the hard part."

"So what's the problem?"

So much for the pride. Mark steeled his resolve to just get the truth out. It wouldn't become any easier if he put it off. He blew out a deep breath. "I had a dream last night that I was being arrested again. They said I had something to do with the bomb."

"And so you *ran*?" His dad pushed off the bench, his hands fisted on his waist.

Mark straightened, his muscles tensing. "I had no choice."

His dad sighed and turned, pulling open a drawer in the bench. "I suppose you came out here looking for this?" He withdrew the container and tossed it on top of the bench.

He should have known nothing would be safe from discovery in here. This was his father's domain--he knew every nook and cranny.

Mark simply nodded and reached for the container. "Yes. After the crap I've had to deal with the last few years, I thought it might be a good idea to have emergency funds in various places." He opened the container and withdrew the money, shoving it into his pocket. "One thing I learned from Kern, is that he had at least a half-dozen aliases. I didn't have time or connections to do that, but at least I was able to put aside some money."

"So what are we looking at? What kind of time frame? What do you need from me?"

To Mark's shock, his dad didn't sound angry, just concerned. Confused, he took his time to consider his reply. He'd been prepared to defend himself, not ask for help. "I...I don't really know." His confusion cleared and he shook his head. "Actually, Dad, I do know. I can't accept any help. That would only get you and Mom in trouble."

He wanted to add that it was enough that his father wanted to help, but the words lodged in his throat.

His dad cleared his throat, the sound loud in the small shed. "Come on into the house. At least say good-bye to your mother."

Mark met his father's eyes, wincing at the pain lurking--pain he'd caused. "I'm sorry."

His dad grasped him by the shoulder. "Don't you *dare* be sorry, Mark. That would mean you were sorry for saving those people on the train. Do you regret that?"

"Of course not."

"Then don't worry about it. You have to do what you have to do. Just remember, *you're* the good guy." He motioned for Mark to precede him out of the shed, sliding his arm to rest across Mark's shoulders.

The yellowed grass and the scattering of brown leaves became a wet blur as he walked with his father to the house. He didn't dare raise his head as his chest burned with emotion. This would be hard enough on his mom. He had to hold it together for her sake.

They stopped just before opening the door. His dad squeezed Mark's shoulder. "You okay?"

Sucking in a deep breath, he blinked hard and said, "Yeah. Fine."

"I was about to come searching for you guys." His mom entered the hallway leading from the front door back to the kitchen, wiping her hands on a dishtowel. "Gene, did you show him your newest project?"

"I did." His dad's arm fell from Mark's shoulders as he went ahead of Mark into the kitchen. He headed to the cupboard, pulling out three coffee mugs.

"It looks great, Mom. I noticed the bench out front too." Mark washed his hands, drying them on the towel his mom handed him. He ambled to the table, drawn by the scent emanating from the pan of rolls in the middle of it. Poking a finger at a roll, he popped his finger in his mouth and licked off the icing that clung to it.

"Oh that's right. Your father finished the bench a few weeks ago." She slid a plate in front of him, and he helped himself to the roll he'd already touched.

His dad brought coffee for all of them. Mark took a sip. The best he'd had in ages. The first bite of roll flooded his mouth with a burst of sweet vanilla frosting and cinnamon while filling his mind with memories of Christmas mornings. It was their tradition. No gifts could be opened until his mom popped the rolls she'd prepared the day before into the oven. As a child, he'd been so impatient, but the scent of them baking while they opened presents was indelibly intertwined in his Christmas memories.

His mom dabbed her mouth with a paper napkin and said, "Where's your car? I didn't notice it outside."

He shot a glance at his dad, who gave a slight nod. Mark took a sip of his coffee, stalling as he decided how to start the conversation. "Mom, there's something I have to tell you."

When he finished telling her, he took another gulp of his now lukewarm coffee as he attempted to ignore the tears in her eyes. "You and Dad should go somewhere. Take a trip. Mo threatened you guys, and if anything happened to either of you..." The coffee threatened to come back up as he imagined the worst happening to his parents. Mark's knee bounced as he gripped the coffee cup. He would find Mohommad first. That was all there was to it. And when he did, Mark vowed to make him pay for the hell he had put everyone through. His father's voice snapped him out of his fantasy of retribution.

"Norma, it'll be okay. This time, Mark has a chance to prove his innocence." His father reached for his mother's hand, holding it in between both of his.

She wiped her eyes, and then glared him. "This is wrong, Gene. How can they let the real terrorist waltz away and instead go after Mark? Instead of slapping handcuffs on him, they should be pinning medals to Mark's chest."

Standing, she snatched her hand away and gathered up the dirty plates, setting them in the sink with a crash that made Mark wince.

His dad sighed, shoved away from the table and crossed to where his mother stood at the sink. She stared out the window as she clutched the edge of the counter. He wrapped his arms around her from behind and rested his chin on top of her head. "It'll work out. I promise you."

Mark averted his gaze from the scene as a wave of guilt washed over him. He was close to drowning as he treaded water in an ocean of it. His dad promised his mother everything would be fine, but Mark knew better. When he was a kid, he thought his dad could fix everything, but he was grown now and knew his dad's limitations. This time, as much as his father might wish he could make everything better, he was even more powerless than Mark.

He glanced at the clock. It was noon. The longer he remained here, the more risk he took of capture. "I have to get going."

His parents turned to him, his mother's face streaked with tears, but she nodded. "Yes, you have to find that bastard, Mohommad."

Mark cracked a tiny smile at his mother's terminology. "Will you guys go somewhere? I don't know if I can focus if I'm worried about Mohommad paying a visit here."

"Don't worry. I've got my hunting rifles, and I'm still a damn good shot."

"He could break in during the night or something. What good is a rifle in close quarters?" The phone rang and his dad gave him a look of relief as he rushed to answer it, as though glad he had a good excuse to avoid the question. Mark turned to his mother. "Mom, talk some sense into him."

At first, she appeared as stubborn as his father, but she caved after a few moments. "Fine. We're not afraid of him though. I just can't say no when you look at me like that."

His dad strode back into the room. "Mark, you have bigger worries than Mohommad. That was Special Agent Sheridan, from the F.B.I. Isn't he the guy who—"

"Yeah, he's the interrogator from the brig," Mark cut in. He could sense his dad about to going off on a tangent and he needed to know why Jim called. "What did he want?"

"That's the thing. He didn't seem to want anything. Just said he was looking for you, and that we should let you know that."

Shit! Had they found him already? "Did he ask if you had seen me?"

His dad shook his head and rubbed the back of his neck. "No, that's what was so strange. I was prepared to lie, but he didn't ask me anything I had to lie about."

Was Jim trying to send a warning?

"I gotta get going." Mark pulled his mom into a hug, and planted a quick kiss on her cheek. "And you guys have to get out of here too. I'm just going to run up and get some of my things from my old room. I couldn't risk taking anything from my loft. I wanted to buy as much time as I could and hope they'll just think I'm out in the city somewhere. I guess my strategy didn't work."

His old backpack he used when hunting with his dad was in the closet, and he stuffed a change of clothes into it along with a sweatshirt. As he closed the dresser drawer, the empty spot from where the sweatshirt had been caught his eye. He quickly re-arranged the drawer so it didn't look like something had just been removed. Just in case the F.B.I. made a surprise visit here.

Next, he went to the bathroom and opened the linen closet and found the shaving kit he kept here and tossed it into the pack.

By the time he went downstairs, his parents had composed themselves. His mom handed him a brown bag. "Just sandwiches and cookies. I also wrapped up a couple of the rolls."

It was almost his undoing. He took the bag and pulled her close, burying his face in her neck. "Bye, Mom." He wanted to reassure her, but his throat closed up.

His dad stood beside them, and Mark turned to him, ready to shake hands, but his dad drew him into a quick hard hug, then thrust him at arm's length and shoved another bag at him. "Here."

The bag was heavy. Heavier than it should have been for the size. He unrolled the top and peered inside, his mouth dropping open as he realized what it held. A gun and a box of clips. He pushed the bag back into his dad's hands. "I can't take this." He stared at his father. "Where in the hell did you get a handgun? And why?"

"It doesn't matter where I got it. After that cult incident, I bought one in case one of those nuts came up here. Or some other nut."

"I can't shoot anyone, Dad."

"I'm not saying you should, but you already said that Mohommad threatened you with a gun. What are you going to do, just find him and ask him to give you the camera back, pretty please?"

Mark tried to ignore his dad's tone. His intentions were good. He attempted to force him to accept the bag back, but his father ignored it. "I don't know what I'm going to do yet, but if the FBI knows I'm armed, they'll probably shoot me on sight."

His dad blanched, but then shook his head and gripped Mark's shoulders. "Then, you can't let them find you. I can't let you face a terrorist unarmed. Last time, Mohommad let you go, but do you really think he'll do that again? He already has the camera, and he must know by now that you had a hand in preventing the bombing of the train track. Don't you understand, Mark? You are a liability." He released his grip, but stabbed a finger into Mark's chest. "You make the camera useless to Mohommad and whomever he works for, if every time they use it, you dream about their atrocities and try to prevent whatever they have planned."

Mark considered his dad's words. He was right. Reluctantly, he took the bag and buried it in the bottom of the backpack. "I hate to involve you any more than I already have, but do you think you could drop me off at the bus station?"

"Sure, but where will you go?"

Mark hesitated. It wasn't that he didn't trust his parents. He knew they would never betray him, but if confronted with either authorities or, god forbid, Mo, he thought it would be better for them to be able to claim innocence. "I can't tell you."

"Listen, Mark. If you get in trouble, nobody else in the world will have an inkling of where you are. You don't have to give me your whole itinerary, just a hint."

"Fine." He ran a hand through his hair and sighed. "I wish I had an itinerary, but I'm flying by the seat of my pants here, Dad. Mo had a sister in Schaumburg. If I can remember where her house is, I'll see if she's seen him or has any idea where he might be. They used to be close. I don't know what, if anything, she'll tell me, but it's my only lead." He thought for a moment and said, "I'll get one of those cheap cellphones and call you when I get a chance. It's the best I can do."

His dad nodded and reached into his front pocket, pulling out his key ring, pressing it into Mark's hand. "Take my car. We can use your mother's. In the meantime, I'll take your mom to your cousin Debbie's house, until this is resolved. She's been begging your mom to come and see the new baby. I'm coming back here though in case the F.B.I. or police stop by. I don't want it to look suspicious. I can handle Mo." His tone brooked no argument. "Call my cell phone. You know the number?"

Mark nodded.

His father rubbed his chin and switched topics. "The police may spot my car and I'm sure they'll put out an APB on it, but, it's a common make and model. You should make it back to Chicago with no problem. You're also in luck. I just filled it up yesterday. If you have to, just leave it in a parking lot somewhere."

Mark clenched the keys until the metal dug into his palm. He blinked hard and said, "Tell them I stole it, Dad. Promise me that. I don't want you getting in trouble for me."

"That's my worry, now get out of here."

CHAPTER FIFTEEN

Jim strode through the office, briefcase clutched in one hand, a tall black coffee in the other. He stifled a yawn, wishing he could have napped on the plane while taking the eight a.m. flight home from D.C, but a crying baby two rows over had made it impossible. Poor little guy kept tugging on his ears, so Jim couldn't be angry, but still, some rest would have been nice. He'd counted on the nap, in fact. He should have known better.

It was only mid-morning, but he felt like a tardy schoolboy, even if he did have an ironclad reason for coming in late to work. In fact, he wasn't supposed to be here at all. By rights, he was supposed to still be in D.C. attending several more meetings, but with the bombing attempt, he had requested permission to return to his office today.

If he had come back the same day as the 'L' train incident like he'd wanted to, he was convinced none of this would have happened. Instead, since everything had turned out okay in Chicago, he had been forced to remain and complete his business. The president himself had ordered a task force to see if the FBI and CIA could cooperate and join together to form a new unit that would oversee interrogations. Jim had been handpicked to be on the task force due to his experience in the CIA, interrogations, and now as head of the Chicago FBI. He had a unique perspective of both agencies, so he'd been required to remain. That didn't mean he didn't chafe at the order to stay in D.C. while his city was in danger.

That thought brought a brief smile to his face. Since when had he considered Chicago home? It had only been a few years, but he supposed he had more true connections here than he had anywhere since he was in college. He set his briefcase beside his desk and removed his jacket, draping it over the back of his chair before sitting. The task force stuff could wait. Peeling back the plastic on his coffee lid, he took a sip, savoring the rich taste and the heat. It was colder here than it had been in D.C. and he hadn't brought an overcoat. Walking out to the parking area at the airport for his car, the wind had been brutal.

A stack of papers was piled in the inbox, and he grimaced, but otherwise ignored them, checking his email instead.

His assistant knocked on his door. "Good morning, sir. I have your messages."

"Good morning, DeMarcus. Or what's left of the morning." Jim smiled and nodded to the inbox. "Looks like I'm going to busy for awhile."

"That's an understatement. I tried to weed through it and prioritize the stack for you." The young man held up the small pile of post-it notes. "Sorry to add to your workload." He entered and placed the pile on Jim's desk. "Also, Special Agent Bishop was by earlier looking for you. She said it was important. I told her you'd be busy all morning, but she said you'd want to hear the news from her."

"What news?"

"I'm sorry, sir. She wouldn't tell me."

Jim sighed. "Okay. Call her for me and tell her I can see her in about thirty minutes. That should give me time to at least read through my email." He waved a hand at his stack of work. "A few minutes won't make much difference."

DeMarcus nodded and left.

Jim pinched the bridge of his nose. It was going to be a long day and the few hours of sleep he caught on the plane had done little to prepare him. Already, a nagging headache had set up shop between his eyes. What could Jessica want? If she was just coming to give him a hard time about Mark being cut loose, he didn't have the patience for it today. She was new here, so he'd cut her some slack, but it surprised him that she would try to take advantage of their friendship to get in to see him during working hours. If others saw her jumping over heads to speak directly to him, it wouldn't sit well with her immediate supervisors.

His email inbox was full, of course. He skimmed the correspondence. Most had to do with the bomb, mostly congratulatory memos about preventing an attack and tragedy. When were they going to learn that preventing one wasn't supposed to be something to gloat about like they had won the Super Bowl? It was their job. It should be business as usual.

Jim had been briefed on the bomb, but he'd been in a meeting with the National Security Advisor in D.C. when the news had come in. On one hand, he'd been ashamed that a terrorist act had almost taken place in his city on his watch, on the other, he was proud that it had been thwarted. The meeting had ended, as everyone headed back to their offices so they could follow what was happening, and the NSA could brief the President, but not before putting Jim on the hot seat with a barrage of questions. Jim thought he'd weathered it well, considering he'd been in the same room as the NSA at the time they had both learned of the bomb.

Jim had since heard conflicting stories on what exactly had triggered the alert, but as long as the bombing had been prevented, he figured he could sort through the details when he got back. So, now he was back, and pissed that so much crap was in his email.

Clicking through, he sipped his coffee, grateful that at least he didn't have to reply to most of the emails.

At a knock, he looked up to find Jessica at his door. He glanced at his desk clock, surprised that a half hour had already passed. "Come on in, Jessica. Have a seat." While he tried not to allow his annoyance to show, he didn't attempt to sound overly warm either.

"I know you just got back and you're probably swamped, but I wasn't sure if you had been made aware of a situation yet."

"A situation?" Jim leaned back in his chair and gestured to his computer. "I have a whole inbox full of 'situations'. You'll have to be more specific." He folded his arms over his chest. "Enlighten me. Please."

"Yes, sir." Jessica adopted a more formal tone. "It's about the 'L' bombing attempt. Mark is the one who discovered the bomb. His discovery was filtered through the Chicago P.D. The official story is that a pedestrian spotted the object in the girder, but Mark called me about it that morning. He'd had a dream."

Jim absorbed the information. Jessica was right, he hadn't known, and he was going to find out exactly why that type of information had been withheld by the police. He had kept up to date on the situation via phone and email, but there had been no mention of Mark Taylor. That struck him as odd. It also worried him about the claim of a dream even without the camera. He would have to call Mark and inquire about that.

"Do you know exactly who investigated Mark's suspicions?"

She nodded. "It was my former partner, Dan. You remember him, don't you?"

"I do. Seems like a very competent detective."

"He is, which is why I was so surprised when I found out about the cover-up."

Jim raised a hand and said, "Hold on, just back up a minute. Leaving Mark's name off the report is hardly a cover-up. There could be a very valid reason for it, or just an oversight.

Jessica's eyes narrowed and she looked like she was going to argue, but at the last minute, remembered where she was and clamped her mouth into a hard line.

Good. He couldn't have her bucking his authority as though they were hanging out at O'Leary's having a few drinks. "Thank you for bringing this to my attention. I'll look into it."

After a moment, she rose and crossed to the door, taking the hint of dismissal from his tone, but she faced him again. "One more thing. I understand that I'm new here and all, but I know the Chicago Police Department, and I know there's something about the situation that smells rotten. I'm worried for Mark."

She had lost the defiant expression and he saw the truth of her worry. "I understand, Jessica. I meant it when I said I'd look into the situation."

"I appreciate it." She glanced at her watch. "Well, I guess I better go. I'm supposed to tag along on an arrest. My first with you guys."

He nodded. When she was gone, he searched his email for Mark's name, and several memos were returned. All had been sent last night or early this morning. He had last checked his email yesterday afternoon, reasoning if there were any emergencies, he would be contacted by phone. As he read the first one, a feeling of disbelief shrouded his initial reaction. This couldn't be right. No damn way. Jim read it again, and quickly clicked to the next memo, sure it would be a correction. *"Shit!"* His chair hit the wall with a thud as he scrambled to his feet, tugging his jacket off the back of his chair and shrugging into it in almost a singular motion.

DeMarcus rushed into the room. "Is everything all right, sir?"

"No, it's not. Get me Harris on the horn. Send it to my cell."

"Craig Harris? I think he just left with a group about five minutes ago. I heard they were making an arrest in connection with the bomb attempt."

"Yes, I only now had a chance to read the memos. Just do as I say."

"Right away, sir."

Jim shouldered his way through the crowd waiting for the elevator. He didn't have time to wait for another car. A few people started to protest until they saw who it was. They stood aside, and when the doors opened, only a few dared to enter it with him, the rest saying they would wait for the next one.

Fifteen minutes later, he pulled up in front of Mark's studio. It was surrounded by Chicago Police vehicles and a few agency cars as well. He was hoping to beat them to Mark's, but he was too late. At least he was here to straighten the mess out. He brushed past the police line, flashing his badge when a cop approached him.

Before he made it past the office, he was met by Craig Harris and several other agents, including Jessica. He craned his neck to look past them, searching for Mark.

"Jim! I didn't know you were back yet." Craig strode up to Jim, putting his hand out. "Welcome back. You missed all the excitement."

Reluctantly, Jim shook the other man's hand. "Well, apparently, I didn't miss all of it. What's going on?"

"The suspect wasn't home."

"What do you mean? Wasn't he under surveillance?" It was standard procedure. At least this would buy Jim a little time to find out what was going on.

Craig's brow furrowed in irritation. "Of course. Chicago P.D. had a man out front in an unmarked car, but somehow the suspect made it past him. We're checking it out. I feel confident we'll get him when he returns."

Jim noted the circus atmosphere of flashing lights, a crowd gathering across the street to see what was going on, and knew that if Mark had just gone to run an errand, as soon as he caught sight of the commotion, he would hightail it in the other direction. Not that Jim could blame him for being a little gun-shy in crowds—not after what happened with Kern, but apparently Harris hadn't considered that possibility yet. Disgusted, Jim almost bit his tongue in half to keep from reaming out Harris in front of the other agents. He inclined his head towards the front of the studio. "I need to speak with you for a moment."

"Sure." Craig pointed to the office desks and instructed the other agents, "Check the desks carefully. There might be something there. I'll be right back."

Glancing around, Jim led Craig around to the side alley, seeking some privacy. When he deemed it safe to talk, he spun to face Harris. "Just what the hell do you think you're doing?"

Harris retreated a step before straightening his jacket and squaring his shoulders. "We're here in support of the Chicago P.D. at their request. They initiated an investigation into Taylor's activities and felt they had enough evidence to make an arrest. Due to Taylor's name popping up on the Watch List, they requested us to assist with the arrest if necessary."

"Taylor shouldn't be on the list. I personally petitioned for his removal over a year ago."

Shrugging, Harris said, "Maybe one of the other agencies listed him too. You know how complicated that can make the process."

Jim nodded, rubbing his hand down his face in frustration. Why hadn't he checked to see if Homeland Security had also put Mark on the list? They were the most likely guilty party. This was going to be a lot harder to clear up than he had anticipated. Before he could address that problem, he had to deal with the immediate one. "Okay, never mind. I'll deal with that later. What were the grounds for arrest today?"

"I sent you several memos."

"Yes, I saw them about twenty minutes ago, but I don't believe it for a minute. Taylor is no terrorist."

"I'll spell it out for you. I know you CIA guys are more used to dealing with prisoners after they've been arrested, but in the FBI, we tend to follow procedure and go by the book, so grounds for arrest are SOP."

Jim crossed his arms, letting the slur slide for the moment. There would be plenty of time later to remind Harris that while he was indeed C.I.A., right now he was still in charge of the Chicago Field Office of the F.B.I. He wasn't sure, though, how long that kind of arrangement would last now that Homeland Security was trying to coordinate intelligence efforts.

Harris began ticking off the evidence on his fingers. "Taylor 'discovered' the bomb out of the blue. He told a CPD detective that he'd dreamed of the bombing. We have a tape of him calling in a bomb report to the police, before he even supposedly found the bomb, and we just did a preliminary search on his computer's history. The guy really needs to learn how to cover his tracks better. Your boy had been Googling bombs and explosives just hours before he found it."

Jim had to concede the evidence appeared damning, but he still wasn't convinced. "On paper, it looks suspicious, but it's all speculation. There's no law against internet searches about explosives, and until you've questioned him, you won't be sure of the timeline. If he spotted the bomb earlier, I am aware of some very good reasons he might hesitate to share the information right away. I know this guy. He wouldn't do something like that. Believe me, if Taylor had any predilection for this kind of activity, I would have discovered it in my dealings with him."

"That may be, but you weren't here and I was in charge. Based on the evidence at hand, I have to at least bring him in for questioning."

"You could have run it by me first. You knew of his former status as my asset. Hell, just a few weeks ago, we had a crew out here when he was roughed up by a much more likely suspect in this case."

Harris glanced down the alley and took a step closer, his voice low, "What do you want me to say, Jim? If you were me, what would you have done? I have no evidence against the suspect in the other case. In fact, Jim, has anyone other than Taylor even seen the guy he claims broke into his studio and assaulted him?"

Jim clenched his jaw, unable to give an affirmative answer, but he kept his eyes locked on Harris'.

Harris nodded. "Yeah. I didn't think so. How do you know he didn't start planning this then? Perhaps he intended to frame this phantom Mohommad."

"Mohommad Aziz isn't a phantom. I've…met the man and he does have a history with Taylor."

"Okay, I'll buy that, but wasn't he exiled back to Afghanistan?"

"Yes, but there are plenty of ways to get back in--you know that."

Jim heard a scuffling behind him and turned, hoping it was Mark so he could straighten the mess out, but it was Jessica, coming from the back of the building. She carried an evidence bag and marched past, not sparing either man a glance.

Jim wasn't fooled by her apparent detachment. Shell-shocked was the expression he was searching for. He felt a little baffled as well.

He rubbed his forehead and turned back to Harris. "Anyway, when you find him, let me know right away. I want a chance to talk to him. And, I don't want any violence, you hear me?"

"If he's armed, we're going to have to do what we have to do. You know that."

"Look, I know Mark. He's not going to be a threat to anyone. Just call me ASAP with any updates. Is that understood?"

"Yes, sir. Anything else? Because I'd like to oversee the collection of evidence."

Jim made a face and shook his head. "No. Go on. I have some things to attend to." The second Harris rounded the corner to the front of the building, Jim pulled out his phone. "DeMarcus? I need you to pull up Mark Taylor's file." He slipped his pen out of his shirt pocket along with a small notepad. Pacing, he waited for his assistant to find the file. "Great. Now, could you give me his parents' phone number?"

CHAPTER SIXTEEN

Mohommad examined the photos again. This time, he had taken snapshots of the pictures right after he'd developed them, and while the original photos of Mark being arrested had changed to simple images of the front of the studio, the one he'd photographed the night before still showed Mark being arrested. He shook his head with a tight smile. Incredible. So, somehow Mark had escaped being arrested--at least for now. Not that it mattered as far as his plans were concerned. The train bombing had been just the warm-up. The real show was still on schedule.

He glanced from the photos to Mark's studio across the street. It had been risky to show up, but he had wanted to watch Mark get arrested and hauled away. The activity proved that the photos had been correct, but something must have changed the outcome. That something might have been a dream. Mark must have dreamed of his own arrest and fled. That ability could prove a hindrance to the next phase of the operation. What if Mark had a precognitive dream of the next event? Would he be able to stop it like he had the train bombing or would he be ignored like he had been on 9/11?

Mohommad pulled the hood of his sweatshirt a little tighter as he strode away from the studio. They couldn't take a chance. He had given his word that the operation would go off without a hitch and he was fortunate that they hadn't sent a replacement. Of course, there were only so many replacements who were as familiar with Chicago as he was.

Now he had to think like Mark. Where would he go? There was his girlfriend, or rather ex-girlfriend. She had connections, but those very connections made her dangerous. She would be obligated to arrest him, especially as she was now an FBI agent.

Mark might not leave the city, but Mohommad didn't think that scenario was likely. Every cop in the city would be on the lookout for him, and after the media exposure Mark had experienced during the cult fiasco, plenty of citizens would recognize him if the authorities went public with his status as a wanted man. Only an idiot would hang around waiting to be recognized. He could always alter his appearance, by growing a beard, cutting or dying his hair, but that would take time. Even a haircut took time unless he had clippers handy and simply shaved his head. Even so, he recalled how the women would flirt outrageously with Mark. Women found him attractive and Mohommad didn't think even shaving his head would change Mark so drastically that he would slip by un-noticed.

Mohommad kept his head bent as he ambled, affecting an easy, unhurried gait. It was difficult when all he wanted to do was race to the train station to get out of town as quickly as he could. He imagined Mark felt the same way. It would make sense that Mark would seek out someone he trusted completely and as much as Mark had grumbled about his parents, his father in particular, that would be where he would go.

He only had to wait a few minutes before the next train to Waukegan left Ogilvie Station. This was the worst part. Trains made him feel trapped, but he hadn't wanted to chance driving and getting a parking ticket or traffic violation in Chicago. That could blow the whole operation. The plates to his car were registered to a deceased man in Lombard and if a cop decided to run the plates, that was it.

With the train overly warm, he had to lower his hood or risk standing out from the crowd. He kept his face averted, watching the passing towns slip past. The wealth of Chicago's northern suburbs sickened him, especially when he compared it to the hovels in which so many of his countrymen lived. What had these people done to deserve so much? Even the poorer towns further north would have been considered rich beyond comprehension to most of the people of his uncle's village. The unfairness was what drove Mohommad. If he succeeded with this mission, his uncle's village would be rewarded. That was the promise.

With the second phase scheduled in three days, Mohommad planned on abandoning his room above the laundry tomorrow. Most of the things he'd need were already packed, and he needed only to get his computer, and wipe everything down. He'd do that tomorrow morning, and then meet Hazim at the barn to complete the final preparations.

Eventually someone would figure out he had lived in the small studio apartment but by then, it would be too late. He wondered if people in the neighborhood would remember him. Would be described as a loner who occasionally bought pizza across the street? When he did speak to anyone, it was in Spanish or broken English. They would say how he had paid his rent on time, and didn't cause any trouble. That would be an accurate description, but it wouldn't include that he could be a lot of fun. Or, at least he used to be. He shook his head. It didn't matter. That was another life.

He worried about Mark finding out about the second phase of the operation. It was apparent that he had foreseen his own arrest even without the camera in his possession, and he must have done the same with the planned train bombing. Who was to say Mark wouldn't see the next attack and prevent it? It was a chance Mohommad wished he didn't have to take, but there was still so much to be done to prepare. He just hoped that the police would keep Mark too busy running to have time to dream.

As the train passed Great Lakes Naval Base, he noticed rows of sailors standing at attention. Imagining target practice from his months of training, he pointed his finger at them and 'pulled the trigger'. A quick glance around assured him that nobody had noticed his action. He shoved his hands into the front pocket of the hoodie to keep from making the same blunder again, but he still scorned the easy training and state of the art weapons the sailors used. How would they fare training on a cold, dusty mountainside? He had prepared as well as possible, even going so far as to take Mark's incredible camera out of the equation.

Had his training prepared him to pull the trigger on Mark if he saw him again? It was one thing to kill nameless infidels, but Mark had shared meals him, had been a welcome visitor in his home, had met Mohommad's family, and had invited him to meet his own family. He slammed the trunk, and stared unseeingly at it for a few moments, imagining Mark dead at his feet. He winced. He should have let Hazim kill him when they'd had the chance. If he had, the first phase would have gone off without a hitch and the second wouldn't be in jeopardy.

Mohommad shook his head, breaking out of his reverie. Somehow he'd get the job done. He stood as the train neared the Waukegan station and moved to the exit of the nearly empty car. If only Mark hadn't meddled with the 'L' track bomb.

***

Jim read through the bomb case file again. So far, evidence consisted of the bomb itself, its components, the bird's nest and fishing line. It was a simple set up, but it would have worked if it hadn't been defused before exploding. If a train had been on the tracks above it, which would have been likely, loss of life could have reached the hundreds.

Harris had hit a nerve with the comment about nobody seeing Mohommad Aziz, but unlike Harris, Jim didn't take it as a sign that Mark was lying, but as proof that his office had failed. They had failed to turn up any suspects other than Mark, although, as he studied everything gathered and analyzed so far, he had to concede that every angle led right to Taylor. There were no fingerprints on the explosive, or the girder, however, the nest was still being examined. It held the most promise. A few dark strands of hair had been found tangled in the twigs. It could belong to someone from the manufacturer, or a clerk or even someone who happened to pass by the nest as it sat on a shelf at the store. It was the type of evidence that could rule a suspect in, but not out. He put it aside.

Jim glanced at up at a quiet knock on the open door. Jessica leaned against the doorframe. She opened her mouth to speak, but closed it and shook her head.

"Jessica. Come in and have a seat. Close the door, please."

She sat, her arms hugging herself as though cold, but the office was warm. "I can't believe this has happened again. He would never bomb a train. You know that, right?"

"I'm not ready to say he's guilty, if that's what you're asking, but I do have questions."

Jessica's eyes narrowed. "Seriously?"

"He ran, Jessica. I have to question why he would take evasive action. Why an *innocent* man would run. It's my job." He didn't add that it was hers too. She wouldn't have been hired if she hadn't been an excellent detective.

"Remember when Mark was in prison, and he wrote down exactly what was going to happen to him? He said he'd dreamed it?"

"Of course."

"Well, that's what happened with this bombing. When he called me early in the morning of the bombing, I wanted to help, but there was nothing I could do. I'm new here, and you were gone. I had meetings to go to. I only just got out of orientation yesterday. I should have brought it to someone's attention. If I had, perhaps this would have turned out differently.

"I understand, but I also have to consider the possibility that he just told people he had a dream. What if—and I know this won't go over well with you--but what if Mark planted the bomb and then claimed he had the dream to be a hero?"

She recoiled as though he'd slapped her. "Mark isn't crazy and he's not looking to be a hero. He never sought the limelight."

Jim studied her tense posture and came to a decision he'd hoped to avoid. "Jessica, you're too close to him to be objective about this case, so I'm sorry, but I'm going to have to order you to work on other cases while this one is being investigated."

Her expression went from anger to shock.

Jim hated what he had to do next, but he had to ask, "Do you know where he might have gone?"

Confusion replaced the shock at the turn of events. "Are you questioning Jessica Bishop, the special agent, or Jessie, ex-girlfriend of the fugitive?"

"Don't make it harder than it has to be. The sooner we find him, the sooner we can get this all cleared up."

Jessica stood, smoothed the wrinkles from her shirt and looked him square in the eye. "I have no information on Mark's whereabouts. If that changes, I'll let you know. Now, if you're done questioning me, unless you're going to arrest me too, I'm going home."

"Wait. Please." Jim blew out a deep breath and relaxed back in the chair, tilting it until he was gazing at the ceiling. He was screwing this up. Right now, Jessica was probably the only person who might have an idea of what Mark's pattern of thought could be, and here he was about to let her go home and ban her from the investigation.

She stood with one hand on the doorknob, appearing as if she was ready to slam the door behind her, but she checked the motion.

He hadn't lost her yet. Jim steepled his fingers, resting his chin on top as he chose his words. "I know you find this hard to believe, but Mark is my friend too. Right now, I want to find him so we can prove that he's not the terrorist Harris is labeling him. As it stands, officially, I'm behind Harris because as much as I hate it, if the suspect were anyone else, I'd be telling Craig he did a great job." Jim reached for the folder he'd been studying and raised it, giving it a little shake. "The evidence is damning, to say the least, but I think *we* can explain it."

Her eyes widened. "We?"

With a nod, he stood and circled the desk to stand before her. "Yes. You and I are going to track him down. We're his best shot at coming out of this unscathed."

"But I thought I wasn't allowed on the case?"

"I changed my mind. You know him better than anyone and you were a damn good detective, so let's see if you can track a fugitive as a Special Agent."

She looked dubious, but shrugged. "I guess I don't have a choice in the matter?"

Jim smiled. "Not really."

CHAPTER SEVENTEEN

Mark circled the block, trying to recall which home belonged to Mo's sister. When he'd been here before, it had been daytime, but he recalled that a fire hydrant had been in front because he'd had to move his car when he parked beside it. The home was in a cul-de-sac in an upscale neighborhood. The houses varied in size and style, but overall, there were only a handful of styles. It oozed upper-middle class suburbia with every manicured lawn and meticulously edged sidewalk.

He stopped a few doors down from the house and glanced at the dashboard clock. Not quite nine o'clock. The lights were still on so somebody should be awake, but he hesitated. What if the FBI had come to her already? They could be waiting inside the house for him even now. Drumming his fingers on the steering wheel, he rationalized that the FBI would be too busy trying to track him down to worry about Mo--at least, not while Mark undoubtedly ranked much higher on their Most Wanted list. Of course, that didn't mean the FBI wasn't on his tail even now, but it was a chance he'd take. Plus, his was the only car parked on the street, all the others were in garages or in the driveways. The thought didn't comfort him as it should have. It meant that someone might be watching him, wondering who he was and why he was there.

Mark moved the car to right in front of the house and yanked the key out of the ignition. Caution was good and necessary, but paranoia would get him nowhere. He stole a look in the side view mirror and at the houses on the other side of the small circle. So far, everything was quiet. He opened the door and stepped out, doing his best to act like he belonged. As he strode up the sidewalk, he wracked his memory for the sister's name. Something with a Z. Zoey? No. Zaira. That was it.

A jack o'lantern decoration grinned at him from the door, and a mechanical black cat, its back arched, hissed in the corner of the porch. Halloween had just passed. Other than Christmas, it had been his favorite holiday when he was a child. Despite the scary nature of the decorations, the ones on Zaira's porch had the opposite effect on Mark. He drew in a deep breath and pushed the doorbell.

A deep bark, toenails clicking and a rush of footsteps mixed with shouting and a woman trying to talk over the commotion followed the sound of the bell. Mark took a step back and turned to see if the racket had attracted any attention from neighbors. It crossed his mind to dash back to his car. This was completely insane. In his moment of hesitation, the door opened. Two little girls, one about nine, the other four, wrestled for control of the door while Zaira rushed up from behind, admonishing them that they shouldn't open the door to strangers. He couldn't blame her as he backed even further from the door in an attempt to appear non-threatening.

"Girls, stay back and take Gypsy with you." Her words were flavored with a light accent, a feminine version of Mo's. The girls protested, but did as told. Zaira remained inside, the screen door a barrier, but she smiled as she said, "May I help you?"

Mark cleared his throat. "Zaira? I don't know if you remember me, but I was a friend of your brother's."

Her shoulders stiffened and she pulled on the handle of the door. "Well, if you're looking for him, you've come to the wrong place." She reached behind her for the heavy storm door.

"Wait! Please." Mark spread his hand over his chest. "I'm Mark Taylor. We've met before, remember? I think it was a birthday party?"

Zaira paused with the door partially closed as she peered out. "Mark?"

"Yes. I went to Afghanistan with Mohommad."

Recognition splashed across her face and with a cry, she opened the door. "I remember you. My brother's lies sent you to prison. Please, come in. I need to apologize for him."

Taken aback at the declaration, Mark didn't enter the house until she beckoned him. He rubbed a hand over the top of his head and glanced over his shoulder before he crossed the threshold. "No need to apologize. I just…well, it's complicated."

She closed the door behind him and extended her hand towards the sofa in the front room. Canned laughter from a sitcom drifted into the room from farther back in the house. "Please, have a seat. Would you like something to drink? I have iced tea or soda."

His mouth still dry from nerves, he nodded. "Sure. Pop would be great--whatever you have."

Too keyed up to sit, he wandered to the fireplace, drawn by the array of framed photos lined up along the mantle. He smiled at the cute pictures of the girls at various ages, and noted the stern-faced man in Zaira's wedding photograph. Mark vaguely recalled meeting him and wondered if he was the one watching the sitcom. Somehow, he didn't seem the type.

Zaira returned and set a tray loaded with two glasses and a plate of snack crackers on the coffee table. "Come. Sit and talk to me."

"Thank you." Mark crossed the room and sat on the chair flanking the sofa. He sipped the soft drink, then set it on the table, taking a moment to decide what he wanted to say. Leaning forward, he rested his elbows across his knees, hands loosely clasped, and said, "Zaira, I have to be upfront with you. I believe at the moment, I'm wanted by the FBI. I don't think they'll track me here, at least not so soon, but I thought I should give you fair warning."

The carpet beneath his feet, with its blood red designs, were reminiscent of rugs he'd seen in the Afghanistan bazaar where he had purchased the camera. The camera had led him down a path that was as twisted and complicated as red trails cutting through the sand colored fibers.

His life now intertwined with so many, and he must be crazy to add Zaira to the mix. Would this complicate things even further? Had coming here been a mistake? Mohommad was her brother. Why should she tell Mark anything, or even worse, what if she called the police? Or what if the F.B.I. found him here? She and her children could be in danger. Mark closed his eyes for a moment, blocking out the carpet and mentally putting the rush of *what ifs* behind a barricade. With a small shake of his head, he raised his gaze to find Zaira watching him, curious, but not alarmed.

He added, "I wouldn't have come here if I hadn't been desperate. The last thing I want to do is drag you and your family into my mess. Still, I can't be positive that the FBI won't barge in, so if you want me to leave now, I would certainly understand."

Zaira perched on the edge of the sofa, her legs gracefully angled to the right as she cradled her drink in her hands. Her eyes sparked with anger, belying the calm façade. "I am no stranger to the F.B.I. or the other various government agencies. When Mohommad was imprisoned, they visited me numerous times and read my letters to my brother. The few I received from him were almost impossible to read, so much of them had been blacked out. Rest assured, Mark-- I have no love for these agencies." Regret dimmed the anger as she added, "However, I will not lie to them."

Mark straightened. "No--of course not. I wouldn't want you to. Not for my sake, anyway."

She tilted her head. "So why are they after you...this time?"

"It's a long story." He sagged against the cushions, the stress of the last few days taking a toll. Rubbing the back of his neck, he strove to organize his thoughts, but weariness added a layer of fog to his thinking.

He barely knew Zaira. Would she side with her brother or listen with an open mind? For that matter, she didn't know him either. Why should she believe anything he said? So far, she had hinted that she knew about Mo's betrayal, but still, Mo was her blood, her family.

"I'm listening."

He glanced at the ceiling as the light patter of small feet raced overhead. It set his mind at ease that the girls wouldn't overhear. Zaira must have caught his look and said, "I sent the girls up to get ready for bed. I will have to go settle them in a few minutes, but they know better than to come down and interrupt."

Mark nodded. "I bolted before they could arrest me, but my guess is..." He hesitated, his future hinged on her reaction to what he was about to reveal. He took a deep breath before plunging ahead with the rest. "They believe I had something to do with the attempted 'L' bombing."

"Why would they think that?"

Her matter-of-fact tone caught him by surprise. Best case scenario, he'd expected her to toss him out after admitting the magnitude of the crime he was wanted for. Worst case, she'd call the police immediately. "I think they'll always be suspicious of me after the 9/11 accusations."

"But you are free now, so they must have cleared you."

"Cleared? Not so much. More like they couldn't force me to confess, and had very little evidence." He sat forward with his elbows propped on his knees and hands clasped in front of his mouth as he decided how to broach the subject of Mo and his role in Mark's imprisonment. "When you invited me in, you mentioned that Mohommad's lies had to do with me going to prison before. Why did you say that? Have you spoken to him?"

She set her glass down, and rubbed her hands together. "No…well, not for a few years. When he was first released, he called me from Afghanistan. He wanted me to move my family back there." She shuddered. "I said no way would I ever take my daughters to Afghanistan. They were born here. Our father brought us here when I was about twelve, but he was even younger, which is unfortunate." Zaira sighed.

"Unfortunate? How?"

"He doesn't remember what it was like. I do, although as a boy, it was different for him, so maybe he just doesn't know any better. He has this idealized vision of a powerful Afghanistan, and blames the U.S. for all its problems. Our uncle encourages Mohommad's anger. He's stuffed my brother's head with talk of violence."

Tears filled her eyes when she lifted her gaze. "Our father would be so ashamed and disappointed. He worked and struggled so we could have opportunities. He risked everything because he thought we were worth it, and my brother has thrown away this great gift." She wiped her eyes, but the corner of her mouth curved up as she chuckled. "I'm sorry. I guess I've had no one to talk to about this and I got side-tracked. Mohommad told me you were still in prison because you had traveled to Afghanistan with him, and introduced him to the leaders of an al-Qaeda group. He said he tried to stop you, but you had agreed to photograph Chicago sites for the group in exchange for money and wanted him to do the same."

Mark dropped his head and twined his fingers behind his neck, surprised that Mo's lies still hurt so much. It was one thing to hear Mo's accusations from an interrogator, but it was a totally different ballgame to hear it from Zaira. Despite what Mo had done recently, Mark had clung to a sliver a hope that his former friend hadn't betrayed him, but had only made up the accusations under the duress of torture. Zaira had no incentive to lie to him.

He buried the pain beneath a deep layer of anger as he stood and paced to the window. Sticking a finger between the slats of the blind, he surveyed the cul-de-sac. His car remained the only one on the street. Mark turned back to Zaira. "None of it is true. I know he's your brother, but I swear I never spoke to anyone from al-Qaeda." He took a few steps towards her. "No way would I do anything like that."

Zaira nodded. "I don't know why Mohommad said those things. When I tried to question him, he cut me off, and said I had forgotten my roots and had become too American." She stood and wrapped her arms around herself as though chilly. Picking up a framed photograph from an end table, and as she gazed at it, an expression of grief flashed in her eyes, and she hugged the photo to her. "He even insinuated that my husband's death was my punishment."

"I'm sorry. I didn't know." Mark felt like an insensitive idiot. His own troubles were insignificant compared to the loss of a spouse.

Zaira set the picture down. "Thank you. Of course you didn't know. How could you? It happened three years ago, and I believe you were still in prison then."

"I was." He jammed his hands in his pockets. "I have to get going. I shouldn't have intruded."

A look of puzzlement in her eyes, Zaira moved towards him. "But you haven't asked me whatever it was that brought you here."

Mark hesitated. She had enough to deal with. Adding to her burden was the last thing he wanted to do. "It's not important. I should get going."

"Mark, you took a big risk coming here with the FBI on your trail, the least you could do is ask the questions that brought you to my door."

It came out in a rush. He hadn't lied about having to go. He was already feeling like he'd stayed in one place too long. "I just wanted to know if you'd seen Mohommad lately or knew where he might be."

"Why?"

The question was so short and blunt, it took Mark by surprise. "He has something of mine that I need back."

"You're not going to hurt him are you? He's still my brother, in spite of the way he's behaved."

"I don't intend to hurt him. I don't want any of this to be happening, but it's very important that I get back what he has."

Her brows rose in question. "What does he have that is so important?"

"It's a camera—a very special camera. If I don't get it back, there's no telling what might happen."

Clearly confused, she put her hands on her hips. "What's so special about this camera, and why does Mohommad have it?"

Mark gestured towards the sofa. "Maybe we should sit again. This isn't going to be quick."

Zaira resumed her seat on the edge of the sofa and Mark took the side chair. "I know it's going to sound nuts, but this camera shows future images, and when it's activated, meaning, when someone uses it, I get dreams of whatever is on the film. Future photos, but it's always a picture of a tragedy. A kid hit by a car, or a man shot in a robbery, accidental electrocutions—pretty much any kind of tragedy you can imagine. I don't know how or why it happens, and why some tragedies are shown and others aren't, but when I realized what the images and dreams were, I began to intervene. I didn't expect that I could change anything. I mean, it sounds crazy, right?" Mark shrugged. "But as insane as it sounds, when I use the camera, between the photos and the dreams, I usually have enough information to stop what's shown to me."

"Usually?"

"Yes. Usually. Sometimes, the event is too big for me to stop it alone. That's what happened on 9/11 and sent me down," Mark tilted his head to the right, "...*that* road."

He didn't have time to get into all that had happened to him before, so he cut to the chase. "Mo visited me a few weeks ago. Only it wasn't to renew our friendship, it was to acquire the camera. He'd learned of it while he was in prison too. Apparently, interrogators are free to share information with other prisoners." He tried to joke about the last part, but failed when bitterness leached into the words in spite of his intentions. Picking up his abandoned glass, he swallowed the rest in a long gulp, as though hoping to wash the resentment away with the sweet drink. The ice clinked as he set the glass down. "He forced me to turn over the camera. It's bad enough that I don't have it anymore—already a few people have died that I might have saved—but he's using it too. Only I don't imagine he's trying to save anyone, and I'm still getting the dreams. I suppose he could be dreaming too, but I don't think so. I dreamed about the 'L' bombing, and had just enough time to find the bomb and show police—only now they think I had something to do with it."

"Do you think Mohommad was behind the bomb?"

Mark scrubbed a hand down his face and sighed. How could he tell Zaira that he suspected her brother was not only behind the bomb, but was a full-fledged terrorist? "I don't know, but I do know that if there's another attack, I'll never get anyone to believe me without the photographs."

Zaira rose and moved to the mantle, staring at the knickknacks decorating the shelf, but didn't seem to see any of them. She crossed her arms, one hand to her mouth as she nibbled on a fingernail. Finally, she lifted one shoulder in a shrug, the mannerism a feminine version of Mo's. "I have not heard from my brother in months. He's not allowed into the country." She chuckled, but there was no amusement in her eyes as she faced Mark. "I guess he got around that requirement somehow. You see, he was released, but it was on the condition that he remain in Afghanistan. If he's caught here, I'm afraid they'll lock him up again, and this time, he'll never get out." Tears welled again. "Even if I knew where he was, how can I turn him in when I know there will be no trial? He's my brother and the closest family I have left."

The image of the cell he'd called home for fifteen months flashed in Mark's mind. He could almost smell the stale stench of sweat, urine and disinfectant that had permeated the stark room. His breathing quickened and his hands clenched as he fought off the flood of memories before they sucked him into a full-blown flashback. He stood and crossed to her, the pain in her expression hitting him like a blow to the chest. "Zaira, I only want the camera and to talk to Mohommad. Maybe I can get him to go back to Afghanistan. He somehow stole into the country; he can sneak back out if he wants to. I swear I won't tell anyone." He meant it too. As much anger as he held towards Mo, he couldn't sentence him to more time in hell.

Zaira shook her head. "He won't want to go back. My uncles have turned him against the U.S. and if I know them, they will have made him feel like a failure for being taken alive the first time. I'm afraid he's on a suicide mission now." The tears tracked down her cheeks and Mark wished he'd never come and caused her this pain.

"I'm sorry." He reached out and touched her shoulder in an attempt to comfort her, but let his hand drop to his side, unable to complete the gesture. Already he'd caused enough grief; he didn't think sympathy from him would be welcome.

She noticed his attempt and gave him a wan smile. "It's okay, Mark. It's not your fault, and I don't blame you." Wiping her eyes, she crossed to an elegant desk in a corner of the room. "I'm not sure if what I have will help you find Mohommad, but it might. He had a lot of friends...before." After poking through a few drawers, she withdrew a small spiral notebook. "I have some addresses of people he knew in here. I compiled them for the FBI when Mohommad was first imprisoned, but they never came to collect it. I guess they got their answers elsewhere. Now you can use it to possibly find him. Kind of ironic, don't you think?"

Mark took the notebook, but could only manage a nod in response. His throat felt swollen and it hurt to swallow. He took several deep breaths, before he was able to speak again. "Thank you."

"You're welcome. I'm doing it for my brother as much as you.

She nodded and turned away. He took that as his cue, went to the front door, checking the street for any cars or observers, but only friendly jack-o'lanterns watched his departure.

CHAPTER EIGHTEEN

After leaving Zaira's, Mark was at loose ends and had no idea what to do next. It was almost ten P.M and fatigue burned his eyes. He wasn't sure what he'd hoped to learn from Zaira, but perhaps some part of him suspected that Mo would be hiding out there. Stupid idea. Of course Mo wouldn't stay with his sister, and as soon as Mark had seen the little girls, he had known it in his gut.

One thing Mo had cherished was his family. When he and Mark had traveled through Afghanistan, Mark had been appalled at the treatment of the women in the country, and while Mo had seemed to share his sentiments, he had also pointed out that Americans weren't perfect. Mo had spoken of the tough time he'd had when his family first emigrated to the U.S. Kids in school had made fun of the way he and his sister dressed and their thick accents. Consequently, they had become champions for each other. There was nothing Mo wouldn't do for his sister and his nieces, or at least, that had been the case before September 11th. Somehow, Mark didn't see Mo taking the risk of bringing danger to Zaira's doorstep.

Regretting the lost time with nothing gained but a few addresses, Mark continued to drive aimlessly, but when a cop ended up beside him at a stoplight, it hit him what a chance he was taking. All it would take would for him to forget to signal a turn or roll through a stop sign, and he would have no chance at all of getting the camera back. He almost pulled into a parking lot for a bar, just to get the car off the road, but he dismissed the idea. Police kept an especially close eye on cars leaving bars. It would help if he had a plan and knew where to go, but there hadn't been time to draw up a plan. If only he'd had a chance to speak to Jessie this morning. Things had just been starting to get back to normal, or at least as normal as anything could ever be for Mark, and when Jessie had met him for dinner, the spark was still there.

Jessie had been his sounding board in difficult situations before, but she was not just a cop anymore, now she was literally the enemy. His other instinct was to consult Jim, but that was out for obvious reasons. Still, it didn't stop the longing to call one or both of them. Would Jessie turn him in? He was certain she wouldn't think he was a terrorist, but she might try to convince him to turn himself in and trust in the system. Mark pounded a fist on the dash. If only it was that simple, but he'd been there, done that and got the orange t-shirt.

His heart nearly stopped beating when lights flashed in his review mirror, but his heart resumed pumping, even adding a flurry of extra beats when he realized the lights were the red lights of an ambulance, not the blue of a CPD patrol car. When the pounding in his chest eased, he ran a shaky hand through his hair and resumed his death grip on the wheel. He had to get off the damn road before he was either pulled over or had a heart attack. Deciding to hide in plain sight, he followed the squad, but he turned right into the emergency room lot and found a parking space not too close to the hospital, and tucked between two sports utility vehicles. He'd be out of sight of the road, and not easy to spot from anywhere but directly behind the car. Reaching down, he flicked the radio on and found a news station. Fingers drumming, he listened through a weather report. He made a mental note of a cold front moving through. He might need to acquire some warmer clothes, but for now, he was more interested in whether or not the police had gone to the media with the story. If they had, his chance of finding Mo and retrieving the camera would be next to nil. It had only been the last month or so that he'd been able to walk down the street or go into a store without someone recognizing him from the Kern debacle and if this story went public, he might as well wear a flashing neon target on his back.

The news segment returned from a commercial and he listened, clenching the steering wheel as the deejay covered world news, then moved on to national, before finally coming back to local news.

"Local authorities confirm they have a person of interest in the thwarted 'L' platform bombing attempt. They are not releasing any more information at this time. Anyone with information is still urged to contact the police."

Mark released a long shaky breath, his arms loosely draped over the top of the steering wheel. So his name wasn't out there. He wondered at that. Had his dream been wrong? Had he fled for no reason? Uncertainty and confusion plagued him. Should he just go back to the loft? If only he could contact someone, but his cell phone was out of the question even if he had brought it with him. It was sure to be tracked, and he'd foregone even carrying it in case they could follow his movements by cell phone towers. Mark was far from a tech expert, but he remembered how an older couple who had made a wrong-turn in a snowstorm out West somewhere in the mountains, were finally found, in part, because the cellphone signal had given rescuers a general location on where to carry out the search.

He turned and looked out the rear window. A few people entered the ER, but nobody was exiting. His gaze dropped to the notebook Zaira had given him. It lay on the passenger seat where he'd tossed it upon entering the car. He flipped it open and read from the list of names. Some he recognized as fellow photographers, and others he'd even seen recently at various shoots. While he supposed they could have made contact with Mo, he thought it unlikely. Other than the names and some addresses, there was nothing else. Who were these people?

Resting his head against the back of the seat, he tried to put himself in Mo's shoes. *Think!* What did Mo absolutely require? Food and shelter. Okay. Food wouldn't be much of an issue. Mo could probably walk into any fast food restaurant or grocery store and buy whatever he needed. Unlike Mark, Mo would be able to come and go freely in complete anonymity.

Shelter. Once again, Mo had the advantage over Mark with the ability to blend in. His face had never been splashed across all the various media. He had never given a press conference, as Mark had been forced to do after being released from the hospital.

Wait a minute. Mo had been arrested as an enemy combatant before Mark. He would have had at least some mention in the news. So, maybe he was doing his best to fly under the radar too. Would he seek out help from the Muslim community? Mark knew there was a sizable one in the area, but since Zaira seemed genuine when she had professed no knowledge of her brother's whereabouts, and she was active in the community, Mark had a feeling that Mo was steering clear of them. Of course, Zaira could be covering for him. It would be understandable given how close Mo had been to his sister, but he hadn't picked up on any hesitations on her part that would point to dishonesty.

Mo had threatened a large scale attack against the city. It was possible the train track bombing was the big event and Mark had disrupted it. Did that mean Mo would give up and get out of Dodge, so to speak? On one hand, Mark hoped it was the case. If Mo didn't flee, it was because he had a reason to stay. The only reason Mark could think of was because Mo was planning another attack. That would mean people, potentially a lot of people, were at risk. On the other hand, Mark wanted Mo to stick around at least long enough for Mark to get the camera back somehow.

Okay, focus on practicalities. The guy had to sleep sometime. Mark rubbed his eyes, wishing he had his own hideout where he could catch a few hours of rest. Had it only been this morning that he had awakened in his bed after the dream of capture? It seemed like a week ago.

With a sharp jerk of his head and a few hard blinks, he returned his attention to the notebook. The orange light cast by the vapor lamps gave the interior of the car a surreal glow and he had to squint to make out the names. Several were Muslim names, and he noted the addresses as not too far away from Zaira's. Those might be the most logical place to start.

If he were Mo, that's where he would go. If the list was accurate, Mo had quite a few friends in the Muslim community. Mark opened the glove box and fished around until he found a pen buried under the auto manual. He'd known his dad would keep a pen there. With another sweep of his hand, he found a small notebook that almost matched the one Zaira had given him, and as a bonus, he found a roadmap of Illinois. A smile tugged at the corners of his mouth. His father hated driving in the city and even after so many years with Mark living in Chicago, he still checked the route with the map before he and Mark's mom drove down to visit.

Sending a silent thank you to his dad, he spread the map open, then took another look outside to make sure nobody was paying attention. Satisfied that his car hadn't attracted undue notice, he circled and numbered areas on the map that corresponded to the addresses in the notebook. He understood best with visuals and seeing the locations on the map helped him to form a plan.

After he located all the approximate addresses, he studied the map, noticing a pattern. It became immediately apparent there were two concentrations of dots. Some on the west side of Chicago not too far from Zaira's home corresponded to the Muslim sounding names. The other cluster was north of the city in the Waukegan area.

Most of those names in the second concentration were Hispanic and the thought triggered a memory of Mo talking about an ex-girlfriend who had been Hispanic. Had she been from Waukegan? He couldn't remember if Mo had ever told him. He'd said that the first time he'd gone to her family's home, they had been talking about him to each other. Some of it had been complimentary, but some, not so nice. It had given him a kick to reply to one of the not so nice comments with one of his own in fluent Spanish. Mark jotted that fact down as something to keep in mind. If Mo had remained clean-shaven since the last time Mark had seen him, he could be mistaken for Hispanic with his dark hair and eyes. His features, if someone looked closely, would give him away as Middle-Eastern descent, but if he spoke Spanish people might not look too closely. Mark figured people generally saw what they expected to see.

His musing was interrupted when the owner of the car beside his returned. Mark hadn't even been aware the people were there until the door slammed just a few feet from his car. Startled, he jerked the map down and tossed it on the passenger seat. He'd been here an hour already. Damn. Jamming the car into reverse, he backed up and left the hospital lot.

He had to find a place he could park and get a least a few hours of sleep. Parking on the street in Chicago was out of the question. He'd either get a ticket, or someone would notice him. Street parking was at a premium in many neighborhoods, and his car, with Wisconsin plates, would attract attention. Although he hated to do it because it felt like he was driving away from where he needed to be, he headed north. Wisconsin plates would be more common up there, and he was sure he could find a dark road to park on. Thirty minutes later, he found what he was looking for in Highland Park. A tree-lined dead-end street with a few cars on it. Not too many that Mark would be taking anyone's spot, but not so few that his would stand out. There was even an alley that cut through to another street if he needed an escape route. Seeing nobody around, he quietly got out and popped the trunk in search of a blanket. Once again, his father hadn't disappointed him. There it was, along with a gallon of water, flares, some kind of energy bars and a flashlight. Taking the water and the blanket, he started to close the trunk, but stopped and grabbed three of the bars as well, tucking them into his coat pocket.

Mark's sleep came in fitful spurts. The blanket was itchy and smelled of exhaust, and his legs cramped from their awkward position. In order to fit comfortably, he sat propped against the driver's door and angled his legs across into the passenger seat leg area. It allowed him to extend his legs fully, but he grimaced and reached for his lower back. He'd definitely be stiff in the morning. The back seat looked inviting, but with a last longing look, he decided against it--too much chance of being trapped. He wasn't sure who would trap him, but all it would take was one cop, curious about a car with out-of-state plates, running the plate number and at a minimum, he'd be questioned. At least in the driver's seat, he could drive away if he had to.

He had parked facing out of the dead end, and after taking a last look around, he closed his eyes and tugged the blanket tight over his shoulders.

Mark wasn't sure if it was the longest night ever or the shortest. Every time he opened his eyes, the dashboard clock had jumped ahead an hour or so, but the frequent awakenings made the night seem to last days. In between waking moments, he had vivid dreams. Were they camera triggered dreams or just regular ones? It was hard for him to determine because of his fatigue. Instead of having one dream from start to finish, he seemed to be starting and stopping the same dream over and over through the night. Mohommad appeared in the dream. He and Mo were on a sidewalk somewhere, and Mohommad carried the camera as he strolled away from Mark towards a black Ford. Mark jogged to catch up and called out to him. Mo turned, one hand going to his pocket and there was a glint of metal an instant later.

Mark awoke with a start. Pink streaked the eastern sky and the interior of the car was lit with a soft pink glow. Stiffly, he pulled his legs onto the driver's side and turned to face the steering wheel, pounding his hand on it. *Shit!* He'd woken up too soon. Where had Mo been, and what had he been going for in his pocket? A gun? Knife? Cell phone?

As he stretched in the limited confines of the car, Mark tried to piece together the dream. A huge yawn overtook him as he dug through the accumulating mess on the passenger seat and found the notebook Zaira had given him. Swiping the map to the floor, he found the pen and jotted down everything he could recall about the dream. There had been a hospital, but it wasn't the one he had left last night. This one was beside a park, but in the dream, he saw it only in passing as though riding in a car. As he dredged up the remnants of the dream, a cop car approached his car from the other direction. As Mark held his breath, the patrol turned right, and continued on its way, but not before spooking Mark.

He made it back to the highway and headed north again. Waukegan was only twenty minutes away, so he decided to investigate some of the names he'd found in the notebook. Mark rubbed a hand across the prickly stubble on his jaw. Before he approached anyone, he needed to change clothes and clean up. His stomach growled too, so when he noticed a diner along the road, he turned in. He was far enough away from Chicago, he didn't think anyone would be looking for him up here and since his name hadn't been released, he decided to take a chance.

Thirty minutes later, he left the restaurant and continued north. He wasn't sure exactly what he was going to do when he got there, but he could at least check some of the addresses, and besides, something in the dream had triggered an impulse to head to Waukegan.

* * *

As soon as Mark exited the highway, he knew he'd been right. Although he'd never been to the town before, the hair on his arms rose and a sense of déjà vu washed over him. Trusting his instinct, he cruised the street, slowing when he recognized the Italian restaurant. He spotted an empty parking space in front and pulled into it. He wiped damp palms on his jeans and sat for a moment. He wished for the hundredth time since he'd woken up, that he'd seen the end of the dream. Since he didn't know the outcome, he didn't know if he should be here or not. Maybe this was where Mo killed him and he had unknowingly driven himself right to his own execution.

The spotted the car that Mo had been heading for, and it was parked in the same spot he'd seen in his dream, so Mo was somewhere around. He dismissed the dentist's office, and the car was parked too far from the restaurant if Mo was inside eating lunch. It wasn't a far walk, but there was a small parking lot across from the restaurant so it didn't make sense that Mo would park down the street and around the corner if he didn't have to.

The house on the fourth corner was a possibility, but just as Mark considered it, a mother and a small child exited. The little boy wore a backpack that was almost bigger than he was but it didn't seem to slow him down as he hopped down the sidewalk, apparently trying to miss the cracks. The duo didn't go far, as they waited on the corner and a few minutes later, a city bus stopped and picked them up. Mark let out a sigh of relief. At least he didn't have to worry about a small child in the vicinity if things turned ugly.

Ruling out the house left just the laundromat or the apartments above it. Mark opened the door and stood beside the car, getting his bearings. Tugging his ball cap down, he headed towards the laundromat. Timing had been his biggest uncertainty. The dream had been so disjointed, he could only hope he could deduce the correct time by gauging it as late morning based on…what? The light? The sun was hidden behind a thick layer of steel gray clouds, and it could just as easily have been late afternoon instead of late morning. Still, this looked right and so far, his dream had been correct. The town was the one from his dream and this was the exact corner. He'd trust his gut once more and bet that any minute, Mo would show up.

He crossed the street to be on the same side as Mo would be when he appeared, and no sooner had his foot hit the curb, than a door on the side of the building opened and Mo stepped out, the camera dangling negligently from his hand by the neck strap. Almost as though he was expecting Mark, he turned towards him.

Of course. Mark mentally slapped his forehead. Mo had to have used the camera to create the pictures that Mark had dreamed, so he would have known Mark would be here. Even after dealing with the camera for several years, the concept didn't come naturally to Mark, and having the camera in someone else's control while he still had the dreams threw all of his prior knowledge about how it worked into a blender and mixed it all up into a fine puree. Right now, it was like he and Mo each held half the pieces of a puzzle. Who would fill in the blanks first?

"Mark." Mo wore a ragged pea green Army surplus jacket. He held a set of keys, occasionally twirling the ring around his index finger in a nervous habit Mark remembered from before. Had the keys caused the glint?

Mark stopped several feet away, his hands ready at his side. "Give me the camera back."

Mo's eyebrows shot up and then he grinned. "Really? And you think I'll return it to you just like that?" He snapped his fingers.

"Listen, I'm still getting the dreams. I can still prevent whatever you might plan so the camera isn't really any use to you. I had a dream last night," he pointed at the sidewalk, "about finding you, and here you are."

"Ah, I wondered how the police were able to find the explosives so easily. I guess you dreamed that too? And here I thought my idea was genius." His tone held no hint of anger, and if the topic of conversation had been different, they might have been trading jabs about favorite football teams instead of casually discussing thwarted terrorist attacks. "I could just stop using the camera." He smirked.

Mark inched closer. "Can you really *do* that?" It was a wild guess, but he knew first-hand how the urge to use the camera was almost irresistible and hoped it had captured Mo in its spell too. "Are you getting the dreams?" He was almost certain Mo wasn't. At least, he hoped that was the case. The only other experience he'd had with something like this was when he'd been in prison and Jessie had used the camera, causing Mark to dream of the photos even though he was a thousand miles away.

Anger darkened Mo's features for the first time as he held the camera up by the strap and gave it a shake. "I don't need dreams when I have the photos."

"Why do you need the photos at all, Mo? Why are you doing this?"

"I have my reasons and you would never understand."

"You're right. I don't understand. You have a sister and nieces here. Do you realize what this could do to them?"

"This has nothing to do with them."

Mark shook his head. "Really? You don't think so? How many times is the FBI going to have to visit Zaira?" He tried to appeal to Mo's sense of honor. "Your nieces—they're the sweetest little girls—and now they're going to have to live with the stigma that their uncle murdered innocent people. Hell, some of their friends could be victims of whatever you have planned."

Mo glanced away for a second, and Mark saw a look of regret cloud his features. It was gone in an instant, replaced by rage. "My sister and her daughters will go back to Afghanistan with me. And there, I will be a hero."

"*How?* How the hell are you going to leave with your sister and her girls? It might be a little difficult for you to book a flight to Afghanistan."

"Mexico."

Mark gave a shake of his head and tried not to glance at the camera. Mo had lowered it, and the camera dangled by his knee. "Mexico? I don't get it."

"That's what my sister will have to do. I'll meet her there, and then we can all four go back to Afghanistan." He spoke as if it was the most logical thing in the world.

"You're crazy." The slur came out before he could stop it. He wished he could reel it back in, but he couldn't so he went with it. "Your sister wants nothing to do with Afghanistan. Her home is here. Her daughters were born here."

Mo's eyes narrowed in fury and he jabbed a finger against Mark's chest. "How do you know so much about my sister? Is that how you found me? What did you do to her? You must have forced her to betray me."

Sensing that Mo had forgotten about the camera for a moment, Mark lunged and grabbed the straps, wrenching them from Mo's grasp. Before Mark could turn to run, Mo tackled him, sending both of them slamming onto the pavement. Mark thrust the camera to the side to protect it from the fall, but immediately pulled it close to his body, ignoring the scrape of concrete against his cheekbone. The punch to his right kidney was more difficult to ignore as the pain made him arch away from it.

Mo yanked Mark's shoulder, causing him to turn onto his side.

"Give it up! It's mine now!"

"Like hell I will!" Mark swung his free arm and shoved it up under Mo's chin, snapping his head back with a loud clink of teeth. It stunned the other man just long enough for Mark to scramble out from beneath him, but Mo recovered in time to snag Mark's ankle, giving it a savage twist and Mark stumbled forward, catching his weight on one hand. With a grunt of pain, Mark tried to yank his foot away, but Mo held fast, so instead of pulling, Mark reversed his tactic and shoved his foot against Mo's chest, knocking him backwards and causing him to lose his grip on Mark's ankle.

Regaining his balance, Mark turned to run to the car, and in the process, ran into a woman carrying a basket of clothes. She apparently had stopped to gawk at the altercation. He mumbled an apology before bolting for the car. As he crossed the street, the whoop of a siren close by spurred him to power past the pain in his ankle.

He flung open the door and tossed the camera onto the passenger side as he jumped in and started the car. With a quick check of the mirror to make sure there were no cop cars approaching from behind him, he gunned the engine and did a U-turn, miraculously missing the cars parked on the other side of the street. Where was the highway from here? Reversing his route here wasn't easy to do in his full-blown panic, but he managed to find the road back to the highway more by luck than any conscious effort on his part. At a stoplight, he reached up to touch below his eye. His hand came away smeared with blood. Damn it. The scrape would attract attention and that was the last thing he needed. He found a paper napkin in the glove box, wetted it from his water bottle and dabbed at the blood. After he cleaned it, it looked a little better. He tossed the napkins on the passenger seat and flipped the visor up as the light turned green.

Ten minutes later, he was on the highway and prayed he wouldn't get stopped for speeding. Slowing until he was keeping up with the flow of traffic, he took a deep breath and tried to form a plan. First, he needed to get some film, and then take some photos. Without future photos, the police would just assume it was an old camera. Jim had dealt with the camera as an extension of his duties as a CIA officer and Mark wasn't clear on how much, if anything, the FBI knew about it. Would Jim divulge the secret to the FBI or the Chicago PD? Given the agency's notorious secrecy, Mark had his doubts, so, he tossed that hope out of the water. If Jim was going to protect him, he would have done it by now. His immediate concern was getting film, finding a place to develop it, and doing both without getting caught. He glanced in the rearview mirror, on alert for any cop cars. The woman outside the laundromat had seen him. She could give a good description and there was no way she hadn't seen the car he got into. He'd have to ditch it somewhere. Scrubbing a shaky hand through his hair, he finally dared allow a little hope to enter his mind. He picked up the camera, immediately feeling the tingle of energy. Despite the throbbing of his ankle and the fear of capture, he smiled.

CHAPTER NINETEEN

Mark ditched the car in the long-term parking lot at O'Hare. It seemed the easiest solution. It wouldn't be towed, at least not for awhile, and he took the 'L' back into the city. At every stop, he worried someone would recognize him, but nobody did. Exhausted, his ankle swollen inside his shoe and aching in every muscle of his body, he wanted only to find a place to sleep, but he didn't have time yet. He needed film and then he'd have to use it. Running into a corner drugstore, he purchased the film and in his hurry, forgot to buy any snacks. At least he'd eaten a big breakfast, and his pack held a few of the energy bars from his dad's emergency supply.

After snapping off the roll of film at the first park he came to, he returned to the drugstore, hoping to have them developed in one hour, but the clerk told him it was too late in the day. Frustrated, Mark bought a roll for the next day. *It's just one more day,* he told himself. He could deal with that. No problem.

Hiding in plain sight once more, he sat on a window ledge of a sporting goods store and ate an energy bar. Most of the pedestrians ignored him, and the few who noticed him sitting there gave him a wide berth. He supposed he looked like just another vagrant. The bar barely put a dent in his hunger, but he levered up, gritting his teeth as he put weight on his ankle. The brief rest had caused it to stiffen. As he limped past a rundown motel, the kind that rented by the hour, he was tempted to get a room. He still had plenty of cash, so that wasn't a problem; the motel looked disreputable, and he'd bet the night clerk wouldn't even remember him. He'd just be another scruffy guy looking for a bed. If he slurred his words or picked up a prostitute, he'd probably fit right in. With a tired smile, he shook off the idea of the prostitute immediately. He already felt dirty enough and he'd hate to get anyone else involved. Rubbing his heavy five o'clock shadow, he knew it wouldn't take much to fit in with the regular motel clientele and the scrape along his cheekbone only added to the affect.

He longed for a hot shower and a shave and he'd be able to get those, plus a good night's sleep. Washing up at the tiny sink of the diner this morning wasn't enough to make him feel clean. Decision made, Mark stepped into the parking lot deciding that the benefit out-weighed the risk. Already anticipating the shower, he strode between two parked vehicles and was about to cross the lane when a police cruiser turned into the other end of the motel lot. He stepped back, hunkering in the shadows until the car passed. In all likelihood, it was just a coincidence, but spooked at the near-miss, he about faced and left the lot. Tugging his baseball cap low over his eyes, he hurried from the vicinity.

* * *

Mark shivered and pulled the blanket tight under his chin as he curled on his side, the camera safely in the crook of his arm like a beloved teddy bear. The floor of the abandoned house was cold and hard beneath him. Even sheltered from the blast of the wind, it was freezing in the house. The broken window in the back didn't help, although it had allowed him access.

He just hoped nobody else decided to use the building as a shelter. The scattering of empty liquor bottles and trash attested to the use of the house on previous occasions. His eyes felt gritty, but after a half hour, he found he was still too keyed up to sleep. Sitting, he grabbed his pack and dug around in the outer pocket for a granola bar. He finished all but the last inch of water in the bottom of the bottle, saving it for morning. Too bad there wasn't running water in the house, but then he supposed it wouldn't be abandoned if it had utilities.

Mark attempted to take his mind off his own problems by wondering about the people who used to live here. A naked Barbie doll did the splits in one corner of the room, and he imagined a little girl like one of Mo's nieces playing with the doll. What he knew about toys and Barbie dolls in particular wouldn't fill a pixel, but he was pretty sure that Mo's nieces would have the doll dressed in regal splendor. Did the girl who had lived here just forget the doll or had she outgrown it? He climbed to his feet, leaving the blanket around his shoulders and jumped a couple of times, one hand steadying the camera to keep it from smashing him in the nose. If he could just get his blood pumping, he would warm up.

He glanced at the ceiling. Perhaps one of the rooms upstairs would be warmer. Grabbing his pack, he navigated by the light from a streetlight streaming through the windows. With no curtains, it was surprisingly bright in the front room, but the stairs were deep in shadow. At the base, he hesitated. Going up would mean being trapped if anyone else came in, but staying down here would mean spending the night freezing. They said heat rose, so if any had built up during the day, it might still be trapped up there.

It was late and he was bone tired. He felt his way up the steps and turned the corner when he reached the top. A stench hit him like a slap to the face and he covered his nose. He'd been correct that it was warmer, but it smelled like something had died. Hesitantly, he went forward. He wasn't sure about sleeping up here any longer, but he had to know what caused the foul odor.

Please don't let it be a body.

Four doorways opened into the hall; all of them open. He peeked in the one on his left, but it was too dark to see, and the scent was less intense. After another forward step, he glanced in the room to his right. He fought not to gag as he scanned the room. Light filtered in from two windows and he spotted the source of the smell. It was a body, but not a human one. The tail gave it away as a raccoon. Relieved at finding the source, Mark closed the door to the room.

He returned to the first room at the top of the stairs, the one with the least odor, and settled in a corner. It was far from warm but better than the room on the main floor. Occasionally, he'd doze, but a sudden shudder would awaken him with a start. The isolation and frigid air took him back to his time in prison and the days he'd spent with nothing but a thin t-shirt and pants to keep him warm. To soften him up for interrogation, they had made the cell so cold, he had been convinced he would die although, he conceded, he would have welcomed it at that point.

Mark pulled the blanket up to his ears, leaving only his eyes exposed. His breath helped warm his cocoon. There had been a lot of things to hate from his time in the brig, but worse than the cold, and even worse than the waterboarding, had been the complete lack of contact with anyone, not even guards. His meal would slip through the slot at the bottom of the cell door, and often, they'd be so quiet, he'd not even hear them until they were gone. With no way to tell time, he'd been disoriented and they had exacerbated his confusion by staggering his meal times.

He blinked, pulling his mind to the here and now. He wasn't in prison and he wasn't going to go back. Ever. He rolled over, facing away from the wall. His eyes grew heavy and finally, he slept.

Mark awoke with a start, his heart galloping in his chest, and he jumped to his feet, camera still clutched in his arms. Something had woken him, but he wasn't sure what. He snatched up his pack but left the blanket so he could move faster. The soft pink light of dawn filled the room so that must mean it was close to 7A.M. As he headed for the stairs, he froze at the voices he heard coming from the porch. The next sound, a key in a lock and a doorknob turning, sent him scrambling down the steps.

"Hey!"

Mark paused for a split second, undecided whether he should push past the men who blocked the door, or race for the back. The uniform of the second man made his decision for him. He bolted for the back of the house and dove through the window he'd come in the night before. His back scraped the top frame and he felt a burning sensation even through his jacket. He ignored it and tucked his head and turned so his shoulder would absorb the impact of the ground. The camera swung up and hit him in the chin. The window was only about five feet high, and a carpet of leaves broke his fall. He rolled to his feet, ignoring the shouts for him to come back.

He cut through alleys and backyards until he was at least six blocks away. He slowed to a fast walk, but adrenaline still raced through his veins and he couldn't control his shaking. Why the hell had a cop come to the house? There was no way anyone could have known he was there. Out of breath, he staggered into the recessed back doorway of a restaurant and sank onto the top step. It was too early for the business to be open and a dumpster hid the steps from the road. Gasping, he released the pack, almost shocked to find he still had it with him. His hand was stiff from gripping the strap so hard and he opened and closed his hand a few times. After moving the camera down, putting his arm through the strap so the camera would angle across and rest on his side, he found the bottle of water. He guzzled it, but the meager amount remaining was just a tease. He stuffed the empty bottle back in the side mesh pocket, hoping to find a place to refill it soon.

A sharp throbbing in his back reminded him of his dive through the window. He removed his jacket and turned it over, grimacing at the jagged tear in the leather. A fragment of glass clung to the lining, and he plucked it out, flicking it into the dumpster. He recalled the shards of glass he'd avoided last night when he'd climbed through the window. It felt like he hadn't made it through unscathed this time, but at least the leather had given him some protection. A deep scratch in the jacket above the actual tear attested to how much worse it could have been. He winced as he tried to stretch to find the cut, but it was beside his right shoulder blade and he couldn't reach it. Putting the coat back on, he cringed as his shirt clung to his back with a clammy coldness that he hadn't noticed before. He just hoped it didn't bleed too much and wasn't visible through the rip.

His stomach growled and he knew he'd have to go somewhere to get something to eat. A fast food restaurant would offer anonymity, but there were security cameras. He knew that nobody would scrutinize the tapes unless they had a reason, but if the police suspected he was in the area, they would question businesses and if anyone remembered him, they'd look at the tapes. A small diner might not have security tapes, but the waitress would be more likely to remember him. It was a toss-up, and so he decided to see if he could find a very busy diner in hopes that he'd just blend in with the morning rush.

As he lifted his pack, it occurred to him that wearing it would cover the rip in his coat, so he slipped it over his arms and shrugged to get it into position. It rubbed against the cut, but if he held the shoulder straps so the pack didn't bounce, it was bearable.

Cautiously, he surveyed the street before exiting the alley. Morning traffic was picking up and included pedestrians. He joined the flow, avoiding eye contact and on the lookout for a place to eat while he planned his next move. Two blocks later, he found a tiny eatery that was busy enough to allow him to fade into the crowd. He stepped through the door and saw the sign for self-seating. Perfect. Even better, there was a table in the back corner next to a hallway with a sign above it pointing to the bathrooms. He sat down facing the front of the diner, setting his pack on the floor beneath the table. Reaching for the plastic menu which was tucked behind the salt and pepper holder, his mouth started watering. He was so hungry, he felt like he could eat the mega meal that included eggs, pancakes, and the rest of the works, but if he had to run again, he'd never make it with all that in his stomach. When the waitress came to take his order, he settled on scrambled eggs and toast, juice and coffee.

After ordering, he made a beeline for the bathroom, camera and pack in hand. He scrubbed his face and hands and rummaged in the pack until he found his clean shirt. As fast as he could, he stripped off his shirt, but took a moment to turn to look at the cut in mirror before putting on the clean one. The cut appeared deep, but only an inch or so long. Satisfied he would live, he dipped the cuff of the ruined shirt into warm tap water and then draped it over his back, catching it near his waist with his other hand. With a gentle see-saw motion, he cleaned off some of the blood. He used the dry sleeve to swipe the drips and put on the clean shirt, not feeling dressed again until the camera was once again safely around his neck. A few drops of pink-tinged water had splattered the ground so he mopped them up, finishing just as another man entered the restroom. Mark stuffed the dirty shirt in his pack and nodded to the man. Better to act normal than to avoid any interaction.

He returned to the table to find his juice and coffee waiting. He sipped the coffee first, craving a burst of caffeine and when his plate arrived a moment later, it was all he could do not to attack it like an animal. These eggs were nothing like the reconstituted ones he was served in prison. These were steaming hot, fluffy and piled high on his plate. Hash brown potatoes came with them, and he used the corner of his toast to scoop them onto the fork. For five minutes, he ate without taking his eyes off his plate, so it didn't immediately dawn on him that the diner had become very quiet. He stilled, praying that it was only because everyone was eating, but it was more, he felt it in his gut.

Outside the diner were two police cruisers and two dark sedans. Men in suits exited the sedans, and with a sick twist of his stomach that threatened to bring up the food he had just eaten, he recognized Jim. Should he wait and confront Jim? Now that he had the camera back, he could prove to the police how he had been able to predict the 'L' track bombing. Except he needed some future photos first, and if he was in custody, he would never get a chance to produce them.

He just needed a little more time. Mark grabbed his pack, and looked over his shoulder for a back exit. Glancing back to the front, he tried to judge if he could make it out the back before they entered the diner. An instant later, he decided he'd have to try no matter what. The alternative was capture and time in the brig again. The front bell tinkled as the door opened and Mark jumped from the booth and darted down the hallway. After that, all hell broke loose.

"Mark!"

"Freeze! Chicago PD!"

Rationalizing the police wouldn't risk shooting in the crowded diner, Mark ignored the command and raced on, tossing his pack behind him in hopes of tripping any pursuers in the narrow hallway. Bursting through the back door, he found himself in a tiny parking lot surrounded by an eight- foot stockade fence. A delivery truck was parked alongside the fence and he bolted for it. Reaching for the grab bar, he used it to scramble onto the top of the cab.

"Mark! Wait!"

Jessie?

Crouching, he turned to see her standing in doorway, and an instant later, Jim rushed up behind her.

"Come on, Mark. Get down from there and let's talk this out." Her gun was in her hand, but pointed up.

"Listen to her, Mark." Jim came up alongside Jessie. He was empty-handed, but the cops racing around the side of the diner were another matter. The camera dangled, banging into the roof of the cab.

"I didn't do anything and I'm not going back there."

He grabbed the camera to steady it and made a leap for the fence, twisting to catch the top as he vaulted over. Gunshots echoed, splinters sprayed against his face, and light burst in his vision as something burned along the side of his head just above his ear. He fell in a heap onto the ground on the other side of the fence. Pain shot up his sore ankle when he hit. A garbage truck was leaving the lot, and Mark ignored the pain and burning as he lurched to his feet and caught the grab bar on the back as it passed right in front of him. The truck was moving slow, but he still was half-dragged until he managed to jump onto the running board just as the truck rumbled onto the street. He stole a peek around the back of the truck and saw Jim and Jessie looking over the fence for him while the police officers raced around the fence, stopping in befuddlement. Then the garbage truck turned a corner and Mark lost sight of them.

CHAPTER TWENTY

Jessie started to climb over the fence after Mark, but Jim pulled her back. "No, go the other way."

He ignored the scathing look she gave him before she leaped off the truck and raced around the fence. Jim jumped down, wincing at the impact that jarred up his legs. He wasn't thirty anymore, that was for sure. He marveled that Mark had managed landing in presumably one piece after dropping an estimated eight feet onto pavement on the other side of the fence. How the hell had the guy recovered and hidden so quickly? The way Mark had dropped after the gunshot by one of the police officers, he almost hadn't wanted to look over the fence at all because he'd been certain Mark would be dead on the other side. Why the cop had fired was something he was going to question and question hard. Mark had presented no threat and if the officer had gone immediately to the other side of the fence instead of stopping to shoot, they might have Mark in custody already. Worried about what might happen to Mark if the police found him first, Jim jogged to catch up, stopping when he rounded the corner into the lot. The cops gone to the far side to check around some parked cars. Jessie was catching up to them, but Jim headed for the dumpster at the back. It was closer to where Mark had entered and there hadn't been more than ten or fifteen seconds between when he dropped from sight and when they had looked over the fence. If he was behind or in the dumpster, they would be able to corner him and take him into custody without anyone getting hurt.

Cautiously, he approached the garbage bin, listening for any sounds and scouring the ground for clues. Near the base of the fence, he spotted bloodstains and his jaw tightened. Had Mark been hit or had he been injured in the fall? The drops of blood darkened the pavement for about twenty feet, and not heading towards the dumpster. Confused, Jim searched for more, but there weren't any. It was as though Mark had snapped his fingers and vanished.

* * *

He blinked as his eyesight threatened to go dark. When the truck stopped to empty a dumpster, Mark dropped off the running board, using one hand on the ground to catch his balance. If the driver of the truck saw him, he never let on. Limping away as fast as he could, Mark searched for a place to hide. His ankle throbbed and his head pounded in time to the beating of his heart. He found a side street and headed down an alley. A pothole tripped him up and he knocked over a garbage can as he tried to regain his balance. At least it was a plastic can, not a metal one. He crossed another street, grateful for the lack of traffic because his vision was dimming on the edges. He had to find some place to rest and find it fast. He tried a few garage doors, but found them locked. Leaning against one, he tried to think, but his head throbbed with every beat of his heart, distracting him. He pushed away from the door and continued until he saw the side door of a garage gaping about an inch.

Cautiously, he looked into the backyard of the home. Not seeing anyone, he opened the garage door wider and stuck his head inside. The interior was dark and dusty. Car parts and rusty tools strained an overloaded workbench on one side. On the other side was an old car. It looked like it hadn't moved in years. With a final check over his shoulder to make sure nobody was around, he entered the garage. Lawn chairs hung from hooks on the wall and he started to reach for one, but stopped and tried the car door first. If he had the energy to smile, he would have when the door opened with a low-pitched squeak. Finally, something went his way. He sagged in relief for just a split second, unable to believe his luck as he climbed in. A cloud of dust rose as he settled in the driver's seat but it settled quickly and he found the lever along the side of the seat, and reclined. Within seconds, he either passed out or fell asleep, he wasn't sure which, but his last thought before the darkness took him was that Jessie had a gun in her hand just before the shot was fired. Had she shot at him?

* * *

Jessica strode towards him but Jim knew from lack of police activity that they had come up empty too.

"What do you think? I know Mark likes to jog, but this is crazy. He should have been caught before he got out of the alley." Jessie pointed from the fence to the exit. "That's about thirty yards, and the others should have crossed his path as he ran out. It's the only way out of here." She turned and studied the back of the lot. "Unless he used the trash bin to get over the fence into the lot behind here."

Jim nodded. "Possibly, but look here." He indicated the blood. "He's injured, and left a trail, but it only goes about twenty feet, then just disappears."

Jessica's face blanched as she followed the blood spattered trail with her eyes, then raised her gaze to his. "You think it's bad?"

He shrugged and when he spoke, his voice had a hard edge. "I have no idea. I can tell you this much though. He's not going to show his face again if he can help it. Not with cops shooting first and asking questions later. I'd like to know why the hell they and you had your guns out to begin with? Mark presented no threat and was, in fact, running in the other direction."

Her eyes glittered with anger and a trace of tears. "It's instinct, damn it! These are Chicago cops and they've seen too many guns aimed at them to take a chance."

"But Mark wasn't aiming a gun." To his mind, there was no excuse. No gun, no just cause to shoot.

"Yeah, well I guess the cops got carried away. They made a mistake."

"Listen, Jessica. You're not a Chicago police officer anymore. Now you're a federal agent. It's not your worry what they do, you just have to do things the way we do them now."

Color returned to her cheeks as she nodded. "You're right, of course. Some habits are hard to break."

"Forget it. Here they come now, and we're going to need their cooperation if we want to find Mark. Just pray that he's in one piece." Jim strode to meet the approaching police officers. "He's gone, but he's injured so he may not be too far away. We'll have to spread out and search the surrounding neighborhoods."

The officer in charge, a big man who sported a thick mustache that had gone out of style at least twenty years before, nodded. "We're on it already. I've notified dispatch and we have a few extra patrols on the way."

"Excellent, and you'll also need to find out which one of your officers fired his or her weapon. There was no cause."

The cop bristled. "My man saw the suspect reaching for something. He fired before the suspect could bring a weapon to bear."

Jim crossed his arms. "Really? I didn't see it that way at all." Jessica threw him a look as though trying to caution him. He ignored it.

"You didn't have the same angle my guy had." The Chicago cop crossed his arms as well, mirroring Jim's pose.

Angry, but unable to disprove the other police officer short of calling him a liar, Jim let it drop…for now. At the moment, he needed their help. "We'll table this for the time being, but of course there will be an investigation."

The cop said, "Absolutely. It's standard procedure when a police officer fires his weapon." His tone indicated that Jim was ignorant for asking.

Jim brushed by the man, hating the pissing contest that always seemed to happen when FBI and police had to work a case together. He heard footsteps in his wake and confident that it was Jessica, he swept his arm out and said, "We have to cordon off these two lots and question the people in the diner. I want to know how long the suspect was here, what he ate and if he spoke to anyone. Don't let anyone leave until they've been cleared of having any contact."

It was all standard operating procedure, but the fact that Mark was the subject of the investigation made it harder for Jim to achieve his normal matter of fact tone. He had to dredge up the stony mask that he had last worn when he worked as an interrogator.

"I'll get right on it, Officer Sheridan." Jessica's formality surprised him, but he didn't let it show, he just nodded.

He was pleased to see the CPD treating the scene correctly and gathering the spent casing along with the weapon of the cop who had fired the shot. Other police officers returned to their cars and headed into the neighborhood across the street. Seeing that everything was going smoothly, Jim returned to the diner.

Jessica was already speaking to a waitress when Jim entered. He nodded to the customers, surmising from the way they were all seated that they had already been instructed that they would need to be questioned briefly before they could leave.

As there was just him and Jessica, Jim pulled out a notepad and, feeling almost like a waiter, went from table to table. Most didn't recall seeing Mark, and those, he allowed to go. One man had seen Mark in the bathroom and had noticed blood in the sink after Mark had left. He hadn't thought much of it.

Lastly, Jim approached the booth where Mark had been sitting. The meal was half-eaten, and some of the potatoes had spilled off the plate, probably when Mark had jumped up to flee. Other than that, the table was unremarkable. He recalled having to leap over a book bag of some kind as he'd chased Mark down the short hallway to the rear exit. He found it shoved to the side and knelt to open it.

On top was a damp bloody shirt. Jim spread it out and saw a tear on the back that was surrounded by the darkest stain. The rip wasn't too big, so Jim hoped that the size boded well for Mark and it was just a minor wound. If they were lucky, that was the source of the blood they had found outside, but Jim had his doubts. The blood on the shirt, except where the sleeve was wet, was dry and the shirt stiff indicating that it was at least an hour or so old, at the minimum. What they had seen in the lot was fresh. Of course, he could have re-opened a wound with that fall. In his mind, he saw Mark duck his head, then drop like a rock at the time the shot had gone off and he just knew that the blood was from a new injury, but how bad was it?

Jim set the shirt aside and dug deeper, finding power bars, a flashlight and a full water bottle. In an outside pocket, he found a small notepad. He flipped it open to discover a list of names and addresses. None of them looked familiar, but they'd run them all through the computer database to see how they connected to Mark.

"I finished with the diner staff, and I saw you had spoken to all of the customers, so I let them go."

Jim glanced at Jessica. She had composed herself, and all traces of anger and emotion had disappeared. Apparently she had her own stony mask. He sighed, wishing neither of them had to do this. "Good. I found his pack and other than a bloody shirt and a notebook, there's not much to go on."

"Bloody shirt?" Her mask cracked a tiny bit.

"Yes. It doesn't look too bad, and he was well enough to sit in here and order a meal without anyone noticing, so I'm not too worried about it."

Relief flashed in her eyes, and he hated to have to add a new worry, but there was no getting around it. "However, after seeing this, I'm even more certain that the shot must have hit him. He went down like, well, like he'd been shot." Sometimes the reality didn't need a metaphor. "But the amount of blood was minimal and he got away, so it must have been a graze or he might have just been nicked by some debris from the fence. I saw wood splinters fly."

It took her a few seconds to respond, and when she did, the mask was firmly back in place even as she said, "I hope you're correct, sir." She cleared her throat before speaking again. "Also, you might want to head outside. There are news vans in the front and reporters are everywhere. They're asking for a statement, and the Chicago PD says it's your ballgame."

"Damn it." He carried the pack to the front of the diner and surveyed the scene. The Chicago officer had about six microphones shoved in his face and even through the glass, Jim heard him say that the FBI was running the case, and they would give a statement momentarily.

One reporter asked if the fugitive was armed and dangerous.

"At the moment, we are assuming he is. That is why my officer felt the need to defend himself. The public needs to be aware and be on the lookout. This man is wanted in connection to the thwarted 'L' bombing. He was suspected of terrorism after 9/11, and was only released due to legal pressures."

"That asshole," Jim muttered. It was going to be a witch hunt for Mark. He could see it coming. He had to take control of the situation. He turned to find Jessica peering over his shoulder, and if the fire in her eyes meant what he suspected it did, she had heard and was just as angry, possibly even more so since she had spent so many years with the CPD herself.

"I can't believe they're bringing up the 9/11 crap." She stood with both hands on her hips, her eyes narrowed as she glared out the window. After a few seconds, she turned the look on Jim. "Mark should have received a medal, but instead, you guys kept quiet and didn't tell anyone how many lives he'd saved."

"*'You guys?'* Check your badge, Agent Bishop. You're one of us now." He hadn't intended to sound so harsh, but she hadn't exactly been so all forgiving with Mark either. Hadn't she dumped him because of his preoccupation with the camera and the dreams? At least, that was how Jim had read the situation. Nobody was completely innocent here, except possibly Mark.

Jessica's face flushed and she broke eye contact.

He had an idea. "You want to help Mark?"

"Of course."

"Okay, then you need to go out there and throw some water on the fire, and toss a lifeline to Mark. Tell the reporters that we believe there's been a misunderstanding, and that the arrest warrant had been executed prematurely, before all the facts had been gathered. Mark is not a suspect, we just want to talk to him." Jim pointed to the TV in the corner of the diner. "There are televisions all over the place. If you plead with Mark to turn himself in, there's a good chance he'll see it, or hear about it on the radio."

"I'm not going to go out there and lie just to get Mark to trust us."

"It's not a lie."

She crossed her arms in disbelief. "You're really not going to arrest him? What about Agent Harris? Isn't he going to have a problem with you naysaying him to the press?"

Jim's jaw clenched. She had a point, but he had one too. "I don't give a damn what Agent Harris says. If it's the last thing I do as director of this FBI field office, I will see to it that Mark gets treated fairly."

Her face softened. "Then why don't you tell them all this?"

The same thought had crossed his mind, but he shook his head. "This is your town. You know these officers. For all intents and purposes, I'm the outsider. Don't worry about Harris. I'll make sure he can't retaliate against you."

She pulled back, irritation crossing her features. "I'm not worried about him."

Jim smiled. "I didn't think so, but just the same, I'll take the heat for this. I just think you'll come across better on camera than I will."

With a tilt of her head, she spread her arms out before letting them drop to her sides. "I won't argue with that logic. Okay. I'll do it."

CHAPTER TWENTY-ONE

Mohommad dug the cellphone out of his pocket and, with one eye on the road, he dialed Hazim. He should have shot Mark yesterday when he had the chance. Or better yet, he thought again, he should have allowed Hazim to finish him off back in Mark's office when they had first taken the camera. He had felt generous at the time, but no more. His generosity had come back to bite him. He gripped the phone, pressing it to his ear. It never paid to be merciful.

Hazim finally answered, and Mohommad told him that the job had been moved up. They would have to proceed as soon as possible. His associate didn't sound pleased, but this was Mohommad's call. Too many months of planning had gone into these attacks, and already, one attempt had failed. He could not allow another failure. Now that Mark had the camera, their element of surprise could be lost, but he calmed his nerves with the knowledge that not every event showed up in the pictures. While the camera had been in his possession, plenty of Chicagoans had died in various accidents that never appeared on Mo's film.

He shoved the phone back in his pocket and rubbed his jaw, still not used to the smooth feel of his skin. There were so many things he needed to do and small details to attend to. It wasn't supposed to be like this. The first attack was supposed to strike terror, and this next one was supposed to not only inspire fear and awe, but further disrupt everyday lives of Chicagoans. He didn't want them to feel safe anywhere, but now, half of his plan had been destroyed, and the second part was in danger of being thwarted as well. What would his uncles say? They would feel shame, and Mohommad felt his face burn at the thought of having to confess his failure. No. There would be no conversation about failure. He would succeed or die trying.

He accelerated, passing on the right of the little old lady doing fifty in the left lane and vowed that the only conversation with his uncles would be one of pride and success. Before he could focus on the task at hand, he needed to take care of some personal business.

Twenty minutes later, he parked in front of his sister's home. A little pang of something that felt suspiciously like homesickness stabbed him in the gut as he took in the Halloween decorations. He shook it off and tried to summon the anger that had sustained him since yesterday afternoon, when Mark had stolen the camera and implicated Zaira.

He knocked on the door, resenting the fact that he no longer had a key to her house. As her brother, it was his right. Of course, Zaira couldn't be blamed for that as he had never come to claim a replacement key, but he held onto the anger anyway.

The door opened, and his sister's face showed mild curiosity before recognition dawned. Her hands came to her mouth in surprise. "Mohommad?"

Mohommad grabbed the door handle and entered, his very presence forcing her to take a step back and allow him entry. "Zaira. It's been a long time. Have you missed me?"

She nodded, but her eyes were shadowed with caution.

In his mind, he had played this differently. She would be crying tears of joy, and he would have gently asked her why she had turned against him, but instead, she didn't appear happy to see him. Instead of the gentle question, he stepped closer and put his hands on her shoulders. "Why, sister? Why did you betray me?"

She shook her head in confusion. "What are you talking about?" She wore a sweater and skirt and that angered him also. Where was the traditional dress? Their mother had worn it her whole life, even here in America. He took a deep breath attempted to rein in his anger. At least Zaira hadn't cut her hair and had it properly covered even if she didn't wear the traditional hijab, but instead wore some kind of scarf. Perhaps all was not lost after all. Perhaps she would consent to helping him.

Mohommad strode past her to the family room. Part of him hoped to see his nieces, but then he remembered they would be in school. A laptop was open on the breakfast bar, a glass of orange juice beside it, and the TV across the great room droned with an insipid daytime talk show. "You know what I'm talking about, Zaira."

She crossed her arms and lifted her chin. "No, I don't, dear brother. I have always been here for you, but you have not been there for me. Where were you when my husband died? I needed you, but you were so busy trying to impress the uncles who never cared for us when we were children, that you never even considered the difficulties I faced. You are the one who always flaunts tradition, but where were you when tradition called on you to take care of things?"

The wind completely knocked out his sails, Mohommad stood with his mouth gaping before snapping it shut. She was right, but that still gave her no right to betray him. "You helped Mark Taylor."

Her eyes slid away for just a split second, but it was enough for Mohommad to realize the truth.

"Am I not your brother, Zaira?"

Zaira moved to the breakfast bar and closed the laptop. "You will always be my brother, but I hate what you've become. Mark wanted his camera back, and you had stolen it."

"You believed him?"

She studied his face until he was hard-pressed not to squirm like a guilty little boy.

"He was honest from the moment he came to the house, and I had no reason not to believe him."

Mohommad shook his head in disgust. "Do you know where he got the camera?"

She shrugged.

"From Afghanistan. He conned it from some old man in a bazaar. It rightfully belongs to our people, not some American. They already take everything from us. They bomb our homes and kill our children, and now they even steal our national treasures."

"An old man in a bazaar cannot be conned. Do you think I have forgotten how those men love to haggle?" Zaira leaned against the counter and crossed her arms. "I think you have also forgotten that I am American. You were American too."

Mohommad glared at her. "No longer." He stalked to the sliding glass doors overlooking the backyard. An elaborate jungle gym took up a good portion of the space. He remembered pushing his older niece on the swing the last time he had been back there for some party. It seemed like a lifetime ago. Or like it had been another life entirely. He had been American back then, before his uncles had talked sense into him. Now he scorned all the trappings of American suburbia.

His uncles would be proud of him and he would restore the pride in the family. Growing up, he had never realized that his father had been somewhat of a family outcast for moving to America.

"Oh my goodness!"

Mohommad turned from the window to find Zaira staring at the television. He followed her gaze. It was a breaking news report, and Mark's picture graced the top left hand corner of the screen with the word, 'Fugitive', beneath it.

The woman speaking seemed familiar, and he missed half of what she was saying as he tried to place her. The news report listed her as Special Agent Jessica Bishop, but the name meant nothing to Mohommad.

It wasn't until she spoke directly into the camera and said, "Mark Taylor, if you're watching this, please turn yourself in. You will be treated fairly, we all guarantee it. We want to talk to you and give you a chance to tell your side of the story." She emphasized 'your side' and sent an angry glance at the Chicago Police officer beside her. As she paused, he finally placed her. There had been photos of her in Mark's loft when he went to retrieve the camera from him. Now it made sense to Mohommad when her voice cracked just a little when she continued, "But if you continue to evade police, we can make no guarantees."

Zaira made a small noise, like a stifled gasp, and he shot her a look. Her expression reflected her despair at the news. It didn't surprise Mohommad. Women had always liked Mark, only half the time, his former friend had been oblivious. It rankled that even his sister had fallen under his spell.

A news crawl across the bottom of the screen contained contact numbers and urged people to call if there were any sightings of the fugitive. Mohommad listened to the rest of the report and got the gist of it. Mark had run, and he could see that there was some kind of small restaurant behind Bishop. He recognized the area. At least he knew Mark's last known location and that he was being hunted by the police. That was great news. A man on the lam wouldn't have the time or resources to develop photos. That made Mohommad's decision to move forward with the next phase of the plan even more imperative.

* * *

Jim stayed at the diner long after the police and Jessica had left. The police didn't have the manpower to tie up so many officers when other areas of the city needed them, and Jessica had paperwork to do. She didn't want to leave, but there was no reason for her to stay and she was low man on the totem pole. Other agents would cry foul if she got preferential treatment. Already he was sure someone would complain that she had been the agent in the limelight on the news. Jim found he didn't give a shit what anyone said. Was this what burnout felt like? It was close to what he had felt when he had left his position as an interrogator.

He ordered a cup of coffee to go and took it outside. There had to be something he had missed, and he sipped the hot brew as he surveyed the back parking lot again. Metal had flashed just as Mark had turned to look at Jessica. For a second, Jim's own instinct had been to go for his weapon, and no doubt, it was what the police officer and Jessica had acted upon. Only something had dangled from his neck as it happened. It had been visible only for an instant, but Jim thought it might have been a camera.

It was even more urgent that they find Mark.

He was convinced he couldn't be far away. A guy didn't just vanish in front of a half-dozen officers.

* * *

Jim tried to concentrate on the report in front of him, but it was a routine budget analysis and his focus wandered. If his trip to Washington hadn't put him behind, he would have let it slide another day or two. Instead of neat columns of numbers, in his mind, he saw the diner parking lot. He had itched to do his own search, not trusting the police, but DeMarcus had called and told him about the pile of messages waiting for him. After returning the important ones, especially the one to his superior at Langley, he had tried to put it out of his mind. He had already called Chicago PD three times for an update on the search, but there had been no news. He was almost glad when DeMarcus buzzed him on the intercom. Anything had to be more interesting than the monthly budget crunch.

"Sir, there's a gentleman out here who says he needs to see you. I told him you were busy, but he insisted. Said he won't go until he talks to you. Should I call security?"

Jim stared at the intercom in puzzlement. It would take a fool to barge into a FBI field office and start making demands, especially to see the SAC. "Does he have identification?"

"Yes. His name is Gene Taylor and—"

Jim cut him off. "Send him right in, DeMarcus."

"Yes, sir."

Jim stood and took his suit coat off the back of his chair and shrugged into it, remaining on his feet as the door opened. He had never met Mark's father but had remembered details of the man from reports he had read about Mark early on. The man who marched past DeMarcus was almost as tall as Mark, slightly stockier and had thick salt and pepper hair. He could see the resemblance to Mark immediately in the eyes, although Gene Taylor's were darker, more hazel than green.

Jim stepped forward, his hand outstretched. "Dr. Taylor, I'm Jim Sheridan. It's a pleasure to meet you."

Gene Taylor stared at Jim's hand and for a moment, Jim flashed back to Mark's release as an enemy combatant and how he had refused to shake Jim's hand. Gene Taylor wore that same look of revulsion on his eyes, but after the hesitation, he clasped

Jim's hand in a firm shake. "I'm sorry the pleasure isn't likewise, Special Agent Sheridan."

"I'm sorry to hear that because Mark has told me wonderful things about you, and I'm honored to finally make your acquaintance." It was a stretch, as Mark wasn't overly talkative about his father, but Jim recalled the emotional phone call Mark had made before the Wrigley Field incident. Whatever their differences, there was a connection between the father and son. "Please, have a seat." He gestured to the chair on the other side of the desk before resuming his own seat behind the desk.

"I'll cut right to the chase. I'm worried about my son, and I need answers. I thought, given your past association with Mark, that you might have them."

"What is your concern, specifically?" Mark's role as Jim's asset was supposed to be confidential, but it sounded like Mark had shared the information with his parents.

"I hope I won't get Mark in more trouble, but he tried calling us today and sounded terrible. He called to tell me where he had parked my car, but—"

"Your car?" This was an interesting bit of news. They had been assuming Mark had been without a mode of transportation that wasn't public.

Gene waved dismissively. "That's not important. I loaned him my car a few days ago, and this morning, he calls and tells me the car is in the long term lot at O'Hare. So, I took a bus down here to come and get it. What concerns me is I found bloody napkins inside, and when he spoke to me this morning, he sounded..." His voice cracked, but Jim pretended not to notice and just waited for the other man to continue. Gene cleared his throat and finished, "He just sounded so exhausted. Beaten."

"Dr. Taylor, I'm not at liberty to discuss ongoing investigations—"

Gene stood and leaned on the desk, his eyes rock hard as they bore into Jim's. "Now look here, buddy. Don't you dare go all official on *me*. You and I know exactly what role you've played in my son's imprisonment, and how he was treated. I came to you because for whatever reason, Mark seemed to trust you, as crazy as that sounds." He pointed his first two fingers at Jim in a stabbing motion. "You *owe* him."

Jim kept his voice low and calm when he replied, "Dr. Taylor, I certainly understand your feelings and concerns, but I assure you that I have no information. In fact, if you loaned Mark your car a few days ago, you've spoken to him much more recently than I have."

Gene sank back into the chair and raked a hand through his hair in a gesture that spoke of where Mark had picked up the habit. "My wife is frantic. The only reason she isn't up here right now is because I sent her back to her sister's house. I told her that Mark might try to call again, and she wouldn't want to miss it." He closed his eyes briefly and when he opened them, Jim almost flinched at the pain reflected in them. "Look, Mr. Sheridan…Jim, I'm going to be staying at The Blackstone for a few days. If you hear anything, would you please contact me?"

"Of course, but before you leave, can you answer a few questions for me?"

Wariness stole over Gene's face. "That depends. Ask away, but I may not answer them."

"Fair enough." Jim leaned his elbows on the desk, hands clasped, while he formed the questions in his mind. "Can you share anything that Mark told you when you saw him? Was he at your house or were you here?" Seeing the hesitancy in Gene's expression, he added, "Unofficially. Believe it or not, I'm trying my best to find Mark so I can help him. Right now, I'm his best bet at getting all of this straightened out, but I can't help him if he's running away."

"He took a bus up to our place. We live just outside Madison, in a small town called—"

"I have your address on file." It sounded callous but Mark's file contained all the standard information, and while Mark had been an asset, it was more than just intelligence information. It was for notifying next of kin in the event of injury or death, but Jim didn't mention that part. "Did he say why he ran?"

Gene rose and threw his arms wide. "Why he *ran*? Are you *dense*? Mark knew he was going to be arrested. He dreamed it."

Jim was only human and couldn't hide his irritation at the slur. It wasn't every day someone dared to call him dense. In his own office no less. When he thought of it that way, he almost smiled. In the last few years, he'd seen Mark becoming more outspoken but had assumed it was in response to all that had happened. Now he wasn't so sure. Just possibly Mark's attitude was genetic. "I suspected as much, but I was hoping for confirmation. Did he say what his plans were?"

"He wanted to find that schmuck, Mohommad, and get his camera back so he could prove he gets future photos. Mark felt they would have to believe him if he had proof. He never had a chance to show anyone his camera after 9/11, and that didn't turn out so well, now, did it?"

"No, I agree. That wasn't a good situation, but his running now just makes him look guilty. I can't help him if he isn't here. He needs to turn himself in, and instead of talking him into doing that, you lend him your car so he can get farther away." More than a little worried that Mark had been badly injured this morning, Jim took his frustration out on Gene. He stood so he could be eye-to-eye and hoped to regain control of the conversation. "Frankly, he's a grown man and needs to face his problems so we can get it taken care of."

Gene leaned forward and tapped a finger on the desk top for emphasis. "Damn straight he's a grown man, and I'm proud as hell to call him my son, but he's just that—*my son,* no matter how old he is, that's how I'll always think of him."

Jim nodded. "I apologize. I didn't mean to imply that Mark had done anything you shouldn't be proud of." He gave a shake of his head, his anger draining as he let out a wry chuckle. "In fact, I know first-hand that you have every right in the world to be proud of your son. In other circumstances, he'd be receiving medals, but unfortunately, it's complicated." With a sigh, Jim pinched the bridge of his nose and organized his thoughts. Emotional outbursts always scrambled his ideas, and it was why he constantly strove to be cool and impersonal. Damn Taylors. First it was the son, and now the father. Letting his hand drop, he said, "I really just want to help Mark. I know he's not guilty of the bombing, but if he's not here, I'm going to have a difficult time convincing anyone else of his innocence."

Gene visibly relaxed, but he still wore a guarded expression. "I'm sorry if I'm questioning your motives. You say you want to help him, but you weren't always in his corner, and from the little Mark confided to us recently, you had basically left him high and dry in regards to the camera. You never even looked for Mo, did you? You let the real terrorist run free but hound my son as though he's Osama Bin Laden himself. Now you claim to want to help Mark, but what if you're just trying to further your career by arresting Mark for the bombing attempt? That would look pretty damn good on your resume wouldn't it?" He paused, his eyes drilling into Jim. "What is it you really want, Special Agent Sheridan? Or is it Officer Sheridan? What hat are you wearing today? CIA or FBI?"

Ignoring the last question, Jim said, "I told you, Dr. Taylor. Believe it or not, in the last year, Mark and I have become pretty good friends, so this is personal for me too. Yes, Mark had the camera and was an intelligence asset, but once the camera was gone, I had no choice but to let him go. We talked it over and came to an understanding. In fact, I thought he was a little relieved to be rid of the camera. You have no idea how chaotic his day-to-day life was. The camera and resultant dreams basically controlled him, and he wasn't free to do what he wanted."

Gene had the grace to nod in response to Jim's observation as he sat back down. "You're correct. Mark hasn't had a normal life for a few years."

Jim also resumed his seat, leaning back with one ankle resting atop the other knee. He rubbed his chin in thought. "You said he had dreams though? Even without the camera?"

"That's what he told us. He said that he dreamed that he was going to be arrested in his loft. He woke up early, grabbed a few things and took a bus up to our house. Apparently he'd been stashing money at our house the last few years in case he needed to get away."

"Yes, that makes sense. We checked his accounts, and there hasn't been any activity on them. Can you think of any other friends or relatives Mark might go to for help?"

Eyes narrowing, Gene replied, "I thought you knew everything there was to know about Mark. You know…in the file?"

Jim felt heat rush up his face but whether it was anger or embarrassment, he wasn't even sure. "The file stops pretty much at Mark's release. We didn't keep tabs on his personal life after that. What I know about him was learned only as a friend."

Gene shook his head. "I'm concerned. I mentioned the bloody napkin right? Could he be in a hospital somewhere?"

"One thing I can confirm is that Mark was sighted this morning, and at the time, he appeared okay. Unfortunately, we lost him after that, which was why I was hoping you'd know of someone he might turn to."

"Then you should know about his ex-girlfriend, Jessica Bishop. He was close to her, and I think they're still on friendly terms. She's a Chicago detective though, so she might be the last person he'd approach."

Jim cleared his throat. "Actually, she's an agent here now."

"Ah. Well, then, that's it. I don't think he'd go to her. He's probably tracking down Mohommad alone, unless you can find someone who can lead you to Mo. If you do, you'll probably find my son."

Not wanting to worry Dr. Taylor, Jim didn't mention the encounter earlier in the day. The blood they'd found could just be a minor cut. After all, he had escaped yet again. If he'd been hurt badly, he would have been lying in that parking lot instead of vanishing into thin air. It had been Jim's hope Mark would have some other friend that no one else was aware of. Some childhood friend that only parents would know.

Jim stood and stuck out his hand, effectively ending the meeting. "If I hear anything, I'll contact you at the Blackstone. You have my word on that, Dr. Taylor."

"Gene. You might as well call me Gene."

Jim nodded. "It's been a pleasure meeting you finally." And he meant it. Even if he and the older man had exchanged harsh words, he respected Mark's father.

"I look forward to hearing from you."

CHAPTER TWENTY-TWO

"Hey!"

Mark started awake. Disoriented, he turned his head and came face to face with an old man peering at him through the side car window. He jerked away from the door, his heart slamming against his ribs as he pressed into the seat. Casting a wild look around the interior of the car, he had no idea where he was or whose car he occupied. His head throbbed, making thought next to impossible, and the effort exhausted him.

The man rapped his knuckles against the glass and said, "I don't know who in blazes you are, but if you don't hightail it out of here, I'm gonna call the cops."

Police? Not good, although the reason why escaped him at the moment. "No, it's okay. I'm going." He touched the side of his head, just above his ear, wincing. His hand came away sticky with blood which he wiped on his jeans. "Jus…just give me a second." His stomach did a flip, and he had to swallow. His memory of how he came to be in the car filtered into his muddled mind in a series of non-sequential images. A garbage truck, a diner and he vaguely recalled scrambling on top of a box truck. Cops had been there too, and that memory came with a jolt of panic. Jim and…Jessie…and… a gunshot. *Shit!* They had *shot* at him. Was that the source of his injury? Mark pressed the heel of his hand against his forehead. If only he could think through this splitting headache. He gave up the effort to remember. Right now, he had to get out of the car before the old guy followed through on his promise to call the police.

As Mark grabbed for the door handle, something clanked against the steering wheel. *The camera!* By some miracle, it still hung around his neck—maybe there was still a chance he could escape from this mess.

"I mean it, mister. Get outta my car!"

Mark opened the door. "I'm sorry, sir. I…I'll be going." He stepped out but had to lean heavily on the door as the garage did a slow loop-de-loop around him. Head hanging, he squeezed his eyes shut until the spinning relented.

"What's the matter with you? Ya got blood on your head."

"Just bumped it, I guess. Sorry. I hope I didn't stain the seat."

The old guy broke out laughing and slapped a hand on the hood of the vehicle. "This jalopy hasn't run in years. I ain't worried about the seats. I only keep this old clunker because my son wants me to get rid of it, and I don't like taking orders from him."

Mark tried to block out the rambling as the man's voice sent shards of pain slicing through his head. He closed the car door but found that without something to hang onto, his knees buckled.

"Whoa there, buddy." Surprisingly strong hands caught Mark under his arms and eased him down to sit with his back against the car. The cold of the metal felt good against the back of his head, but made him shiver. "Just sit tight. I'm gonna call 911."

"No! I'm fine." Mark grabbed onto the man's arm. "Please, don't call." He reached up for the door handle, grateful that the car had the older handles that stuck out from the door. Pulling with all his strength, he managed to get upright again.

"Well, somebody's gotta come and help you. I don't drive no more, so I can't take you to the hospital. Besides, what if you die in here? A possum died in here one winter, and I didn't find him for months--not until he started stinking up the place. I found his carcass right underneath *here*." He thumped the hood of the car again, the sound blasting through Mark's head. He cringed and put two fingers to each temple. If the old geezer did that again, Mark was going to have to hurt him. "The thing was half-rotted by then and stunk up the whole garage. I don't want to have to clean your remains out of here next spring."

Mark tried to think past the pain and fog that shrouded his brain. "Yeah, that probably wouldn't be a good thing."

"You got *anyone* I can call for you? A friend or someone?"

"Um…" If he hadn't felt like vomiting, he would have laughed at the question. The whole reason he was in the predicament was because of his so-called friends. His knees wobbled when the garage renewed its rotation around him. If he didn't give an answer to this old man soon, the next time he woke up, he'd be in jail. He had to make a plan. Running was out of the question. With the way he felt, he wouldn't get ten feet before collapsing, and if that happened, the old guy would have to clean up his rotting carcass in the spring after all. His mouth turned up in a ghost of a smile. That would teach the guy to bang on the car. Organizing his thoughts into a cohesive plan was like trying to wade through quicksand. The faster he tried to think, the worse his head hurt. "Yeah, I have someone."

Okay. He had the camera now, so he didn't really need to run. Getting a future picture had been his goal, but he was going to need help to get it now. The only person who might give him half a chance was Jim. At least he believed the camera existed, and he had the power to get others to listen. Jessie might have helped while she was with the police, but with her new position with the FBI, he knew she wouldn't have the authority to help him.

He reached for his wallet when his attempts to extract Jim's phone number from his memory resulted in a wave of nausea. Struggling to focus in the dim garage, Mark fished around in the billfold until he found one of Jim's cards and handed it to the man. His voice felt as thick as molasses, and his tongue a couple of sizes too big for his mouth as he said, "Here. Call this number and ask for Jim Sheridan. Tell him the call is from Mark." He paused to take a breath, then added, "He'll come by or send someone." Probably with a bunch of his FBI friends in tow, but Mark didn't add the last bit. The game was up and a surge of anger gave him a dose of energy, making him contemplate escaping again, but as quickly as it hit him, the adrenaline dissipated. His only hope would be that he'd be given a chance to demonstrate the camera to authorities before they locked him up.

The man held the card up, an arm's length from his face and squinted at the print. "Special Agent in Charge, Jim Sheridan?" His mouth hung open for a second or two. "You didn't like my idea to call 911, but you think calling the FBI is a *better* one?"

"He's a friend. Sort of." It occurred to him he had no idea how long he'd been in the garage. He'd been at the diner in the morning. "What time is it?"

"About two o'clock." He grinned and raised the card a fraction. "I never called the FBI before. I'll be right back."

Mark attempted to roll his eyes at the old man's enthusiasm, but the motion made him retch. He leaned against the car, and slid down until he plopped onto the cold cement again.

It seemed he'd only just sat down when someone shook his arm. "Mark! Wake up!"

"Huh?" Mark opened his eyes to find himself on his side on the floor with no memory of lying down. Jim squatted beside him, gripping Mark's upper arm. "Jim? How'd you get here so fast?"

"Fast? It's been at least thirty minutes since Mr. Dudek called me. I got caught in traffic."

"Mr. Dudek?" Mark struggled to a sitting position. His headache hadn't subsided at all. If anything, he felt worse. He gripped the sides of his head, his elbows braced on his bent knees as he squeezed his eyes shut when the pain intensified.

"Mr. Dudek is the gentleman who owns this garage, and I promised him I'd remove you from it before his son gets home. So, let's see if you can stand, okay?"

"Okay," Mark agreed, but made no move to get up. He took a deep breath and concentrated on sending the command to rise from his brain to his legs, but the signal seemed to short out before it reached its destination.

"*Today,* Mark." Jim's grip tightened on Mark's arm, and tugged until Mark was forced to use his legs to lever himself upright.

"Good…good. Whoa. Put your arm over my shoulders. *Mark?* Open your eyes and listen up!"

He hadn't known he'd closed his eyes, but they snapped open at Jim's command. "Sorry. Kind of dizzy."

"Yes, I know. You have quite a gash on your head, but you're going to be fine."

"Okay." Jim said it, so it must be true. The guy was always right.

"Just walk along here with me. I'll go slow, but if we don't get going soon, Mr. Dudek is threatening to call an ambulance. I told him I'd take you to the hospital, but if you can't get to my car, I might have to go along with Mr. Dudek's plan."

Mark shuffled beside Jim but balked at the mention of a hospital trip. "I can't go to the hospital. They'll call the cops."

Jim snorted. "I can't believe I'm agreeing with you, but for now I am, so get your ass in gear."

It felt like the walk was miles as they made their way through the backyard to a narrow walkway alongside the house. Mark blinked in an attempt to widen the tunnel of vision he peered through. "Where'd you park?"

"On the street in front. I was afraid of blocking the alley and drawing attention, but I think I should have risked it now. Just keep moving. You're doing fine. That's it."

Mark stumbled when his foot landed on the edge of the walkway, and his sore ankle gave out. Jim pulled him up, but the sudden movement was too much for Mark's stomach. He shoved away from Jim and, with one hand on the wall of the house, leaned over and vomited into a bunch of yellowing and wilted day lilies. His skull threatened to explode, and as if from a distance, he heard Jim speaking, but it was too much effort to decipher the words. He tried to spit the taste out, but his mouth was too dry. "Sorry. Tell Mr. Du…Dude…" He forgot the man's name. *Damn it.* "The old man. Tell him I'm sorry I puked on his plants."

"Don't worry about it. Just a little farther."

Finally, they made it to the car and Mark climbed in, barely noticing when Jim strapped the seat-belt over him. When the car began moving, he groaned.

"You're not going to be sick again, are you?"

Mark almost laughed at the panic in Jim's voice. "No. Nothing left." He tried closing his eyes, but that just seemed to make the dizziness worse, so he kept them opened a slit and fixed his gaze out the front window.

The car swerved suddenly and Mark had to close his eyes and swallow hard. Jim's voice droned, but Mark had the impression he was speaking to someone else, especially when Jim gave out his own address and then said a curt good-bye. Mark was sure that when they reached their destination someone would be waiting for him with a fresh set of handcuffs.

He didn't dare turn his head, but he managed to ask, "What's going on?" He knew he should care, but he just couldn't summon the energy. "I suppose you'll send me back to the brig." The window felt cool against the side of his head as he slumped against the door.

"The brig? Not if I have any say, but don't worry about that now. I'm taking you to my place. I have someone meeting me there who can help you. I hope."

Questions formed in his mind, but he forgot them almost as soon as they took shape. Frustrated, Mark gave up and just tried to keep from vomiting in Jim's car. He didn't want to give the man any reason to change his mind and lock him up.

CHAPTER TWENTY-THREE

Jim clenched the steering wheel, his knuckles white. What he was doing could cost him his career or worse, and his common sense screamed at him to take Mark into official custody. All his life, he'd done things by the book and for the most part, that strategy had worked for him. This one time, he closed his ears to the pleading of his common sense and listened to his gut. The damn book didn't have a chapter that dealt with guys who could see the future. Jim supposed one day he'd be an expert and could write that chapter, but until then, he was forced to improvise.

He took the turn onto his street as slowly as possible, noting Mark's occasional moan when the car would jolt over a pothole or turn at a normal speed. About halfway to Jim's house, Mark had closed his eyes, and now, his head lolled. Only the groans indicated he had any awareness at all.

What if Dr. Taylor assessed Mark's condition and concluded that it was serious and Mark *needed* to go to a hospital? There was no way to hide him as a patient. Not unless Jim outright lied and came up with a phony ID, but even if he might consider going to that extreme, he didn't have any fake IDs close at hand. If he was still strictly CIA, he would have been more prepared for this kind of contingency. It was the one time he regretted taking this job instead of taking a different position offered at the same time. Jim vowed he would do what he could to protect Mark, but once everything became official, those blasted rules had to be followed. Jim glanced at Mark and said, "You better damn well be okay."

After pulling his car into the garage, he jumped out, calling over his shoulder for Mark to sit tight, and he'd be right back. Mark didn't budge. The door into the kitchen opened as Jim reached for it. Startled, his hand instinctively went to his gun. "I see you found the key I told you about." Gene stepped out, gave Jim a sharp glance, but ignored the comment as he barreled past him and around the car to Mark's side.

"What did you do to him? He looks terrible," he said, as he opened the car door and Mark tumbled out. Only Gene's quick action of grabbing the collar of Mark's coat prevented Mark from smashing face first onto the cement floor of the garage.

"I didn't do anything. This is how I found him." Jim rounded the car, as Gene tried to get between Mark and the interior of the door in order to gain some leverage to hold Mark's weight. Jim reached under Mark's arms and locked his own hands across Mark's chest, supporting him. "Come on, Mark. We're here. Time to wake up."

Mark batted at Jim's hands, but only a few times before his head sagged forward and his arm flopped to the side.

Jim sighed, worried about how unresponsive Mark had become. "We're going to have to carry him."

Gene took his son's legs, and between the two men, they managed to get Mark as far as the couch in the living room.

Out of breath, Jim attempted to set Mark down gently, but his back protested and instead, he dropped Mark unceremoniously onto the sofa. Gene glared at Jim. Bent with one hand on the small of his back, Jim just returned the glare, too out of breath to do more, but it was on the tip of his tongue to point out that the end he had carried was a lot heavier. A moment later, he straightened, wincing at the lingering spasm. A second later he was wincing again, this time in sympathy as Gene rubbed his knuckles hard against the center of Mark's chest. Mark groaned and mumbled something as he swatted his dad's hand away.

"That's it, Mark. Open your eyes." Gene removed a small penlight from an old-fashioned doctor's bag. Jim didn't think those kind of bags really existed, but this one was worn enough that it looked like it received frequent use.

Shining the light into Mark's eyes, he frowned but said nothing, although he seemed pleased when Mark turned his head away. "At least he's reacting to the light." He took another instrument out of the bag and checked Mark's ears. The right only took him a moment, but he cursed as he tried to peer into Mark's left ear.

"*What?* What's wrong? Is he okay?"

Gene raised an eyebrow. "Does he look okay to you?"

"Well…no, but he spoke to me earlier and was somewhat alert."

"Sorry. I didn't mean to snap." Gene straightened and set the instrument on the coffee table. "His pupils are a little sluggish, but equal, and that's a good sign. I'm trying to check for signs of skull fracture, but the whole side of his head is just caked in blood, and of course, some of it ran into his ear. I can't tell if he has cerebral spinal fluid in his ears or if it's just blood from the head wound."

Jim looked down at his hands, finding red smears on them as well as more blood on the left sleeve of his suit coat. "I'll get some towels and water."

Gene nodded. "That would be great. Thank you."

Glad to be of some use, Jim practically flew to the linen closet and grabbed the first three towels and all the washcloths he had. He set them on a chair in the living room before racing to the kitchen for a couple of pans of water.

"Here."

"Thanks. We better get a couple of the towels beneath him. This is going to be messy."

After helping to place the towels, Jim stepped back and watched, hoping Mark would wake up any second. What the hell had happened? While Mark hadn't seemed totally with it back at the garage, he'd at least spoken and walked to the car. What if his skull was fractured?

After a head to toe examination, and cleaning the furrow on the side of Mark's head, Gene straightened, wiping his hands with a clean, wet washcloth. "It's hard to say for sure, but I don't think it's anything more than a concussion. He's also moderately dehydrated, and that along with what I'm guessing was considerable blood loss, has him wiped out."

Relieved, but puzzled, Jim said, "But I thought all head wounds bled a lot. I didn't think it was that big of a deal."

Gene shook his head. "It's not a big deal in a minor injury. Even a tiny quarter inch cut can look like someone's bleeding to death, but it usually stops quickly." He tossed the cloth onto the stack of dirty clothes piled on one of the towels. "But, in this case, Mark's been grazed by a bullet and has a two inch gash on the side of his head. Another couple of millimeters and we'd be discussing funeral arrangements." Eyes narrowed, he continued, "I want to know why the hell my son was shot and what you know about it, but first, I have to stitch the wound shut while it's still fairly fresh. The cut on his back too. I just hope I have enough supplies to close them both. Then, I'll have to get Mark to drink something, preferably some kind of electrolyte solution."

Jim nodded. "Fair enough. I'll tell you the whole story, but what about Mark? Will he be okay?"

"I think so. If we can get some fluids in him, that is."

"By electrolytes, do you mean something like a sports drink? I don't have any on hand, but there's a mini-mart just around the corner. I could get some and be back in less than ten minutes."

"That would be perfect. Before you go, we need to turn him on his side and facing the back of the sofa so I can get to his injury."

Mark roused when his father injected the numbing agent. Jim had to get on the end of the couch and reach over to hold Mark's head still while Gene stitched.

"Hold still, Mark. I'll be done in a few minutes."

Jim felt a jolt course through Mark's body when Gene spoke. Jim couldn't see Mark's face, but could sense that he was trying to look over his shoulder to see if the face matched the voice.

"Dad?"

Gene spoke again. "I'm here, son."

Nobody spoke for a few seconds, and then Gene cleared his throat. "This reminds me of when you were about ten, and you crashed your bike trying to jump three garbage cans. Remember that?"

"Yeah." The word was almost inaudible, but Jim caught it and smiled.

"Remember what you were doing that day, Mark? Can I tell Jim? I'm sure he'd get a kick out of it."

Mark's body shook, as though he was trying to suppress a cough, or, Jim noticed the corner of Mark's eye crinkle, a fit of laughter.

"Don't you dare." Mark's voice was stronger.

"You should have seen it, Jim. He and his friend--Paul, I think his name was--were re-enacting Fonzie's jump of the barrels. Or was it the shark? I don't remember, but Mark just about scared his mother to death when he came in with blood gushing down the side of his head." Gene never looked up from his work, but Jim caught him blinking hard as he paused, the muscles of his jaw visibly tightening.

After a moment, he continued, his tone light, "She thought I should take him to the emergency room, but he was fine—just needed a few stitches. Just like today." He snipped the last one and stepped back, nodding for Jim to release his hold.

Mark reached up to feel the wound and rolled onto his back. His eyes darted to his father and landed on Jim. "Where did you come from? How did you find me?"

Jim frowned. "Don't you remember giving that man my card and asking him to call me?"

His brow furrowed in confusion, Mark stared at Jim, but finally, he gave a small shake of his head. "I don't remember much of today. It's all a blur."

Gene put his instruments in one of the pans. "It's a good thing you managed to contact Jim. You need some fluids."

Grimacing, Mark rubbed his forehead. "I don't know if I can drink something now. I'm thirsty, but my stomach's kind of queasy."

"If you drink it slow, you should be fine. If you don't drink, the nausea will get worse, and then we'll have to take you in to an ER for an I.V. I have just the basics in my bag. Lucky for you, I'd already stocked it for my upcoming hunting trip."

Mark sighed and closed his eyes.

"I have one more needle for you."

Mark's eyes snapped open. "No…"

Gene pulled a vial and a syringe out. "Yep. I have to give you a shot of antibiotics. You really should have a course of I.V. antibiotics, but this will have to do."

Not wanting to see yet another needle, Jim gathered up the scattered towels, piled them with the rest of the dirty linens and tossed them on the pile. "While you do that, I'm going to run and get the sports drink. I'll be right back." He thought Mark and his dad might need a moment to talk too. Jim picked up one of the pans. "If you're done with this, I can empty it in the kitchen before I go. Just toss the towels and stuff in the hamper in the bathroom."

"Yes, I'm finished. Get at least a few bottles of the drink." Gene reached into his pocket and pulled out his wallet.

Jim passed him with the pan, ignoring the twenty Gene extended. "I got it."

"You're sure?"

He knew it shouldn't, but the offer angered him. "Yes, I'm sure." Jim emptied the pan and put it in the dishwasher. It crossed his mind to wonder if Mark and Gene would be here when he returned. Now was their chance. Gene would have a car, although he'd followed Jim's advice and parked it around the corner, and if they left there wasn't much Jim could do to stop them. Reporting them would implicate himself, and they were smart enough to realize that. Jim considered Mark's state of mind. Well, at least Gene would realize it. At the moment, he wasn't sure Mark even remembered why he was running.

Chances were slim that his condo was under surveillance, but just in case, Jim took a meandering route to the mini-mart, checking his mirror to see if he was being followed. He even doubled back to check to make sure no suspicious cars lurked about, watching his home. Satisfied that it was only his inherent caution and that there was no real threat of discovery, he didn't rush into the mini-mart but instead, ambled in like he didn't have a care in the world. After choosing a couple of flavors of sports drinks, he added some saltines to the purchase after recalling Mark's upset stomach. As he passed the shelves stocked with pain relievers, he remembered that his bottle of ibuprofen was almost empty, so he grabbed a bottle of that too. Was ibuprofen okay to take with a concussion? Jim had no idea, and to be on the safe side, threw a bottle of acetaminophen along with a bottle of aspirin, into the hand basket.

As he waited for the few customers ahead of him to check out, Jim thought over the last few hours and tried to develop a plan. Mark couldn't hide out forever at the house, but he wouldn't be able to go home either. Somehow or another, they had to come up with a way to get Mark exonerated. One thing they had going for them was that the camera was back where it belonged.

* * *

Mark grit his teeth as the needle plunged into his thigh. His dad had given him a choice, leg or butt. It was really no choice at all. Once his dad finished, Mark lifted his hips off the sofa and pulled his jeans up and zipped them. The exertion caused his head to pound, and it was a few seconds before he heard his dad speaking.

"So, what happened to you? Do you remember?" His dad sat on the coffee table, hands planted on his knees, waiting.

Digging his elbows into the leather, Mark hitched up higher on the couch until he was more comfortable. It would probably be easier to pretend amnesia, and truthfully, it wouldn't be far from the truth. His memory of the last day was scattered at best. He remembered the fight with Mo and—Mark bolted upright, ignoring the dizziness, pain and nausea the action caused. "The *camera?* Where is it? I got it back from Mo." He grabbed his head when he couldn't ignore a spear of pain that lanced through his skull.

His dad's hands were on his shoulders. "Lie back down. Your camera is right here. You had it around your neck when we carried you into the house."

Mark slit his eyes. "You *carried* me in?" Oh God.

"You didn't leave us any choice. You wouldn't wake up." His dad leveled a serious look at him. One of the looks he'd seen his dad use on patients. Mark squirmed under the scrutiny.

"What?"

"When I saw you slumped in Jim's car, for an instant, I thought you were dead. I was ready to kill your buddy, Jim."

"Sorry, Dad." Mark sat up, disregarding his dad's admonishment for him to lie down. "I'm not dead, but if I can't get someone to believe that I had nothing to do with the 'L' bombing, I might as well be." He scrubbed his hands down his face, wishing he could wipe away the brain fog. "I need to use the camera and then develop the film. Hopefully, something will show up, and I can show the police so they can see that the photos and dreams were the only connection I had to the bombs."

"Mark, listen. I don't know much about your camera, but I know you're in no shape to go traipsing around taking photos. Do you have to be outside? Is there a secret to getting the future photos?"

"I don't know about any secret to it. I just load the film and shoot. Often, I'll get photos of something that wasn't there when I took the picture. Then after I see the photo, or maybe it's something in the camera...anyway, there's some kind of connection between me and it—and yeah, I know that sounds strange, but it...it's like it triggers something in me, and I dream about it."

"Are you the only one it works for?"

Mark shook his head, but stopped immediately and swallowed as bile rose in the back of his throat. After the nausea subsided, he said, "Not really. It seems like anyone can take the pictures, but I think I'm the only one who gets the dreams. Why?"

"Well, what if I took some photos and had the film developed? You could rest here in the meantime."

Mark raised an eyebrow. "Really? You'd do that?"

His dad shrugged and stood. "Of course I would. Why wouldn't I?"

"Oh, I don't know—maybe because you've always thought the camera and dreams were a bunch of baloney." If he hadn't felt so lousy, he might have succeeded in better masking the bitterness in his tone, but Mark was running on fumes, and it was all he could do to keep his eyes open, let alone try to phrase his response in a more neutral manner.

"I never said that. I just didn't understand the whole concept. It's not every dad who finds out their son has some kind of freakishly bizarre ability to see the future in a photograph."

"True. I guess I never thought of it that way before." Mark attempted a grin. "No wonder you've been so ornery around me the last few years."

His dad raised his hand as though he was going to clap Mark on the shoulder, but at the last second, he must have thought better of it and instead, just patted Mark's shoulder and gave it a slight squeeze. "I apologize for that, Mark. I guess I never really understood the magical part and all the implications, but I finally realized I don't have to understand it. I just have to believe it exists."

* * *

Jim returned, relieved to find Mark and Gene hadn't taken off. He gathered a plate and a glass, and hanging onto the plastic handles of the bag, carried it all out to the living room. "I got some pain relievers, so take your pick, Mark." Jim set everything on the coffee table and withdrew all three bottles of pain relievers and placed them in front of Mark. "I got some crackers too. I thought they might help your stomach."

"Thanks."

"Good thinking, Jim," Gene said as he opened the blue sports drink and poured it into the glass. "It's like you've done this before."

Jim shrugged. "Kind of. My son had a concussion after taking a hard hit in football one season."

Mark reached for the ibuprofen, but his hand stalled halfway there. "Son? You have a son? How come you've never mentioned him before?"

"There are a lot of things I don't mention, Mark."

Mark shook his head. "You're the master of secrets."

"What do you expect? I am CIA after all," Jim said, his tone dry.

"And I suppose your son is classified information?" Mark opened the bottle of ibuprofen, shook three out, and grasped the glass of sports drink, downing the pills in one swallow.

"No, not classified, but I try to keep my personal life separate from my work." Jim picked up the box of crackers and tugged at the corner of the cardboard flap. He scowled as the box ripped. Pulling a sleeve of crackers out, he set the box down and the tore open the sleeve and swore under his breath when a couple of crackers popped out and onto the floor. "We don't see each other much. Not after his mother and I divorced."

Gene handed him the plate. "Where's your son now?"

"What is this? Twenty questions?" He dumped a dozen crackers on the plate and set it down with a clatter.

"Christ. I was only asking out of mild curiosity. It's not like I'm going to go extract retribution on him for what you've done to *my* son in the past."

Jim bristled. "My son and his whereabouts are nobody's business. For all I know, that's exactly what you're planning on doing." The moment the words were out of his mouth, a wave of shame washed over him. Gene Taylor was no threat and Jim felt like an idiot for implying that he was, but pride and habit kept him from apologizing.

"Dad…" Mark rose and put himself between his father and Jim when Gene took a menacing step towards Jim. "Calm down."

Gene had a hand on Mark's chest to nudge him out of the way, but his nudge sent Mark stumbling sideways as his foot caught on the leg of the coffee table. Both Jim and Gene reacted, reaching out and grasping the arm nearest to them. Between the two men, they steadied Mark.

Mark shrugged them off, glaring first at Jim and then his father. A flash of pain crossed his face, and he lifted a hand to his temple before resuming his seat on the couch. "On second thought, have at it guys." He waved his hand towards the middle of the living room. "Duke it out if you want. I'm…I'm just going to lie down for a few minutes." With that, he swung his legs up on the sofa and reclined, his eyes closing as he slurred, "It would be…great if you took the fight away from the couch though. I can't promise I won't puke on the carpet if you knock into it while you're beating the crap out of each other. You've been warned."

Jim felt the corner of his mouth twitch as his gaze moved from an apparently already sleeping Mark, to Gene. The other man looked at Jim, the corner of his eyes crinkling as he rubbed the back of his neck, a sheepish expression on his face. Jim was sure his own mirrored it. "Listen, Gene…I'm sorry. That was stupid of me to say that. My son is a sore spot with me, and I guess I let my anger at that situation color my reaction."

Gene pulled an afghan off the back of the sofa and draped it over Mark. "I know the feeling."

Jim bent and retrieved the dropped crackers. Straightening, he said, "Possibly, but I think only another divorced parent could truly understand." From Mark's bio, he knew his parents had been married a long time. They had never had a custody battle.

Gene might think he knew how it felt to lose custody of his son, but unless it happened to him, he'd only be guessing. The day Jim had signed the custody agreement had been the most difficult in his life.

"It's true that I never had to deal with divorce and all the crap that comes with it, but Mark and I have had our share of differences, and then he was...gone." The last word sounded strangled, and the muscles of Gene's throat worked.

Jim looked away and busied himself with gathering the unused pain relievers and the unopened extra bottle of sports drink off the table. He stuffed them back in the bag and tucked the torn box of crackers under his arm. "Yeah, I guess we never know what someone else is going through."

Gene cleared his throat and topped off Mark's drink before following Jim into the kitchen. "That was the worst thing. We couldn't talk to anyone about it."

Jim didn't want to hear this. How would he ever do his job if every time he questioned a suspected terrorist, he'd be picturing a grieving mother and father wondering where their son was? It wasn't his fault Mark had been arrested, and he'd only been doing his job when he questioned Mark. So why did he feel so guilty?

Jim shoved the crackers in the cupboard and left the pain relievers on the counter in case they were needed again. "It was a difficult time for everyone." There. He had acknowledged Gene without admitting to any wrongdoing. He took the opened bottle of sports drink from Gene and set it on a shelf in the fridge. While he was there, he grabbed a can of beer and lifted another towards Gene in offering. Coffee would be a better choice, so they could keep their heads clear, but one beer wouldn't hurt them, and they needed something stronger than coffee. Too bad he didn't have any Scotch on hand.

Gene took the beer and sat at Jim's kitchen table, popped it open and took a long swig. "I'll tell you what though. We found out who our true friends were, and the list wasn't nearly as long as I'd expected it to be. Norma, Mark's mom," he motioned with the beer towards the living room, "and I had a rough time. Thought we were going to get divorced, but we hung on, and then he came home." He took another swallow and played with the ring on the top of the can.

Jim sat across from Gene and opened his own beer. The role he'd played in Gene and his wife's difficulties wasn't lost on him, so he just sipped his beer and let the other man fill the silence.

"Norma never doubted Mark. Not for an instant." Gene plucked at the ring now, the metallic twang the only sound in the room.

"But *you* did?" Jim had to ask to confirm the silent implication.

Gene lifted one shoulder. "I didn't want to, but…the government wouldn't make an arrest unless they had plenty of evidence. Right?"

Jim shifted in his chair and took a gulp of his beer.

Gene chuckled. "Yes, I know that sounds incredibly naïve. I was in college during the Vietnam War. Hard to believe I'd forgotten some of the lessons I'd learned back then." He shrugged. "But as you get settled, have a family and build a career, you don't focus on the outside world. You trust the government to do the right thing."

"I go by Fox Mulder's advice." Jim couldn't resist and wanted to steer the conversation away from politics. "Trust no one."

Gene laughed and shook his head. "That was one show that both Mark and I enjoyed. He'd already moved out by then, but when he'd come home on a weekend, we'd watch it." Tilting the can, he emptied it. "And now, we're living an X-File."

Jim almost choked on his beer as a laugh erupted without warning. He swiped the back of his hand across his mouth. "Does that make me Fox Mulder? I am working for the FBI after all."

"I suppose it does."

They sat in comfortable silence for a few moments. Gene stood up, turned in a half circle until he spotted the garbage can in the corner and tossed his can in.

"I have a few more cans of beer in there. Help yourself."

"No, I'm good." He returned to his chair. "You know, I really am sorry about the scene in there. It's none of my business, but, like I said, one of the hardest things when Mark was gone was not being able to talk to anyone."

Jim's impulse was to brush off Gene's unspoken invitation, but after hearing Gene's confession about how the stress had almost cost him his marriage and how he'd harbored some doubt about Mark, he decided he was making a bigger deal of it than it was. "There's not much to say, really. My son's name is Chris, and his mom and I divorced about five years ago. He was a sophomore in high school." Jim shook his can, less than half left. "I was gone for my work a lot back then. Sometimes out of the country for months at a time. My ex-wife couldn't take it anymore and divorced me. I wanted to be there for Chris, but not long after that, 9/11 happened, and my workload tripled. I was back in the States, but shortly after the divorce, I was transferred from Virginia—where I was based when not out of the country—down to Charleston. At times, I would have to go to Guantanamo or even Afghanistan. I didn't get to see much of Chris. Just a few times a year. He's in college now and wants nothing to do with me. End of story."

"That's rough." There was no condescension in the statement. "I'm a bit of a workaholic too, so I didn't get to spend as much time with Mark as I wanted when he was growing up. He went to college as pre-med, and although it might not be apparent, he's a smart guy. Pulled A's in class without breaking a sweat, but he had zero interest in medicine. He only went in as pre-med at my insistence, but all he wanted to do was take pictures. I was angry, and even a little bit envious. I struggled through college, and here he could have sailed through and he didn't want to. I was so frustrated."

"Chris is studying theater." Jim finished off the beer and tossed it into the can from where he sat.

Gene threw his head back and laughed. "I hope you don't use that tone when you speak to your son about his major."

"What tone?"

"You might as well have said he was studying shit."

"Is that how it sounded?" Jim replayed his comment in his head. Did Chris hear it like that too?

"You know what? Reach out to Chris and ask him about theater and listen to his reply. You might find that you haven't lost your son at all." Gene placed his hands on the table and stood. "And speaking of sons, I'm still waiting to find out what exactly happened today that almost cost mine his life."

The reprieve over, Jim considered his reply. "A report came in to the Chicago P.D. of a sighting of Mark in a house that was just foreclosed on. It seems he spent the night there. It was bad timing on his part, as today was the scheduled day the Cook County Sheriff had to evict anyone still living there. The sheriff showed up with a representative of the mortgage broker, and Mark ran past them and leaped out a broken window into the backyard. I think that's how he cut his back, by the way. We found a ripped and bloody shirt in the backpack he abandoned at the diner. Anyway, police were on alert and an off-duty cop spotted him in the men's room of the diner. He called police. We picked it up on the scanner and took a run over there at the same time."

"That doesn't explain the gunshot wound."

"Unfortunately, Mark bolted out the backdoor of the diner. The cops split up, some going around the back and some going through the diner. The guys who went around back saw Mark climb up on a box truck parked out there, ready to drop over the fence into the neighboring lot. At that time, Jessica Bishop and I were exiting the back of the diner as well. It all happened so fast, but piecing it together, Mark froze when he saw us. He reached for the camera just before he jumped for the fence, and the officers thought he was reaching for a gun. One of them fired his weapon just as Mark cleared the fence. I have to admit, I thought I'd find his body on the other side, but when we got there, he was gone. I still haven't learned how he did it, but he managed to get a few blocks away and entered an unlocked garage and slept in an old car in there. The homeowner went out to the garage to 'tinker' as he described it, and found Mark sleeping. He called me after Mark gave him my number."

"So you didn't shoot him?"

"No. I didn't have my weapon out, but let's be clear on this--I would have been following procedure if I'd had my weapon in my hand." Jim waited a beat, then added, "Special Agent Bishop followed protocol."

"Jessica Bishop?" Gene's mouth set in a hard line.

"That's correct, but she never fired her sidearm."

"How generous of her."

"It was, actually. If she'd fired at him, she most likely would have been cleared in the subsequent investigation. You have to realize that Mark was fleeing from not just Chicago Police, but the FBI as well. That sudden movement and glint of metal was enough to trigger reflexes when adrenaline is running high. *We* may know he's innocent of wrongdoing, but to others, his running made him look guilty as hell."

"After what happened to Mark before, can you blame him for running?"

"I'm not saying he had an alternative. I'm just stating the facts as they appeared to the others in that parking lot."

Gene didn't appear placated, but after giving Jim a long, hard stare, he simply said, "I'm going to check on Mark, and then I'm going to go out and try to take a few pictures with Mark's camera. We thought it might work for me. He's going to present it as proof that he's been telling the truth all along."

"That sounds like a plan. I'm going to check in with my office. See if there's anything going on that I'm missing. I pretty much abandoned work when I got the call about Mark."

CHAPTER TWENTY-FOUR

Jessie tried to concentrate on the meeting, but all she could think about was Mark's face when he'd turned to see her at the back door of the diner. His eyes had been wide in surprise--or fear, she wasn't sure which. Maybe it was both. Then there had been the gunshot and he'd dropped from sight. It had been hours and nobody had reported any sightings. How could he have just disappeared?

Suddenly she realized the meeting had ended and the other agents were standing, stretching and chatting. Still the new agent on the block, she gathered her notes, and headed towards the door. An agent whose name slipped her mind approached her, a smirk turning up the corner of his mouth.

"So, how did you manage to get picked?"

She crossed her arms. "Picked? What are you talking about?" Simon. That was his name, only she couldn't remember if it was his first or last name. Maybe his first name was Simple. Yeah, Simple Simon. Okay, that wasn't fair. The guy wasn't stupid, but his attitude annoyed her.

"First, Sheridan puts in a good word for you to get hired, and then just a few weeks later, you're chosen to go along to arrest the most wanted fugitive in Chicago? To top it off, you then hold a press conference."

How much should she mention? Would it be better to keep her relationship to Mark a secret or would they feel better knowing that she'd only been given the assignment this one time because of the special circumstances? His smirk bugged her. "First of all, there are special circumstances. I have some information about the fugitive that I acquired as a detective with the CPD. In light of that knowledge, I've been asked to work on the case. As far as the press conference goes, it wasn't a conference, it was just a couple of words to the press, who had already gathered. We didn't call them or anything. I know the local press, and Ji—Director Sheridan thought it might be better for me to speak to them and keep it low key than for him to answer questions."

"Ah, so you're on a first name basis with Sheridan? How'd you manage that? The guy is the most distant and cold director I've ever worked under. I don't think I've ever seen him crack a smile. That's how those CIA guys are. They think they're too good for us."

"If I was interested in your opinion about the director, I'd have asked for it, Simon." She brushed by him, tossing over her shoulder as she passed, "Besides, I look better on TV than the director."

At least Simon laughed at that and it didn't even sound mocking. Maybe he wasn't so bad after all.

Back at her desk, she dropped the notes and checked her voicemail. *Please let there be some information about Mark.* Her shoulders slumped. Nothing. Just a message about a meeting for the next day that had been re-scheduled. She thought there would be more messages as immediately after the press conference had aired, the phone began ringing off the hook. Those were the notes she'd shared at the meeting. So far, none sounded too promising, but it had been just such a tip from someone at the diner that had led them to Mark this morning. As her finger lingered on the number to erase the message, the phone rang, making her jump. "Special Agent Bishop speaking."

"Agent Bishop? Are you the one I saw on the news this morning?"

Jessica tried not to sound impatient. After twenty such calls, it was difficult to do. The switchboard tried to filter calls, but if they were in doubt, they sent callers through. "Yes, how can I help you?" The caller, a woman, had a light accent, possibly Middle Eastern. Jessie sat and pulled a pen from her pen cup."

"I'm not sure how to go about this, but I spoke to Mark Taylor a few days ago--"

"Where? May I get your name?" Callers didn't always want to be identified, but she hoped this one would. The tone spoke of hesitancy, and Jessie had heard the same hesitancy in enough informants' voices to recognize it as reluctance usually expressed by someone close to a suspect.

"My name is Zaira Saleem, but my maiden name is Aziz. My brother is Mohommad Aziz."

Jessie almost dropped the phone. None of the news reports had listed Mohommad as wanted. "I'm listening."

"Two days ago, Mark Taylor came to my house looking for my brother. I don't know if you know about my brother, but he and Mark used to be friends. I know my allegiance should be to my brother, but he stole something very important from Mark

"Go on. What was it he stole?" If she said camera, then Jessie would know it was a legitimate call.

"Mark said Mohommad stole a camera…a special one…and that he needed it back so he could prove that he had nothing to do with the attempted 'L' bomb."

"That's correct. And you think Mark was looking for Mohommad to get his camera back?"

"I know he was."

"And did you tell him where your brother was? From my intelligence reports, your brother should be living in a village in

Afghanistan. That's quite a distance for Mark to go to retrieve a camera."

"My brother is in the U.S. He's right here in Chicago."

Jessie closed her eyes and let out a deep breath. Finally, they had a witness who could place Mohommad here in Chicago. She'd always believed Mark, but without a witness, there was no way to prove his claim that Mo was here. "What is he doing in Chicago?"

Zaira hesitated.

"If you know something, you're obligated to tell us. If you don't, and something happens, you're just as culpable."

"I understand, but that's not it. I just don't know exactly what my brother is planning, just that I think he has something big in the works. He wants to impress our uncles back in Afghanistan."

"What kind of plan? Like an act of terrorism?"

"I don't know, but he's here and he's angry."

"Are you afraid of him?"

"Not for myself, but he was so full of hatred. I'd given Mark a notebook with names and addresses of Mohommad's friends, but the list was old. I was asked to compile it when he was arrested after September 11th, but then nobody ever came to collect it."

"And…?"

"Well, apparently Mark found him yesterday and got his camera back. Mohommad said it didn't matter. He'd be able to carry out his mission even without the camera. It was only going to be used for insurance, but now it's almost like he's counting on Mark to try and stop him."

"Do you have any idea where your brother might be now?"

"I'm sorry. I don't. I'm not sure why I even called as I don't know where anyone is now. I saw on the news that Mark escaped this morning. I can't say I'm unhappy about that."

"Really? And why would you feel that way? He's wanted in connection to the attempted L bombing."

"He told me he didn't do it and I believe him. In fact, he told me about his magic camera and how he had a dream about the bombing, and was able to help stop it."

Jessica hated it, but she had to play the skepticism role. These calls were recorded. "That's what he tried telling us too, but it's just a bit far-fetched, don't you think?"

Zaira must have sighed, as there was sudden sound of air rushing over the receiver. "I suppose it does sound that way, but how hard would it be to put out a message with the media telling Mark that you know he now has the camera and can turn himself in and the camera can be tested."

"Well, I'm not sure about testing the camera, but I do appreciate the tip on your brother. Although he's not wanted in connection with this case, he shows up in my database as banned from the country, so your encounter with him does back up Mark Taylor's claim that Mohommad was back in the country."

"Will that help Mark's case?"

Jessie shrugged, but realizing the other woman couldn't see the gesture through the phone, finally said, "It couldn't hurt."

She ended the call a few minutes later after getting Zaira's address and phone number. Now what? Where was Mark? He had the camera, so why didn't he come forward? It would be a simple matter to prove the future photos. Jessie had no doubt about that, but why had he run this morning? Why had he risked being shot?

***

Mark squinted up at the white ceiling, trying to gather his wits. He recognized Jim's living room and the day's events rushed back to him. Rubbing his forehead, he took mental inventory. The headache was still present, but not as all-encompassing as earlier, and he could at least remember most of what had happened since he'd run out of the abandoned house. Was that just this morning? The shades were pulled, but other than a square of light splashed across the carpet from the kitchen, the room was dark. It could have been early evening or middle of the night for all Mark knew. His mouth tasted like old wood ashes and his first goal was to get something to drink. He risked sitting, arms braced as he teetered on the edge of the seat cushion and waited for the Earth's rotation to catch up. As soon as he could focus, he noticed a glass on the table containing the blue stuff he'd sipped before falling asleep. He tried to ignore the shaking of his hand as he grasped the glass and took a long drink. The liquid was lukewarm and salty, but it tasted like nectar of the gods at that moment. After catching his breath, he drained the glass.

His stomach gurgled in protest, but Mark took a few deep breaths in an effort to overcome the nausea. He was *not* going to get sick again. He swallowed convulsively as cold sweat popped out on his brow. *Damn it.* Standing, he wiped his palms on his jeans and took a tentative step towards the bathroom.

"Hey, Mark, where are you going?" Jim stood in the doorway between the kitchen and living room, a steaming mug in his hand.

"Just to the bathroom. Don't worry, I'm not trying to escape." The deep breaths seemed to be working as the rumbling in his belly quieted to a low growl.

Jim moved to within a few feet and set a mug on the coffee table. "I wasn't accusing you of trying to escape, and besides, you're not a prisoner here."

Mark paused in his journey to the bathroom. "I'm not?" Since Jim hadn't taken him straight to be processed, he'd figured he wasn't under arrest yet, but didn't expect he was free to leave either.

"No, but we'll talk about it after you come back…" Jim nodded towards the bathroom.

"Yeah. Okay." Although he didn't feel the need to rush anymore, he was eager to clean up. He couldn't ever remember feeling so grimy, and wondered if he smelled bad as he felt. "Uh, Jim? Is there any chance I could use your shower?"

Judging from Jim's quick agreement, Mark decided he probably did smell a bit ripe.

"Sure, but aren't you supposed to keep the stitches dry?"

Crap. He'd forgotten about them. He looked over his shoulder to the kitchen door. "Is my dad still around?" What his father didn't know wouldn't hurt him.

"No. He went out to use your camera, then was going to get the film developed someplace that could do it in an hour." Jim glanced at his watch. "So, given he left a few hours ago, he should be back soon. It's getting kind of late and I imagine most places he could get the film developed will close soon."

"Okay, good. I'm going to take a shower and play dumb about the stitches."

Jim shrugged. "It's your head and your father. Towels are in the linen closet. I'll grab you some of my old sweats and leave them outside the door of the bathroom. If you're up to it, I have some disposable razors in the medicine cabinet."

Thirty minutes later, he emerged feeling ten times better. He'd even managed to shave, only nicking himself a few times. He'd patted the stitches dry as best he could and just hoped his dad wouldn't notice.

Jim sat in a recliner, feet up and a file of some sort open on his lap. He glanced in Mark's direction and said, "Feeling better?"

"Yeah. Thanks." He looked for the glass he'd been drinking from, but it was gone. "You mind if I help myself to something to drink?"

"Be my guest. I made some fresh coffee too."

Coffee. He could almost feel a jolt of energy just from thinking about the first sip. He should probably stick to the other stuff, but caffeine was medicinal to his way of thinking. Besides, he felt a lot better since he'd downed the last glass of sports drink. Returning a few minutes later, he cradled the mug as he sat on the edge of the couch, elbows propped on his legs. "So? What happens now?"

"We wait until Gene returns with the photos."

"What if there isn't anything important on them? That happens sometimes." Mark took a sip, set the cup down, and clasped his hands, one in a fist, the other wrapped over it. He couldn't even look at Jim, dreading the answer and not wanting to see it written on the other man's face. No way would he go meekly to be thrown into the brig again. No. Damn. Way. He took a deep breath and said, "What's going to happen to me? Chicago PD wants me dead or alive."

"No they don't." Jim set a paper back in the folder and closed it. "Not the dead part, anyway. They want to question you, of that there's no doubt, but they don't want you dead."

"Really?" Mark raised an eyebrow as he slanted a glance at Jim. "And was there an engraved invitation to meet with them on that bullet they sent to my head? 'Cause if there was, I missed it."

Jim levered the recliner to a sitting position, sat forward and dropped the cream-colored folder on the coffee table with a sigh. "That was just an unfortunate reflex on the part of the officer. You looked to be reaching for something, and that kind of action will put a cop on alert. I think sun glinted off the camera. That, coupled with your sudden movement was all it took. The officer mistook your actions, thinking you were going for a gun, and fired. Pure survival instincts. Besides, it doesn't matter because I'm not turning you in."

"I don't get it. Why would you do that? I don't know much about FBI policies, but I can't believe they'd condone hiding a fugitive."

Jim gave a snort, one corner of his mouth turning up. "That's true, but like I've been told before, I owe you one."

"More than one."

"Don't push it, Taylor," Jim warned, but his eyes crinkled.

"Seriously, Jim. I know what you're doing can't be considered regulation. I'm already screwed, but I don't want you throwing your career down the toilet because of this."

Jim took a deep breath, his expression becoming serious as he tapped the folder. "Do you know what this is?" Before Mark could reply, he answered his own question, "It's my resignation."

Stunned, Mark stared at Jim. "Why?"

"Oh, don't worry, I won't submit it just yet. I want to keep some advantage on our side."

Our side? Had he heard correctly? "Look, Jim. I appreciate everything you've done here today, so don't get me wrong, but I can't let you destroy everything you've worked your whole career to achieve. You're in charge--"

Jim cut in, "I don't need your permission, Mark."

Mark narrowed his eyes, his jaw tensing as he gave a short nod. "Fine. It's your life. Screw it up all you want, but I'm not going to be the cause of it. I'll turn myself in first." He stood and looked for the phone.

"Sit down. Even if you called a SWAT team down here *right now* to take you into custody, I'd still resign—it's not about you. I have my own reasons, but I will admit that all of the…excitement, the last few days, did add impetus to my decision."

Resuming his seat, he tried a different approach. "But I have the camera back and--"

The grind of the garage door cut-off Mark's reply. He started and turned towards the sound.

Some of the apprehension he felt must have shown on his face because Jim held up his hand in a 'calm down' motion and said, "I let him use my car, just in case anyone was watching. He parked his own car around the block."

Even though logically Mark recognized that Jim was probably right, the twenty seconds it took for his dad to get from the garage into the living room were some of the longest of his life.

"Mark…you've cleaned up. I hope you didn't get those stitches wet." His father breezed into the room, bringing with him a blast of cooler air from the garage. He held a photo envelope under one arm and had the camera looped over his shoulder. He set the envelope and a key ring down on the table, his eyebrow arched in Mark's direction.

"Uh…I forgot, but I dried them as good as I could." He ignored the soft snicker from Jim as the other man bent to get his mug from the coffee table.

"Well, what's done is done. You look human again."

Jim sat back in the recliner, feet crossed at the ankle as he droned, "Smells human again too."

"Yeah, Mark. I meant to ask you about that. What did you do? Roll around in a trash heap?"

Thinking he might very well have crashed into a few garbage cans as he stumbled down the alley before spotting the open garage door, Mark just shrugged and reached for his coffee. The rejuvenating effects of the shower were beginning to wear off and he grimaced at the increased pounding in his head. The relative ease between his father and Jim surprised Mark. When had they joined forces?

A wave of fatigue washed over him. Carefully setting the mug down in hopes neither man would see his shaking hands, he said, "Look you guys, I'm not sure I can handle the tag teaming right now, so Dad, if you could just show me the photos you took..."

His dad gave him an appraising look and then moved around the coffee table to stand beside him. He took Mark's chin in one hand and removed a penlight from his shirt pocket with the other. He tilted Mark's head. "Look straight ahead."

Mark winced as the beam of light seemed to pierce his skull. He tried to pull his head away, but his dad's grip tightened.

"Now follow my finger."

Mark sighed and did as directed.

"No, just with your eyes. Keep your head still."

The eye movement added to the pain level, but he must have passed whatever test his dad had given him because he released Mark's chin and sat beside him. He picked up the photo envelope and slid four prints out.

"I think these might be future photos because they aren't at all what I took pictures of. These are the only ones out of the roll of 24 that came out differently. The others are still in there, but I separated these for you."

"This first one is just a bus. I almost left it with the others, but I couldn't remember taking a picture of a school bus, so there you go."

Mark glanced at it, also unsure what it could mean. It was a run-of-the-mill school bus, but there was no company or district name on the side. He set it aside to take the second picture. This one was more interesting. The bus was now in front of Navy Pier at the entrance for the Children's Museum. The sky was bright, but it was going to be a cold day judging from how bundled the Pier visitors appeared. Mark knew the wind could be brutal as it sped unobstructed off the lake, and the American flag on the left of the picture was standing almost straight out, showing proof of the conditions. The angle of the shadows indicated mid-morning.

"Here are the worst ones."

The next photo showed the bus, or what was left of it--just an axle with one melted wheel--alongside the building. A huge crumbling hole scarred the Children's Museum and black smoke billowed out. Sickened, he wanted to fling the photo away, but instead, he clutched it and studied it trying to commit every detail to memory. He couldn't let any clues escape his notice. The photos showed where, and a rough estimate of when, but *who* was still a mystery. Mark felt in his gut it was Mo, but a gut feeling wasn't enough.

Jim took the photo from Mark. He didn't speak for a moment, but the hard glacial expression that settled in his eyes sent a chill down Mark's spine. He'd seen that look before during interrogations, and was thankful it wasn't directed at him this time.

The last print showed the walking wounded, and behind them, laid out on the blocked off road, were rows of body bags. Police and fire department personnel dashed about within a large area condoned off with yellow tape. Debris littered the ground. Thousands of sheets of paper, parts of exhibits and building material littered the area. A piece of debris caught his eye. Mark held the photo closer and squinted, trying to make out a twisted piece of metal with a small wheel sticking up in the air at about waist height. With a shudder, he finally realized what it was--the frame of a stroller. Closing his eyes briefly, he prayed it had been empty when the bomb exploded. He set the picture down and bent his head, resting it on his clasped hands until he worked up the will to force himself to resume his examination. At least fifty bags were visible in the photo and who knew how many more weren't in the picture?

Overwhelmed and feeling like someone was driving a spike into his skull, he let the print slide out of his grasp and onto the table. Elbows on his knees, he cradled his head again and tried to fight the impulse to block the images from his mind. This rivaled the Wrigley Field photos for effect they had on him. Only 9/11 had stunned him more, but with those photos, disbelief at the carnage had colored his view. He was sure he would be able to stop it with a few phone calls, and so the sick fear he had felt had been tempered by his self-assurance that the pictures wouldn't come true. After all, he had been successful in every attempt at changing the outcome of the photos prior to that day.

The couch sagged and a second later, a familiar hand squeezed his shoulder. His dad didn't say anything, but he didn't have to. Never very demonstrative, his simple gesture spoke volumes and filled Mark with a renewed sense of purpose. They would stop this.

For a good five minutes, nobody spoke. Jim continued to examine each photo, and quickly shuffled through the ones that were unrelated, apparently finding nothing of importance. His father sat beside Mark for a couple of minutes more, but didn't look at the photos again. With a final squeeze and pat of Mark's shoulder, he stood with a heavy sigh and went into the kitchen.

"I think we can stop this one pretty easily. We'll just block off the street in front of Navy Pier and put out an APB on an unmarked school bus. Too bad we can't see the license plate or any identifying numbers, but just the fact that there don't appear to be any markings will stand out." Jim held up the first photo and pointed to the blank side of the bus. He pulled the photo in for a closer look. "Hold on. Somewhere around here, I have some reading glasses that can act as magnifiers."

Mark nodded, but he wasn't convinced. It sounded too easy. "I think this is Mo's work. He all but admitted to me that he planted the bomb under the 'L' track, so I know he's capable of it.

If he is responsible, he knows I have the camera and the dreams. He'll be on the lookout for a police presence. If he gets spooked, who's to say he won't turn the bus around and blow it up outside the Art Institute, or even in the middle of Michigan Avenue?"

Jim turned the icy look on him as if Mark had masterminded the plot himself.

Mark shifted on the sofa, but held Jim's gaze, refusing to be intimidated. "Hey, I'm playing the devil's advocate here. I just have a feeling, and I've been doing this long enough now that I trust my instincts."

Breaking eye contact, Jim blew out a deep breath and nodded in acceptance. "I just want it to be cut and dried, but I should know better. While you were sleeping, Jessica called me with some pertinent information. It seems Mohommad paid his sister a visit earlier today. We now have an eyewitness besides you who can place him in the Chicago area. According to Zaira, he was extremely angry and she feared he was planning something, but she didn't know what it was. Oh, and she admitted to speaking with you and giving you an address book."

"Zaira won't get into any trouble for that, will she?"

"No, we can work out something since she came forward with this new information. Don't worry about it." He stood, crossed to the bookshelf and found the glasses. Returning to his chair, he held the glasses a few inches above the first photo. "I thought I saw a shadow that could be the driver."

Mark slid to the end of the sofa closest to Jim and leaned over to see through the lenses too. It wasn't as strong as the magnifying lens he would have used in his studio, but it did enlarge the details somewhat. "I see what you're saying. There's someone there and it looks like a man with dark hair."

"You think it could be Mohommad?"

"I can't be one hundred percent sure, but his hair is short now, and the shadow man has short, dark hair. Of course so do a million other men in Chicago. Hell, *I* have short dark hair."

Jim threw him a speculative look. "Hmmm..."

Mark rolled his eyes. "Knock it off. You have short dark hair too."

"Okay, so what do you propose we do?"

It felt unnatural to take the lead in this situation. He had always been the one delivering the information, but Jim had been the one to act on matters like this. Still, for several years now he had been taking care of the plenty of impending incidents with no help at all. His confidence had grown with each one, but he wouldn't have a clear idea of what to do until after he dreamed. "I can't say for sure yet." He chuckled and said, "I'll sleep on it." His joke fell flat and it was Jim's turn to roll his eyes.

"Here, Mark."

Mark turned to find his father beside him holding a couple of pills and a glass of water. "More already?" As bad as the headache was, he didn't want to risk taking something that might hinder or inhibit his dreams.

"It's just ibuprofen. It should help control your headache so you can get some real sleep."

His dad had a point. The way he felt now, he wasn't sure he'd be able to sleep, as tired as he was. As he reached for the tablets, his stomach growled. His dad pulled back the pills and frowned. "You should take these with food. When was the last time you ate?"

Mark had to think about it. "I guess this morning."

"No wonder you're so shaky. We need to get some food into you."

The thought of food repulsed him. "I don't know if I can eat anything."

"Didn't you say you bought crackers, Jim?"

Jim stood and said, "I did. And I have peanut butter or some cheese. I think I even have a frozen pizza I could toss in the oven. I'm kind of hungry too."

Pizza didn't appeal to him at all, but Mark thought he could stomach crackers and peanut butter. He followed them into the kitchen, sitting heavily at the table. How was he going to be able to stop a terrorist attack tomorrow when walking 30 feet left him feeling like he'd just slogged five miles through a bog?

Jim started the oven and pulled the pizza out of the freezer. "You didn't have to get up, Mark. I'd have brought you a plate."

Mark lifted his head off his hand, surprised and a little suspicious of Jim's hospitality. "Who are you, and where's the Jim I first met in the brig?" The light-hearted tone he'd meant to impart on the question didn't quite match the reality and Jim paused as he tore the cellophane off the pizza.

"Actually, I guess I've changed. It was bad luck for you that you came through the Charleston brig not long after my divorce was finalized. I was…hmm…let's just say I was more than a little bitter." He slid the pizza into the oven and turned back to Mark. "That doesn't mean I did anything I shouldn't have. I followed protocol to the letter."

"Yeah, don't I know it." Mark rested his head on his hand again. "Sheesh, I bet lots of guys would love to have your job after getting a divorce. What a way to work out anger. It was just my luck to draw you as my interrogator." He was only partially kidding.

His dad and Jim both laughed at that and Mark sent his dad a sour look for siding with the enemy. Or former enemy. He would have said something, but his dad set the plate of crackers, a knife, and the jar of peanut butter in front of him and suddenly, he was starving.

After eating, Mark's dad went back to his hotel. Jim had offered him the sofa, but he declined, saying he had to get all of his things anyway, and when he came back in the morning, he would bring some clothes for Mark.

CHAPTER TWENTY-FIVE

The Ferris Wheel shone red and white against the crystal blue autumn sky. The laughter and squealing of children mixed with the occasional scolding of chaperones blended with sounds of traffic to create an undercurrent of joyful energy at Navy Pier. School buses lined up to disgorge their eager cargo at a drop-off area, then, newly emptied, the buses looped around and disappeared into city traffic.

Mark was there and yet not there. Sounds reached his ears, but felt distant, the sights just slightly out of focus. He wandered, avoiding children who didn't seem to see him and the adults looked through him. Feeling like a ghost from A Christmas Carol, *he realized he must be dreaming.*

Seagulls dove, snatching up any scrap of food a child dropped, but it was only mid-morning and most lunches were still safely packed away. In the drop-off area, as one bus pulled away, the next would take its place. As the students exited the buses, they gathered in large groups, before dividing into smaller groups and heading into Navy Pier, most probably on their way to the Children's Museum.

A bus took its turn at the front of the drop-off but instead of sending forth a stream of children, it just sat there. The driver of the next bus in line must have become impatient, for he blasted his horn a few times, but the first bus never moved. Mark's first thought was engine trouble, or maybe a teacher was giving last minute rules to the children. He remembered those days of being a child and practically bouncing out of his seat in excitement and having to listen to the teacher drone on and on about staying with the group, keeping quiet, blah, blah, blah. He chuckled at the memories. Poor kids.

After a few more moments, he stepped closer noticing that something was different with this bus. The windows. That was it. They were empty. No excited faces peered out, no heads bobbed, there was no movement at all. Puzzled more than alarmed, he looked for a group that was already done with their field trip and ready to board the empty bus, but none of the groups paid any mind to the empty bus. The hairs on the back of his neck prickled and without realizing it, he began moving towards the bus, but it was like trying to sprint on a treadmill. He was getting nowhere fast. The door opened and Mohommad appeared in the entrance of the bus, scanned the crowd and appeared as though he was going to exit the bus. Just as he started to step down, his gaze turned towards Mark and after a moment's hesitation, he scrambled up the step back into the bus. Had he seen him? How could he have? None of the other people seemed to notice Mark's presence. Just then, a Chicago police officer strolled past Mark. Mohommad must have been looking at the cop, not Mark. Knowing it was futile, Mark pushed harder to reach the bus, but it was like swimming through pudding. A sudden flash blinded him an instant before the sound blasted through his body. He flinched but strangely, didn't feel anything. The dream slowed to a quarter-speed as the wave of energy lifted people, tossing them like so many rag dolls, only to drop them in boneless heaps on the pavement.

When the image returned to normal speed, the bus was gone, as well the two flanking it. Only the axle of one bus remained. Shock and panic hit him at the same time. Above him, thousands of papers fluttered in the dense smoke-filled air. At first, there was just the sound of debris and the tinkling of glass, but soon, moans, cries and screams filled the air as terrified children and adults registered the explosion. Beyond the buses, on the side closest to Navy Pier, it was even worse. The wall of the Children's Museum had disintegrated and twisted metal beams protruded through the brick and glass.

His instinct was to help someone, but all around him, bodies littered the pavement…or pieces of bodies. He covered his mouth, gagging at the sight of a lone sneaker-clad foot. Unsure what to do first or where to go, he froze until the moans and cries of the survivors spurred him to action. A woman crawled across debris, her goal, the remains of a stroller. One wheel spun crazily in the air. A moment later, the woman screamed. And screamed. The wail pierced into his brain.

Mark jolted up in bed, his hands tight to his ears as he opened his eyes, relieved to find himself in Jim's spare bedroom instead of at Navy Pier. He'd been expecting the dream, but even so, it left him drained, and more exhausted than he'd been before going to bed. Hands shaking he lowered them and swung his legs to sit on the side of the bed. The wail still echoed in his head, amplifying the throbbing from his head injury. Remembering the ibuprofen Jim had bought, he headed to the kitchen to get a glass of water and down a couple more of the pain relievers. Still shaken from the images in his dream, he sat on the couch and flipped the TV on, turning it on low. He knew he should write down the details while they were still fresh, but he didn't think he was in any danger of forgetting them. They were etched indelibly into his mind. An infomercial touting the magical cleaning properties of a hand towel came on and the sound increased. He didn't notice until Jim came out into the living room. Mark did a double-take. Logically, he knew Jim wouldn't sleep in an immaculately pressed shirt and tie, but he still raised an eyebrow at the faded pajama pants the other man wore. It didn't fit the image.

Mark muted the TV. "Sorry. I didn't mean to wake you."

Jim rubbed a hand over his face, creating a sandpapery sound as he plopped onto the edge of the recliner. "What's wrong?"

"I had the dream." Mark's throat tightened making his next words inaudible. He cleared his throat and tried again. "It was…intense."

Jim sighed and sat back, but didn't recline. "Did you notice anything that might help us stop it? A time? A license plate?"

Mark shook his head. "Sorry. It wasn't much different than the photos--just a long line of buses, then one that didn't have any passengers. Next thing I know, it blows up and takes out the wall of the museum."

"Did you get an ID on the bomber? A license plate on the bus? *Anything*?"

"It was Mo." The shock of the dream started to wear off and anger took its place. "I saw him just before he blew the bus." Mark glared at Jim. "How could he do that to a bunch of little kids? Goddamn innocent *babies!*" He rocked forward, rubbing his temples and mumbled, "Damn it! I can't believe I was friends with him. I should have seen signs or…or something." Disgust at his own ineptitude made his stomach churn. "I must be a complete idiot."

Jim didn't speak for a several moments, but finally he leaned forward, hands clasped in front of his mouth, almost like he was praying. "If this is Mohommad, he's been brainwashed in a way, based upon what his sister recounted. He's not the same man you knew and there's no way you could have predicted what he would become. We had him for a year, and we didn't predict it. If we had, we never would have sent him back to Afghanistan."

"So we're all idiots."

Jim's mouth twisted into a wry smile. "Yes, I guess so, but at least we have some warning. That's going to make a difference, Mark. We're going to stop this, just like we stopped the Wrigley Field thing."

"But what if we don't? What if you set up extra security like you suggested, and he just goes and blows the bus up somewhere else in Chicago? You didn't answer that question. What's to stop him? Hell--he could pick any school in the city and just wait for the end of the school day, and then blow all the students to smithereens as they leave the building." He sat back with a growl of anger and gave the table a little shove with one foot. "Why didn't I dream of him getting *into* the bus? We'd know where he started out and that information would have been a lot more helpful."

"I agree, that would have been nice, but we have to work with what we have, which is more than we would have had if you hadn't taken the camera back."

Mark let out a deep breath, reluctant to let go of the self-loathing. His leg bounced, and annoyed at the nervous tic, he fought to control it, already embarrassed he'd lost control when he kicked the table. "Yeah, but..."

"Look, it's only a little after one a.m. Try to get back to sleep so your head will be clear in the morning. We might need you to identify the bus and I don't want your memory blurred by fatigue."

"Yeah." The yelling hadn't helped the headache and he winced as he stood.

"How's the head?"

"Fine."

"Liar."

"I just took some more ibuprofen. It'll be fine soon." Mark turned towards the hallway to go back to bed, but hesitated as Jim remained sitting. "What about you?"

"I have a few calls to make first."

"Okay. Goodnight."

* * *

After jotting down the details of the dream, Mark returned to bed, only to toss and turn for the next couple of hours. Jim's voice carried to him, but he couldn't make out what he was saying. Guilt that he should be out there trying to help instead of lying in bed made sleep even more elusive. Around 3:30 A.M, his limbs became heavy, his breathing deepened and he felt himself drifting off.

The Ferris Wheel shone red and white against the crystal blue autumn sky. The laughter and squealing of children mixed with the occasional scolding of chaperones blended with sounds of traffic to create an undercurrent of joyful energy at Navy Pier.

Mark glanced around and tension coiled in his muscles, but he wasn't sure why. Nobody else looked uptight. Buses unloaded children, and their joyful shouts and laughter should have helped him relax, but instead, it fueled his anxiety. People brushed past him, and he felt trapped, like he needed to be somewhere but wouldn't be able to get there because of the press of bodies.

A bus pulled alongside the curb, but didn't unload passengers like the ones farther down the line were doing. A police officer approached the bus and made a move along gesture. "Yo, Buddy! Unload or move before I have to ticket you."

Whoever was in the bus didn't acknowledge the cop. Feeling pulled towards the bus, Mark edged next to it, running a hand along the side of the bus as he moved from the back to the front. He glanced at the windows, but no eager young faces peered out at him. A sick feeling of dread washed over Mark, but he was powerless to stop his forward motion. He had been here before, only it was different.

The cop rapped on the door of the bus, and glanced over to his left giving Mark a 'Back-off, this doesn't concern you' glare. Mark wanted more than anything to heed the unspoken threat. Not because he was worried about the officer, although he knew he should have been, but because the bus was going to explode. An image of the resulting carnage was imprinted in the front of his mind. He'd seen it. A warning lodged in his throat and no amount of working the muscles of his tongue or jaw would free it. The officer turned his attention back to the bus when the door squeaked open and an instant later, a shot rang out. The officer dropped in a boneless heap.

Shocked at the sudden violence, Mark wanted to recoil, but his feet continued their journey as if of their own accord, taking him right up to the downed officer. The door to the bus remained open and Mark leaped through it. Finally, his feet obeyed his signal and he stopped on the second step. Mo sat in the driver's seat, his eyes wide as they darted to Mark and then beyond, to the body of the officer. He still held the gun, but the barrel was pointing at the floor of the bus.

"He shouldn't have knocked on the door. He made me shoot him."

Mark took another step up, his front foot on the top one, and darted a look into the back of the bus, hoping his earlier premonition was wrong and he'd see little children, but he knew the wish was just that--a wish. Mo wouldn't have stolen into the country just to become a school bus driver. Instead of eager students, lined up as neatly as eggs in a carton, were a dozen gray barrels. Wires snaked along the floor connecting the barrels. "The cop made you shoot him? Then who forced you to make a bomb?"

The next few seconds were a blur as Mark lunged for the gun and knocked it out of Mo's hand. It skittered into the back and he dove for it, but Mo landed on top of him before his hand could close around the weapon. Something struck the back of his head, knocking his forehead into the cold metal floor. Mo's hands wrapped around his neck and fingers dug into his throat. Mark struggled to breathe. Mo's grip loosened when the bus jolted. Mark froze in his efforts to escape and Mo's grip fell away as the other man scrambled up and rushed to the driver's seat. Was the bus getting ready to explode? Had the jolt been a warning? Jumping to his feet, Mark took a step towards Mo, but tumbled back to the floor when the floor dropped beneath his feet. It took him a moment to realize it wasn't just the floor, but the whole bus.

Water poured in through the open door, sweeping Mark hard into the barrels. Pain shot through his ribs on the right. Gritting his teeth, he attempted to stand, but the force of the water kept him pinned with his back against a barrel. Mo had smashed against the driver's side window, equally helpless against the inrush of frigid lake water. Their eyes met and Mark saw fear and confusion that must have mirrored his own. The bus lurched and the water sloshed, changing direction and releasing Mo from its grip. It sucked him, arms flailing, down the stairwell.

The bus shifted again and Mark pushed away from the barrels, half crawling, half swimming as he struggled to reach the door. It felt like an invisible hand pushed against him, keeping him from reaching his goal. The water level rose until Mark's head bumped against the roof of the bus, and the door was below him, fully submerged. No matter how hard he kicked, he couldn't reach it. Exhausted, he tried to catch his breath and rubbed a hand against the window to see where the bus was and if help was on the way. The sliver of window above the water afforded him a view of the Ferris Wheel, the cages gently rocking but otherwise stationary. To his right, he heard the roar of engines. Water lapped at his nose. Panic raced through him as he tilted his head back and with the toe of his shoe pushed against the window ledge to get a few last breaths before his air pocket collapsed. Coughing and gasping, he fixed his gaze on the Ferris Wheel, a small part of him glad the bus hadn't exploded, but angry that he wouldn't ever get to ride the damn Wheel again. He shoved the heel of his hand as hard as he could at the glass, but couldn't seem to make contact. Over and over, he tried to break the window out, but it was if the window was beyond his reach.

* * *

"Mark! Wake up! Quit swinging at me!"

Opening his eyes, Mark found his father leaning over him, one hand up in a defensive stance, while the other still shook

Mark's shoulder. "Where am I?" He turned his head to see the small desk and realized he was still in Jim's guest room. He sat up as his dad backed away, slowly lowering his guard, but still giving Mark a look that mixed concern and annoyance.

"Are you okay? You were shouting and kicking and you damn near took my head off with a wild swing. I didn't think I'd ever get you to wake up."

Mark scrubbed his hands down his face and mumbled, "Sorry, Dad. Oh man. It was a doozy of a dream." He swung his legs over the side of the bed and sat trying to gain his composure as his heart slammed against his ribs.

"I thought you already had a dream last night? Jim's been on the phone since I got here an hour ago. If things have changed, you better let him know as soon as possible. I think he's called in the cavalry. "

Mark shot a look at the clock. It was only 7:05A.M, but it seemed like days had passed since he'd awakened in the middle of the night. "I guess I was dreaming, but it was so real…I was on the bus…"

He thought of the whole dream and recognized that the hazy beginning was classic dream and the longer he was awake, the more unreal the dream became. Was it one of his future dreams or just a dream born of fear of failure? It had the hallmarks of his future dreams and enough similarities to the earlier one, that Mark couldn't be sure. One thing he knew was that in this dream, he was *there*. He wasn't just watching the events unfold, but had been part of the dream.

"I need to do a quick exam, especially since you're exhibiting some signs of a mental status change." His dad touched the wound on the side of Mark's head, causing him to flinch and push his dad's hand away.

"It was just a dream, Dad. I'm fine. I know where I am, who you are, and today's date." So, he was lying about the date, but he attributed that to his days on the run. If he thought about it, he could come up with the correct date. Probably. His head still hurt from connecting with the floor of the bus, and he rubbed it as his heart slowly settled into a normal rhythm.

"If you're feeling so good, why are you rubbing your head?"

"It just hurts from hitting the floor of the bus." The words were out before he thought about them. How could he have pain from an injury sustained in a dream?

"Okay, that seals it. You're going to have to go in for some tests."

Jim strode into the room before Mark could protest his father's suggestion.

"What's all the commotion? I was on the phone with the Chicago P.D. I was able to get them to assign some extra patrols around Navy Pier today."

Mark thought of the officer who had been shot. "Warn them not to approach any buses in the drop-off lane."

"Excuse me? Isn't that exactly what we want to do?"

"I just had another dream." Mark stood, trying not to wince at the various aches and pains from the previous day's flight from the diner. The pain in his head was just residual from the gunshot wound. That had to be it.

"What do you mean, you had another dream? Was it the same one? I've just spent half the night organizing my team and the Chicago P.D. on how to prevent the scenario presented in the first dream, and now you're saying all of that was a waste of time?"

Mark shouldered past the two men, feeling claustrophobic in the tiny room. "I need a few minutes then I'll explain." He headed to the bathroom. As he splashed his face with cold water, his dad knocked on the door. "I brought you a change of clothing. It was too early to buy anything but a package of underwear at a drugstore, but my stuff should fit you okay."

"Thanks." He opened the door and took the bundle. "I'm going to take a quick shower."

"Keep those stitches dry or— "

Mark turned the water on before his father could complete the warning. As he stood under the hot spray, he gasped and his heart pounded. The liquid hit his mouth and nose, making him gag as it triggered a sensation of drowning. He didn't know if it was stress which triggered flashbacks to his waterboarding experiences or if it was the dream, but he rinsed and shut the water off as quickly as possible.

He toweled off, replaying the second dream in his head. His dad had awakened him before he came to the end, but he was pretty sure of the conclusion. Mark pulled on his clothes, trying to reason out a different outcome, but he couldn't overlook the obvious. He braced his hands on either side of the sink basin and let out a long, shuddering breath. He had died in the dream.

"If you got those stitches wet and end up with an infection, don't come crying to me."

Mark cast a glance over his shoulder at the bathroom door as a bubble of wild laughter escaped his mouth. Infection—as if he'd have to worry about that, and the stitches were destined to get wet later in the day. His only consolation was that the bus didn't explode. That was a better result than the first dream, but also meant he had to let the dream run its course without trying to change it.

If they did nothing, except get the police officer out of the line of fire, and let the rest of the dream play out, nobody else would die. Gingerly, he toweled his head, not bothering to comb his hair. He just ran his fingers through the wet strands instead.

His dad had included a toothbrush in the bundle, and Mark was grateful for it, absurdly concerned about not wanting to die with un-brushed teeth. Maybe his mother's lectures growing up had etched into his psyche. Clean underwear was another prerequisite, and he was glad for that too, not that anyone was likely to notice clean teeth and underwear on a corpse. Would his body be bloated when they found it? Closing his eyes, he forced the thoughts to the back corner of his mind, locking them away. Mark finished in the bathroom, tossing his borrowed sweats in Jim's hamper, and went to the kitchen. Before he entered, he took a deep breath and did his best to appear calm although inside, his emotions were a mess.

The smell of frying eggs and bacon made his stomach growl and despite thinking he wouldn't be able to eat a thing, he was ravenous. As a last meal, he could do worse.

His dad stepped away from the stove and pushed a plate in front of him. "Eat up. I'm not the greatest chef, but I've been told I can make a mean fried egg, and you can't save the world on an empty stomach."

Mark took the plate as emotion tightened his throat. He managed a strangled, "Thanks, Dad."

His father shot him a sharp look before turning back to the stove.

Jim entered the kitchen, cell phone pressed to his ear, his attention focused on the conversation for a few seconds before he finished the call and slid the phone into his suit coat pocket. He glanced at Mark as he passed on the way to the coffee maker. "Tell me about this new dream." He took a mug out and held up a second in Mark's direction, his eyebrows raised in a silent offering.

Mark nodded and noticed his father already had a mug in one hand while he wielded the spatula in the other.

After pouring the coffee, Jim handed Mark a mug and sat at the table. He pulled a notepad from his breast pocket, clicked a pen, and held it poised over the notepad. "I got your notes from the first dream, so now tell me about the second."

Mark took a bite of his breakfast. The egg yolk was rich and creamy, the salt from the bacon adding a nice complement. It was the best egg he'd ever eaten and he wished he could eat it in peace. He dipped a corner of his toast into a puddle of bright yellow yolk and took another bite, both stalling and taking the time to savor the meal. He washed it down with a swallow of hot, strong coffee. His attention fully on his plate, he shrugged. "Not much to tell. The bus was there again. This time, it went into the lake."

Jim's coffee cup clanked onto the table. "What do you mean, it went into the lake? Before or after it blew up? Did the explosion catapult it into the lake?"

"No. It rolled into the lake when I jumped in and fought with Mo. We must have bumped the gear shift. The bus never exploded, but a police officer is shot when he threatens to give Mo a ticket for illegal parking, so you might want to warn the police away."

Mark swiped the last yolk off the plate with his final bite of toast. "On second thought, let him make the threat. I'll be close enough to get him out of the way, but I need Mo to open the door of the bus, and if the officer isn't there, I'm not sure he'll have a reason to open the door. If I'm the one who gets shot, I won't be able to board the bus." After he said it, the implication that he was justifying that they allow the officer to be shot, hit him like a bucket of cold water. They had to figure out a different way. "Never mind. Warn him away and I'll figure out a way to get in."

His dad sat opposite Mark, and began eating his own breakfast. Mark gestured to Jim. "Where are your eggs? Aren't you eating?"

"I ate already."

Mark's dad snorted. "He had a granola bar. How he expects to function on rabbit food, I'll never know."

A smile flickered to Mark's lips, but didn't linger. If all went as Mark envisioned, Jim would be able to have a nice fat steak later today in celebration of saving the day. Jim might even receive a bonus for taking Mark out as well. He wasn't going to kid himself that he'd go down in history as a hero. He was still a wanted man, had been friends with Mohommad, and would die on a bus filled with explosives. He didn't think even Jim would be able to protest Mark's innocence when faced with all that evidence. His biggest fear was the fallout for his parents. Somehow, he had to make sure they wouldn't be condemned for his perceived sins. Mark set his fork down and folded his hands on top of the table, leaning forward as he tried to come up with a way to protect them. What if he left a note admitting to the guilt and asking that his parents not be blamed? Americans were forgiving. Maybe they'd feel sorry for his folks and give them a break.

Jim set his pen and paper down. "What aren't you telling me?"

Lost in his own thoughts, Mark jumped at the sudden question, making the coffee cups rattle. "Nothing. Why?"

Arms crossed, Jim scrutinized him as though he could read Mark's mind.

His left foot bounced several times. *"What?"* He glanced at his dad, who was also regarding him with suspicion. Unable to hold his dad's gaze, he broke it off and returned his focus to Jim.

"It sounds too simple." Jim's eyes narrowed.

Mark shrugged, found a stray crumb on the table top and covered it with his fingertip. He circled the finger on the wood a few times, swirling it through a drop of coffee. "It *is* simple. I just have to be at Navy Pier this morning. A bus will pull up as if it's going to unload students, but it just sits there instead, holding up other buses waiting to unload. A cop approaches, threatens a ticket and gets shot. I jump in the open door, confront Mo, and fight with him. Before he can blow anything up, the bus rolls right down the road and into the drink. Nothing to it." Mark lifted his finger to find the crumb embedded in the end. He flicked it onto his empty plate.

"So, I should have help standing by in boats."

Hope flickered in Mark, but died as he recalled how quickly the bus submerged in the water. Even if a boat arrived immediately, he wasn't sure anyone would be able to get him out in time. Still, he nodded. "Yeah, that would be a good idea. The water's pretty cold this time of year." He chuckled as if he didn't relish spending too long in the water, and silently congratulated himself for sounding calm and not overly concerned. "So, I hope my second dream doesn't cause any problems for whatever you had planned." Mark gave himself another pat on the back for the re-direct.

After a hard look, Jim sighed and stood, coffee mug in hand. "I'll look like an idiot, but I can rearrange some things. Say some new information came in. This is all pretty hush-hush right now anyway and it's not like I have what others would consider credible evidence. Mohommad's sister's warning is the main excuse I'm using right now since we have that conversation taped." He took a sip of his coffee. "There are plenty of tour boats docked right there, so getting one to the bus shouldn't present any obstacles." He emptied the last few drops of coffee down the drain. "I did have a report about a fertilizer theft a few weeks ago, so I'm playing that up even though the case hasn't been solved yet. It's very possible it's connected to this attempt since what you describe sounds like the kind of bomb used in the first World Trade Center bombing, and the Oklahoma City bombing. I'm just not sure we can cover all the bases if I don't call in enough help."

Jim rinsed the cup, and set it in the sink. "If I need more manpower, I can call in a Mark Taylor sighting." He chuckled. "Half of the Chicago police force is out looking for you. I could have them at Navy Pier in five minutes flat if I did that."

Mark tried to laugh, but even to his own ears, it sounded forced. He'd seen alternate outcomes of the same scenario. Could there be a third? Would having police swarm Navy Pier result in an outcome that didn't end with hundreds of people dead, or with his own death? Couldn't there be solution that saved everyone? He opened his mouth to confess the real result of the second dream, but snapped it shut. Once he told them, there was no way they would let him play that dream out, and he knew for a fact that if everything went according to the dream, the Pier and everyone on it was saved with the exception of the police officer and himself. Mark hoped his warning would effectively prevent the officer's death, but he couldn't come up with a solution that would allow him to save himself while still preventing the explosion.

CHAPTER TWENTY-SIX

Jim tapped the end of the pen on the notepad as he went over what Mark had recounted of the second dream. It sounded straightforward, but something was wrong. He could sense it. He might not have Mark's power of seeing the future, but he hadn't made it to his position without having an instinct for knowing when someone was lying to him. When interrogating a suspect, he didn't just listen to what they said, he learned as much from their body language, how they spoke and eye contact or lack of it. Based on his observations, Mark was hiding something. He wasn't lying, but he was withholding information and Jim was determined to find out what it was.

Noting the empty plate, he said, "It seems your nausea has passed." He would take the indirect route to the truth.

Mark nodded. "Yeah. I feel pretty good, all things considered." He straightened, rolling his shoulders as if to prove he was fine, but Jim caught the slight wince. A moment later, Jim felt a rhythmic vibration on the floor and knew it was probably Mark's leg bouncing—a sure sign that something was bothering him.

"So, you feel confident that sticking to the facts in your second dream will keep the bus from exploding?"

Another nod, but Mark's eyes only flicked to Jim's face before his attention turned back to the dirty plate. Either he found something fascinating in the waxy smears of yolk dotted with crumbs, or he was purposefully avoiding making eye contact. Jim voted for the latter.

Gene finished his meal and gathered up his own plate and took Mark's away as well. With nothing to study, Mark's eyes roved the kitchen as though desperate to latch onto something just to avoid looking at Jim.

"You aren't leveling with me about everything, but for the moment I'll let it slide. I trust that you'll tell me if my plan to avert the bombing won't work because of whatever you're withholding." Jim decided that beating around the bush was just going to result in wasting time and that was one commodity they didn't have. He would just have to trust Mark.

Although he finally looked directly at Jim, his eyes wide, Mark maintained his silence on the matter. Jim sighed. So much for jarring the truth out of Mark with a direct statement. It was already after eight. According to photos and Mark's dream, the event would happen sometime before lunch. The tourist attraction didn't open until ten, and from the photos and the number of people around, it was apparent the site was open when the bomb went off, and the shadows showed it was still before noon. That left them only an hour to come up with a plan, and another hour to get it in place before Mo and the bus arrived. Jim had already notified the Chicago P.D. to be on the lookout for the bus, but even if they spotted the vehicle, it was no guarantee that they could avoid a catastrophe. Like Mark had said, having Mohommad flee with a bus full of explosives wasn't a best case scenario. It would be better to secure the bus at Navy Pier. The most difficult decision was whether to close the tourist spot down for the day, but if they did that, what was to stop Mohommad from going somewhere else, or coming back tomorrow or some other day?

Jim had arranged to meet his team at Navy Pier to coordinate efforts, but he couldn't very well show up with Mark in tow. Too bad Mark had shaved the day before but if they put him in a ball cap and sunglasses, he might go unnoticed. An idea took shape. The police were looking for a man who was on the run, not a family man with a wife and kid. Jim felt sure it would work, at least for the short amount of time that they needed Mark in plain sight. Now, he just had to come up with a wife and kid to play the role.

"I think I have a way to allow you to roam around Navy Pier and not arouse suspicion. We'll have Jessica pose as your wife--"

"No!" Mark pushed away from the table and stood all in one motion. "No way! You have to keep her out of this!"

Not expecting the outburst, Jim jerked in his chair, but otherwise maintained his composure. He had definitely struck a nerve. "She's part of my team and beyond that, she's the only one I, no make that, *we* can trust to go along with my plan without revealing your identity."

His knuckles blanched as he gripped the top of the kitchen chair, Mark shook his head. "I don't care. I don't want her anywhere near Navy Pier. It's too dangerous."

"You don't get a say so, Mark. She's a Special Agent and this," Jim stabbed the notepad with his pen, "is her job." Why was Mark protesting so hard now, when he hadn't before the Wrigley Field incident? What was different this time?

Mark's mouth set in a hard line, and when his father rested his hand on his shoulder and tried to reason with him, Mark shrugged the hand off. "You don't understand. I don't want her there to see—"A mixture of frustration, fear and anger played over his features. He crossed his arms. "I just don't want her there. *Please*."

Jim wished he could abide by Mark's wishes, but he couldn't. Not unless Mark offered up a hard piece of evidence that Jessica's presence would either jeopardize the operation, or she was in imminent danger of dying, and even then, it wasn't a guarantee he would take her off the case. Mark would have to outright say she would be killed, and there was nothing they could do to prevent it short of keeping her away. "Tell me why, and I'll think about it." It was the best he could do.

"I can't. Just *trust* me." He gave the chair a hard push into the table, while his eyes reflected his anguish. With a groan, he clasped his hands behind his head, tilted his head back, eyes closed his mouth twisted as though in pain and frustration. After a moment, his hands fell limply to his sides and his shoulders sagged in defeat.

Gene sat at the table with a sigh, clearly wanting to side with his son, but as confused about Mark's stipulation as Jim was. His fingers tapped out a rhythmic tattoo on the wooden table as his gaze darted between his son and Jim.

"By now, you must know I trust you, Mark. I wouldn't have you hidden away here in my home if I didn't, but lives are at stake, and I need every available person I have at my disposal. Jessica, while new to us, was hired in part because I know I can trust her implicitly. The way I see it, you had two dreams about the same event. In one dream, the bus explodes and kills an untold number of people."

Jim flipped the page in his notebook and started pro and con lists. "We can concentrate on changing that dream by swarming the area with police and agents, stopping every bus in a mile radius and check for explosives, and also prevent any from coming near Navy Pier. Of course, that means Mohommad could just find another place to set off the explosives." He jotted that in the 'Con' column. He was aware that Mark had tuned him out as he leaned against a counter, arms crossed and his gaze fixed on the opposite wall, but he continued anyway, hoping some of it would penetrate the wall Mark appeared to be constructing. "I don't know about you, but I feel better knowing the where and the approximate when, rather than having all of that unknown." Another addition to the 'Pro' column.

Mark broke off his contemplation of the wall as his eyes flicked to Jim.

Taking that for a good sign, Jim said, "Here are the problems we face—there's no time. I'd love to take Jessica off the case, but we're pressed for time and manpower. That's it. Bottom line. In fact, we're wasting time right now." Jim stood and tucked the notepad into his breast pocket. "Come on. We'll finish talking in the car."

Resignation settled over Mark's features, but he nodded and a moment later, resolve took the place of resignation.

Gene stood. "I'll meet you down there."

Jim paused. It hadn't been in his plan to have Mark's father present during the operation, but if things didn't go well, it might not be a bad idea to have a doctor handy, but on the other hand, he was already putting one civilian in harm's way, but to put two from the same family would be unconscionable.

"Dad, why don't you wait here? Or at your hotel?"

"I have to agree with your son."

Gene glared at Mark and then turned to Jim, including him in the hostile look. "Are you going to arrest me?"

"Of course not, but let me put it this way. I can't look out for Mark to the best of my ability if I'm worried about where you are too. I have agents and police officers to coordinate, and somehow, I have to figure out a way to get Navy Pier visitors out of harm's way without making it obvious."

Gene appeared as though he was going to protest, but then he grinned. "You need a diversion."

"Excuse me?"

"It won't work for everyone, but you can thin the crowd at the front of the Pier by having some kind of diversion at the other end. You need something that will attract as many visitors as possible, but still not arouse suspicion."

It wasn't a bad idea, but what could they use to divert attention?

"What about free lake tours?" Mark suggested. "Most of the boats dock on the other side of the pier."

"It's pretty cold out..." Jim mused aloud.

Mark shrugged. "True, but it's sunny. I bet you can get a few hundred out on the tours. Make sure the boats take an extra-long tour."

Gene was nodding and Jim warmed to the idea. "We might have enough time to get some of the river tour boats to participate too. The hard part would be getting everyone aboard quickly and without raising suspicion." He thought again and shook his head. "On second thought, I don't want to draw anyone to Navy Pier who wouldn't already be there. We'll talk to the lake boat operators and pursue that route, but not expand it."

"Gene, I can't stop you from going, but I want you on one of those boats. If nothing else, you can be my eyes and ears out in the lake."

Mark let out a deep breath as though in relief and once again, Jim wondered what he was withholding. He didn't have time to worry though. "Mark, you need a coat and a hat. I have one in my hall closet. Be right back."

As Jim returned to the kitchen, he overheard Gene caution his son. "Be careful today, Mark."

He stepped through the doorway in time to see Gene extend his hand and Mark clasp it, but then Mark pulled his father in for a brief one-armed hug and mumbled, "Love you, Dad." And then he turned away, rubbing the back of his neck.

Gene's brow was furrowed as his eyes followed Mark. His mouth opened like he was going to say something, but instead, confusion fought with concern and he must not have known what to say. He glanced at Jim, and raised an eyebrow as though asking what the display was all about.

Far from an expert about father and son relationships, Jim could only shrug. Neither man struck him as being overly emotional, but then again, he hadn't seen them together long enough to know if the behavior was out of the ordinary. Not wanting to get involved, he thrust out the coat and hat. "Mark? Here's the jacket and a baseball cap."

Mark turned. "Thanks." He took the items but didn't make eye contact. "Let's go."

Gene left first and Jim noted that Mark kept his eyes on his father's car until it was out of sight.

After they were on their way, Jim pulled out his cellphone. "Jessica? I have a special assignment for you. I'm going directly to Navy Pier. You need to meet me there as soon as possible. Oh, and dress like you're going to spend the day as a tourist."

After a few other instructions, he hung up and glanced at Mark, intending to ask him to spill the beans on what he was withholding, but Mark sat with his elbow on the window ledge, leaning his head on his hand. He'd pulled the hat low, but Jim saw enough of his expression to realize the other man was a million miles away. Whatever had him so distracted, Jim was sure that if it was something that was detrimental to the outcome, Mark would share it with him. He trusted him completely. Mark had already proven himself by taking the risk in the 'L' track incident. He had to have been aware that he could take the rap for the bombing, but he didn't hesitate, even without proof, to bring the bomb to the attention of the police. If he would risk that, he wouldn't risk something going wrong here without enlightening Jim. The rest of the drive was completed in silence.

CHAPTER TWENTY-SEVEN

Mohommad climbed aboard the bus and inspected his payload with a sense of satisfaction and purpose. Hazim and he had put the finishing touches on it just hours before, making sure the wires were all tight and wouldn't loosen on the road.

Originally, Hazim had been designated to ride with him, but Mohommad insisted that he wanted to do the honors alone. Hazim was under the impression that Mohommad would use the timer they had installed and they could meet up later in Afghanistan. Mohommad had smiled at him and shook his head, telling him that the plan had changed. After a brief argument, Hazim had acquiesced to Mohommad's wish and bowed out.

At that moment, the other man should be on his way to O'Hare, booked on a flight to Egypt. From there, he would catch another flight to Pakistan and eventually reach his home village in Afghanistan. Mohommad had reminded him that the icing on the cake would be that with his experience, Hazim would be sought out for advice and he'd be a hero to those who mattered. It was imperative that at least one of them lived to pass on the knowledge. If something went wrong, and Mohommad had to resort to using the emergency trigger, Hazim would at least be able to carry on the fight from Afghanistan. Mohommad assured him that for generations to come, the name Hazim would be uttered with reverence.

They had planned originally to use a timer with Mohommad to pick Hazim up after he parked the bus.

Mohommad was going to head to Mexico and then eventually back to Afghanistan, but when Mark stole the camera, he had forced Mohommad to re-think the plan. It was too risky to park the bus anywhere, but especially in front of Navy Pier because he was worried Mark would know about it. While the bomb was powerful, the timer wasn't especially complicated and a good bomb squad would easily be able to short circuit it. So, instead, Mohommad had volunteered to drive it and use the fail-safe back-up that required a direct gunshot. After he did that, the bus would blow up almost immediately, so it was now a suicide mission. Mohommad shrugged. It was better this way. Afghanistan didn't appeal to him as much as he pretended to his uncles. It would kill them to realize just how corrupted he had become by living in America for so long. Every time he tried to pretend to love Afghanistan, he was overcome with shame. He couldn't live with that anymore.

He made sure he had the pistol and felt his pocket for the disposable cellphone. Hazim had one also, and once he was past security, he would text Mohommad. It would have been better to wait to make sure Hazim had landed in Egypt, but this was the best they could do. With his toe, he pressed a piece of tape more firmly against the floor.

Mohommad sat in the driver's seat and gripped the wheel. He had expected more turmoil in his belly, but he felt surprisingly calm. The hardest part would be actually driving the bus. It was so heavily loaded, he worried someone would notice how low it rode, but most people didn't notice things like that. He glanced at the scattered trash in the barn, feeling a twinge of guilt at leaving the old man a mess, but he didn't worry too much about it. There was no need to cover their tracks anymore.

His bus driving experience was minimal, but he only had to make it forty miles and the first thirty were highway miles. By the time he hit the city, he would be more comfortable. He had practiced driving other large vehicles, but it would have been too risky to take the bus out, so for the last four months, he and Hazim had gathered materials for the bomb and transported them here in small quantities to store in the back of the barn. Although no longer used for animals, the structure was sound and more importantly, had no gaps in the boards to allow prying eyes. Set off the road and behind some newer pole barns, it was hard to see unless you were looking for it.

He had only found it by chance in the summer when the old and faded 'Stalls for Rent' sign had caught his eye. The old man who lived in the farmhouse on the property had been surprised at the interest, assuming that Mohommad's inquiry was in regards to stalls available in the pole barn. He'd been thrilled to rent out the barn when Mohommad had said he wanted to rent it to store some old farm equipment until he could sell them. After paying the rent, he hadn't seen the old man again. He thought it would be difficult to smuggle the bus, bought at an auction, and the fertilizer in, but the owner never paid attention. As luck would have it, the old farmer liked his alcohol, and from the amount of liquor bottles in the recycling bin every week, he was probably in an alcohol-induced stupor every evening when he and Hazim had worked in the barn. They couldn't have asked for a more secluded place to work.

Once on the highway, Mohommad pulled out his phone. Besides Hazim, he wanted to make one more phone call. "Zaira? It's me."

"Mohommad? Where are you?"

"I can't tell you that, dear sister." He smiled, hearing her voice soothed him even more.

There was silence on the other end that lasted for a beat. "Mohommad…what is going on? You're not doing anything crazy, are you?"

"I've never been *more* sane. My mind is crystal clear." He spoke the truth. Never before had he seen the world in such sharp relief. The sky had never been so blue or the sun so bright. It was beautiful and he took it all in as he drove. The forest preserve bordering the highway was a tangle of gray tree trunks and brush, but he spotted a cardinal on a branch, and a hawk gliding in lazy circles. "I just wanted you to know that I love you and forgive you for not understanding. It's not your fault."

"Mohommad, you're scaring me."

"I don't mean to. I just wanted to hear your voice. Give my nieces a hug and kiss from me. Tell them I always loved them." He hung up before Zaira could reply and tossed the phone out the window.

* * *

Mark gave the bill of his cap a tug and turned up the collar on the jacket as he stepped out of Jim's car. He took one look at the area in front of Navy Pier and knew they had a little time. The shadows were too long so the sun would have to move higher in the sky before Mohommad arrived. His gaze moved upward and he stilled at the sight of the Ferris Wheel. Cold tendrils of dread swept from his chest, up his neck and down his arms, making the fine hairs stand on end. He turned away from the ride and caught Jim's eye across the roof of the car. Pushing his fear aside, he said, "I think we have about an hour."

"Damn. I was hoping we'd have more time. We've got to hustle to get everyone in place." Jim strode around the car and Mark fell into step beside him as they walked up to the front entrance to Navy Pier.

"Jim, would it be so bad if you didn't get anyone in place? Why do we need a bunch of people here? Wouldn't it would be better to have less people around. The boat thing is great to get the visitors away from possible harm, but I'm telling you, having agents and police swarming the place is going to change things. I can't promise that the dream will happen like I envisioned it if Mo gets spooked by an unusual number of uniformed officers."

Jim stopped and rested one hand on his waist as the other rubbed across his mouth while he contemplated Mark's advice. He surveyed the area, taking in the light crowd. Mark compared it to what he had seen in his dream. It was early yet, and more people would arrive closer to late morning, but right now, adding a bunch of people who just milled about trying to look like they belonged would attract more attention, to Mark's way of thinking.

Mark couldn't help thinking of Superman as Jim looked from one side of the pier to the other, his fists on his waist. It was fitting. The man had complete confidence that they would stop Mo. After all, they had right on their side.

"Quite a few of our people are here already. Can you tell who they are?"

Casting an eye over the area, Mark had to admit that all he saw were ordinary looking families and couples. "No, but that still doesn't make it right."

Jim pressed his cellphone to his ear and motioned for Mark to follow him. Feet dragging, Mark complied. None of this seemed familiar from his dream, but he reminded himself that he'd entered the dream at what seemed to be mid-scene. Maybe all of this had taken place and he just hadn't seen this part.

A staging area had been set up inside a Navy Pier management office and already, a bank of monitors was in place, showing every angle of the park. Jim's definition of a small low key operation differed from Mark's. The place felt like Grand Central Station. Mark leaned against a wall and refused the cup of coffee someone tried to press on him. His nerves were already jangling. No need to add more fuel to the fire. Agents and officers were dressed as either employees of various businesses, or as visitors. Mark, of course, had drawn the role of visitor. The fact that he was wanted by the very people in the room with him amused him somewhat. Of course, they would never look for him in the midst of their own group.

Jim approached and handed him a Kevlar vest, igniting painful memories from the last time he'd worn a bulletproof vest. Kern had been killed, but not before he had taken another life. The senselessness of the deaths had hit him like a sledgehammer after he'd left the warehouse where they had set the trap. Mark didn't know whether to be sad or grateful that at the end of the day, he wouldn't be around to regret anything. He pushed the vest back into Jim's hands. "I don't need it. Mo doesn't shoot me."

"Take it anyway. Just in case."

"No." Even though he didn't think it would make difference in the outcome, he made a good argument against the vest. "I'm going to be in a bus that is sinking in the lake. Do you really think a heavy vest is going to increase my chances of survival?"

Jim blinked and after a beat, nodded. "Fine."

Regretting his sarcasm, Mark reached to take the protective apparel from Jim. "Sorry. It doesn't matter. If you want me to wear it, I will." It wouldn't make a difference in the outcome, and he hated the thought of being remembered in his last hours as being a sarcastic jerk.

"No." Jim smiled and shook his head. "I just have to remind myself that you've already 'lived' this, so to speak, and I have to do a better job of listening to you."

Mark pushed off the wall and shoved his hands into his jacket pockets. "What should I do now?"

"You're cleared to go out and do whatever it is you need to do. We have cameras in place. I thought about wiring you, but that didn't work so well in the past." His eyes flashed with humor and the corner of his mouth turned up. Mark appreciated his attempt to lighten the mood. "Anyway, it seemed to be more of a distraction, so we'll just keep an eye on you, and have an agent close at hand at all times," Jim finished.

Taking a deep breath, Mark let it out slowly in an attempt to quell his nerves. All humor disappeared from Jim's expression as he extended his right hand. "You'll do fine out there, Mark. When this is all over, I'm going to see that you get your name cleared once and for all, and you get the recognition you deserve."

Jim couldn't have known the effect of his promise, but he must have sensed it from the way Mark gripped his hand and gave it a firm shake. "I appreciate it." Just knowing that his parents wouldn't have to bear the double burden of his death, and him being thought a terrorist, lifted a weight from his shoulders.

***

Mark strolled through an immaculately groomed small park. They said in the last few seconds of living, you saw your life pass before your eyes. Mark wondered if he was getting the double feature since he had more than a few seconds. He wanted to pay attention to what was going on around him, but it was as if he couldn't control his thoughts. A woman with a stroller kept pace with him, and he glanced at her in surprise when she moved up close to him.

"Quit staring at me like you've never seen me before. Remember you're supposed to be a *happy* dad."

"Jessie?" Why hadn't Jim mentioned that she was going to be the agent assigned to him? Was it because Jim knew Mark would protest? He knew he should be angry. While he didn't want her there to see the end results, he selfishly felt a surge of joy that he had one more chance to speak with her. He grinned, and she rolled her eyes, but her lips pressed together as if trying to suppress her own smile. She had obviously taken his silly expression as an over the top attempt to play the 'happy dad.'

His grin faded as he took in the stroller. "Whose baby is that?" Jim wouldn't take the chance with a baby, would he?

"Don't worry—it's not yours," Jessie teased.

"No, I'm serious. You have to take this baby back to its mother." He didn't even know if it was a boy or a girl. Heart pounding, he leaned over and grasped the blanket.

Jessie snatched the blanket away, glancing around as she did and said in a low voice, "Mark, for God's sake, it's a *doll*."

Relief washed over him, followed by a surge of anger. "How was I supposed to know? In my first dream, there was blood and body parts all over. And the one thing that stood out in my mind was what was left of a stroller just like this." He gave the handle of the stroller a hard shake. "What if I can't stop this thing and it means that you blow up? What if some of those body parts are yours?"

Jessie blanched, but her shoulders straightened. "I'm sorry for making light of your concerns, but this is my job. Now, if you don't mind, we need to play our roles. School buses are beginning to arrive."

Mark turned and saw several buses approaching the front entrance. This was it. He faced her again, wishing he could take back his words from the minute before. Her sunglasses hid her eyes from him, and he longed to see them one more time. He touched her cheek, smoothing his thumb over her skin. "I'm sorry." She might think it was for what he had said, and it was, but mostly it was because he was going to ditch her the moment he saw Mohommad's bus.

As if she could read his mind, she lifted her glasses and searched his face. "Mark?"

He broke eye contact and headed closer to the street. "Come on. We have to move closer to the front of the Children's Museum." They had to cross the street before the buses blocked their way. The two buses he had seen were already unloading. They went behind them, cutting in front of a third bus. The sudden influx of children on the pavement made navigation more difficult.

"Here comes a new batch of buses. Anything?"

His senses seemed to sharpen, but everything moved in dream-like slow motion. The laughter of nearby children was louder, the piped music clearer and the acrid smell of the exhaust from the line of buses burned his nose. Ignoring the crowd, Mark searched the line of buses. When he moved through the crowd, he almost tripped over a young boy who dashed in front of him. Catching his balance and lightly gripping the child by the shoulders to keep from falling on top of him. The boy's mother rushed up and apologized to Mark.

His mind whirling, he had a difficult time concentrating. The buses were all pencil yellow with black markings. Standard school buses. School district names or bus company names emblazoned on the sides were the only discernible differences that he could see. He swept the line again. *Concentrate!* He was forgetting an important detail. Wait. It was a slight difference that set the exploding bus apart from the others. The markings. That was it. Markings--or lack of them.

"There's one..." Without finishing, he pushed through the crowd. It was the one. Whatever Jessie's plan had been, apparently he wasn't following it as she called out for him to wait.

Mo's bus was right there--just ten yards away. It hadn't reached the head of the line yet, but was next to move forward.

How could they stop this when the bus was already here? All it would take was Mo doing whatever it was he did to start the explosion. Now, because of his damn dream, not only would all the people originally here die, but also all those who came to stop it. Including Jessie. And his dad. *Oh God.* He wouldn't let it happen. It was as simple as that. He would drive the bus right into the lake on purpose.

The message to the police officer from his dream must have been delivered because although the bus in front of Mo's had moved out, clearing the way for his bus to move forward, the bus just sat there and no officer approached. He wasn't sure whether to be glad for the deviation from his dream or worry about the implications. What if other things changed?

Mark rushed the doors of the bus, digging his fingers into the weather stripping. Another difference. What if he couldn't get into the bus? It could explode any second. Maybe it was his determination or a miracle or maybe it was just the thick cable the snaked out the bottom of the door and ran beneath the bus and broke the seal, but he didn't care, as long as it allowed his fingers to curl around the edge of the door and yank it open.

He turned sideways and squeezed into the small opening before Mohommad could react. Mo grabbed the door lever and yanked on it, causing it to close on Mark's chest, momentarily trapping him, but Mark shoved against the folding door and fell all the way into the stairwell on his side. Clawing his way up the steps, his only goal was to get Mo. Rage blinded him to anything but wrapping his hands around Mo's throat and squeezing the life from him before Mo could pull the trigger on the explosion.

"Get off! You can't stop me!" Mo kicked out, catching Mark in the shoulder. Mark grabbed Mo's foot and twisted it until Mo had to turn onto his stomach or get his ankle broken. Stumbling on the top step, Mark lost his grip on the shoe, but put his hand out, regaining his balance as he caught the handrail that angled down the steps.

Mo recovered, turned and pulled a gun from his pocket, aiming it at Mark. Instinctively, Mark froze, but only for an instant. He had no choice. Whether Mo shot him or the bus exploded, he was going to die. It made his next decision easy. He lunged across the short space separating them and grabbed Mo's gun hand, pushing it down while trying to pull him from the driver's seat at the same time.

"Give it up, you crazy bastard!" Mark yanked Mo from the seat but the backward force caused him to fall against the front of the bus. Something jammed into Mark's lower back and he grunted as he pushed away, using the momentum to knock Mo into the passenger area of the bus, where he fell, his wrist hitting a barrel and knocking the gun from his hand.

The bus lurched and Mark tripped on one of the cables that crisscrossed the floor of the bus. Falling to one knee, he caught his balance on the chrome-covered pole just behind the driver's seat. The gun was between him and Mo. They both made a dive for it at the same time, but Mo beat Mark by a hair.

The bus bumped again and Mark felt the vibration of the bus moving over pavement. It rolled and picked up speed. He ducked Mo's incoming fist, receiving a glancing blow on his head, but it was the same place he'd been shot and he was blinded by a white burst of pain. He sagged, but shook it off as he slammed the heel of his hand up against Mo's chin, feeling the other man's jaw snap shut.

He wrenched the gun from Mo, but before he could bring it to bear, Mo lunged toward him. Mark toppled backward onto the driver's seat and lost his grip on the gun. The bus continued moving forward and Mark tucked his legs against his chest and kicked out, catching Mo full in the abdomen and propelled him down into the stairwell. Still lying sideways on the seat, Mark grabbed the steering wheel, and was able to turn it enough to avoid a group of schoolchildren. His evasive maneuver sent the bus careening down the road. Mark clutched the wheel and tried to gain control while keeping an eye on Mo, who sat up and charged again.

Mark stiff-armed Mo in the throat, and the other man fell to his knees gagging. After a few seconds of recovery, he crashed into Mark's shoulder, sending him hard against driver's side wall. Mark reached for the steering wheel, pulled on it, attempting to take the corner. Beyond the corner, Lake Michigan dazzled on a few feet away. Sunlight glinted off the waves. Unable to make the full turn with only one hand and wedged sideways on the seat, Mark was unable to reach the brake. The bus hadn't blown up yet, so Mo must not have been able to activate it. At least, he hoped that was the case. It could be on a timer, but the first dream had shown it exploding almost immediately. Mark had changed things and the bus hadn't exploded. He had to trust that was the reason.

Hope flared. There was still a chance he could stop it from going into the lake. He braced as the front wheels hit the curb and popped the front end of the bus into the air. It landed with a bone-jarring crash, and he felt blood flood his mouth from biting his tongue. He tried to keep the steering wheel tight in his hand, but lost his grip when Mo punched him in the eye. Suddenly, the bus hung in mid-air while Mark's stomach felt like it flew up to his mouth as the bus rolled across the narrow barrier, and into the frigid waters.

The plunge left him weightless for a fraction of a second before his head hit the roof of the bus. The impact threw Mark back down against the steering wheel, sending shooting pain through his ribs. The breath knocked from him, his head reeling, he lay draped over the wheel, stunned. Out of the corner of his eye, he saw Mo had been tossed against the front of the bus and lay in a heap against the windshield, his head towards the door.

Water rushed into the bus, and already, the stairwell was full. Mark pushed off the steering wheel and grabbed the door lever. The pressure of the water already made opening the door difficult and he was only able to open it six inches before the bus shifted and tossed him towards the door. He slipped down the steps, and reached for the rail in a blind panic to stop his fall. His fingers brushed against cold denim. Mo's leg. Mark's momentum carried him past Mo, and he snagged Mo's foot, slowing his fall, but in the process, spun the other man off the front of the bus to land with a splash in the water rapidly filling the front of the vehicle. Mark hit the door with his shoulder and felt something pop.

Mo floundered, attempted to stand, and shook water out of his eyes, sputtering. Mark watched through a red haze of pain as Mo stood with his head almost touching the ceiling, one foot braced on the dash, the other on the driver's seat.

Turning to look out the back of the bus, Mo sighed, his body sagging. He faced Mark and said, "I failed. Again."

His left arm hanging limp, Mark found the railing and pulled himself out of the stairwell, his feet slipping and sliding on the floor of the bus as he reached for the chrome support bar, but the metal was slippery and he couldn't hang on. If Mo was looking for sympathy, he was searching in the wrong place. "You might plan on going down with your ship, but I don't."

Mo glared at Mark, then burst into laughter and reached down, catching Mark under the arm. Mark flinched, but all Mo did was haul him up to a standing position. Nodding, Mo said, "I guess it is more of a ship now."

Confused at the gesture, Mark just clung to the pole and stared as he tried to catch his breath.

"We need to get out the back!" Mark pointed to the emergency exit.

Mo shook his head. "It won't open. I welded it shut."

The weight of the barrels in the back of the bus pulled that end down, making trying for the emergency exit a moot point. Panting, the water up to his waist, Mark looked for something to break a window out, but there was nothing. The gun. He tried to look through the water to find it, but with all the jostling, it was likely long gone. They had to get the side door open. He slogged past Mo, who still balanced on the wheel and bar, only his feet in the water. He pushed the door lever. It gave another inch. "I think we can squeeze through!" Mark swiped water out of his eyes and tried to catch his breath. Knife-like pains in his ribs made taking a deep breath impossible.

Mo jumped off his perch, landing beside Mark. He jerked a thumb over his shoulder. "It's not going to matter very much if we get out. This stuff isn't stable when it's wet."

Mark tried to see how far away from the pier the bus had floated. He'd felt the sensation of drifting as well as sinking, but he doubted they had gone far. If the bus exploded, at least the water would mute some of the explosion. Not that Mark would ever know if it had. He pushed the thought out of his mind. It hadn't exploded yet, so there was still a chance. "Go!" He gave Mo a shove in the back, pushing him towards the opening. Mo resisted. "Get your ass out of the bus!"

Mo held firm against the push. "Why do you care if I get out?"

Mark didn't have the breath to launch into a speech so he just locked onto Mo's eyes, and gave another nudge. "I'm crazy, that's why, now go!"

A light flickered in Mo's eyes and he finally took the edge of the door and pushed it open wider, slipping out a second later. Mark tried to follow, but the bus shifted, sinking even deeper.

Floating now, his head against the roof, Mark reached up with his good arm and tried to push off the ceiling and dove into the water to reach the door. His ribs protested the deep breath, but he ignored the pain. He found the door in the murky water, but was unable to pull his body through it. The bus had come to rest against an old piling and it wedged against the door preventing it from opening far enough.

Three times, he popped back up to take another breath, only to return to the door, but he was unable to get through. He let out all of his pent-up air and finally squeezed through the small opening. Just as he did, the bus sank further into the lake bottom, and the door slid forward against the piling, trapping his foot in the door. With no breath left, darkness crawled into the edges of his vision. He bent and tried to wrench his foot free, but he had no leverage in the water. He twisted and turned, to no avail. His head felt ready to explode from his efforts to hold his breath. The surface was a silvery white, and so close, he could raise his arm and almost break through it.

A shadow crossed over him. Dimly, he felt the door shift a fraction, and hands tugged at his ankle, freeing his foot. He kicked hard, striving for his goal so close, but the breathing reflex triggered before he could reach it. His mouth opened as if of its own accord and water rushed in.

CHAPTER TWENTY-EIGHT

"Mark!" Someone slapped his face. He turned his head away. "Come on, Mark! I can't do this alone. You have to help me."

Arms gripped his middle and jerked against his upper abdomen. Mark retched. The arms jerked once more, making him vomit again, and sending daggers of pain through his ribs. He groaned and sent an elbow against whoever was holding him. The arms released with a curse. Mark sank, water rushing over his face. He kicked, struggling to stay afloat, but it was the hand grabbing his jacket collar that kept his head above water.

"Mmm..." Awareness filtered in, and his limbs felt leaden. An arm circled his throat, tilting his head back, but Mark clawed at the arm, feeling as if it was going to choke him.

"Stop fighting me, Mark."

The voice. He recognized it and knew he shouldn't trust it, but he had no energy to fight. His teeth chattered and his body shook with cold. He tried to open his eyes, but sunlight stabbed into his pupils and he slammed them shut. Rhythmic tugging at his neck confused him, but he didn't fight it anymore, allowing his body to float. Distant shouting penetrated his mind, but it was too far away. Not his concern. Something grabbed the collar of his jacket again and he moaned when his left arm was pulled up, sending pain lancing through him.

"Grab him and get back! All of you, get ba--"

The earth shook and Mark felt his body lifted as if on a giant wave of air. He landed on top of something soft. He shivered, unable to do more than lie there with his eyes closed. Water splattered all around him, surprising him since the sun had been shining so brightly before. When had it started raining?

* * *

Sirens cut through his head and Mark opened his eyes. A plastic mask hissed a stream of oxygen at his face, and he swiped at it, rebelling at the sensation of having his nose and mouth covered. The movement triggered a cough, and someone pulled Mark's hand away from the mask.

"Leave it on."

He turned his head to see a paramedic leaning over him and placing a stethoscope against Mark's chest.

"Yeah, definitely leave it on. You sound pretty wet in there."

Mark had no idea what he was talking about but, was too tired to argue. Trembling with fatigue and cold, he tried to piece together what had happened. After leaving the bus, it was all fuzzy, except he knew his foot had been trapped, but he vaguely recalled the relief when it had come loose. Someone had been there with him. The sunlight bothered his eyes and with nothing to see but the paramedic and blue sky, he closed them again.

A warm hand touched his right shoulder. "Mark?"

He turned his head. "Dad?" All he could make out was a dark shadow. "What happened?" A cough interrupted his questions, and he swore when the spasm passed. "Were you here? Where's Jessie?" His eyes adjusted and he noticed his dad was all wet too.

"Slow down. She's with Jim. They're meeting with the Chicago Police and clearing your name. Jim told them that you had been working undercover for him the whole time, but he couldn't divulge it and blow your cover."

The tension that had been building over the last several days melted off him. He could go home again. "Sorry I got my stitches wet again."

His dad laughed. "You have to stop giving your old man so many scares. I'm almost completely gray already, but I swear I felt what little pigment I had left in my hair drain right out when the bus blew up."

"Blew up?" Mark struggled to sit up, but his dad maintained pressure on his shoulder, not allowing him the freedom to sit. "When did it blow up?" He pulled the mask off, not caring about the paramedic's warning.

"Just after you got out of the water, but it did very little damage."

Mark craned his head, hearing the activity behind him. "I don't remember." He rubbed his forehead in confusion. He should be able to remember something like that. "Mo said the bomb could be unstable in water…"

"Don't say another word, Mark." The tone of his father's voice startled him.

"What? Why?"

His dad glanced at the paramedic, who had his stethoscope while getting Mark's blood pressure, and then over his shoulder. "I just think you should tell Jim what you know first."

"Know? I don't know anything. Just before we escaped, Mo said—"

His dad snapped the mask back over Mark's face and gave him his most stern look. He wanted to tell his dad that it had been a long time since that look had intimidated him, but instead, he gave a tired smile and closed his eyes again. "Fine."

His dad didn't speak again, but his hand remained on Mark's shoulder as though on guard. Mark let his mind drift. He couldn't ever remember being so exhausted. The background sounds faded.

He awoke with a start when the noise became more than background noise and centered above him. Four paramedics crouched, two on either side of him.

"Okay, on my count, let's move him to the gurney."

Before he knew what was happening, they used a blanket that had been under him and lifted him onto the cart. "Whoa. I don't need a gurney." Where was his dad? "All I need is a hot shower and some sleep."

One paramedic placed a belt over Mark's chest, but before any other belts could restrict him, he pushed on it, sliding it closer to his waist and sat up. "I'm not going anywhere until I talk to Jim Sheridan."

The first paramedic he'd seen tried to calm him down, but Mark was having none of it. "I know I don't have to go if I don't want to. I have rights." Or did he? Was he under arrest?

"What's going on?" Jim stopped beside the gurney. He was wet too, his clothes smudged with dirt. "Are you giving these guys a hard time, Mark?"

Mark struggled with the buckle of the strap. "I need you to tell them that I can't just leave. I have to talk to you first. I have a ton of questions, and I also want you to take me to wherever you're holding Mo so I can ask him why he came back to save me." The buckle finally came undone and he swung his legs over the side of the cart. He was breathing hard but tried his best not to show it.

Jim shoved his hands in his pockets and glanced around at the paramedics gathered beside the gurney. "Could you guys give us a few minutes?"

After the medics stepped several feet away, Jim looked at Mark, and then out over the lake. He didn't speak for so long, Mark wondered if he had forgotten whatever it was he had planned on saying. Sorrow shadowed his eyes when he finally focused on Mark again. "Mohommad didn't make it."

Shock hit him in the stomach, knocking the breath from him. "What? How? I was sure he freed my foot." Mark searched his memory. Was he mistaken? He shook his head and scrubbed his hands down his face. No. He was sure. It had been Mo's voice he'd heard. There was no mistaking that accent.

"I'm sorry, but I don't know how he got you loose, Mark. I was sure you were both dead, but Mohommad surfaced for a moment. After taking a few breaths, he dove back under the water." Jim made a circling motion with one hand. "One of the tour boats was coming around to try for a rescue, the one your dad was on, in fact, but when Mohommad went under, it was hard to pinpoint the location of the bus, and they stopped too far out. I thought Mohommad was escaping by trying to reach the docks over there." Jim pointed to a pier a few hundred feet away. "But then he popped up again with you. He swam over to the ledge right there and we pulled you up just as the bus exploded. The shock wave threw Mohommad into the seawall head first."

"Damn it." It came out as half sob, half growl of anger. He leaned forward, elbows on his knees, hands dangling. He was missing a shoe on one foot, and both his sock and shoe on the other. How would he walk to the car with no shoes? It was a stupid random thought, but he fixated on it. "I need some shoes." He wanted to pay his respects and knew this would be the only time he would get a chance. He owed him that much. "I have to see his body."

"I'm sorry. We haven't found his body yet. It was there immediately after the blast, but the waves were so bad, nobody dared go into the water. Also, we didn't know if there would be another explosion. By the time we felt it was safe to go near the water, he was gone." Jim turned and motioned to the activity near the water. "Divers are searching now. I expect they'll find him soon."

Mark snagged the blanket off the gurney, wrapping it around his shoulders, and stood all in one motion. He was unsteady for a moment, but maintained his balance. "I can't leave until they find him." He brushed past Jim and trudged to the edge. His father was there and beside him, Jessie. They turned at his approach. His dad looked like he was going to say something, but he didn't, instead, he just reached out and pulled the blanket up higher on Mark's shoulder.

Jessie circled him and put her arm behind his back, her eyes roaming his face. "How are you feeling? You almost gave me a heart attack. When they pulled you out, I thought you were dead."

Uncomfortable he avoided her gaze but couldn't resist draping an arm over her shoulders as he kept an eye on the activity of the divers. "Okay. Better than I expected to be, in fact." The cold, dark water swirled as a boat circled and Mark shivered, imagining Mo's body caught in the whirlpool.

Jim moved up beside Jessie. For several minutes, nobody spoke as they observed the recovery attempt. It was strange to think how just a week ago, Mark would have welcomed news of Mo's passing, and now he could only hope that everyone was wrong and his former friend would show up alive, maybe swept farther out and clinging to the end of Navy Pier or something. He flashed to the look of anguish and regret on Mohommad's face just before they escaped the bus. Mark felt relief that Mo had been unsuccessful in his mission, but he sensed that Mohommad's comment about failure hadn't been about the bomb at all.

In a voice raw with emotion, Mark broke the silence. "He seemed…not exactly *sorry* for what he had planned to do, but upset that he couldn't even get this right. It was like he hadn't thought of the consequences of people dying. I know he wasn't doing this for himself." He paused, unable for a moment to squeeze the words past the tightening in his throat. "Mo was trying to prove something to his uncles." I just can't believe that in his heart, he was a terrorist—a killer. I just can't."

Jessie tilted her face up towards him. "Are you saying he didn't know what he was doing? Because I'm sorry, but if you hadn't stopped him, he would have succeeded in murdering dozens or even hundreds of people today, including *you*. Admit it." Her eyes were dark with anger even as tears brimmed.

He stared at her and then pulled her tight against his side, whispering down by her ear, "I'm sorry." Somehow, she had known.

The divers surfaced and between them, they clutched Mohommad's lifeless body. His face was a mottled gray. It was hard to think that less than an hour ago, they had faced each other in the bus. Had Mohommad prepared himself to die like Mark had this morning? Or had he expected to live and escape back to Afghanistan? Feeling empty and sick, Mark bowed his head. "What a waste."

His dad's hand wrapped around the back of Mark's neck and he gave a little squeeze. "At least he did something good in his last few minutes. That has to count for something."

Jim made a sound of agreement as Mark turned to his father in puzzlement. "Ask Jim what your buddy's last words were."

Mark looked over Jessie's head to Jim, who nodded and said, "His last words were for us to grab you and get you back--for all of us to get back. I think he knew the bus was going to explode."

Mark turned that over in his mind as a kernel of warmth grew inside his chest and spread through him. "So, he warned all of you, and he could have saved himself, leaving me to die, but instead, he saved me and warned all of you. What kind of terrorist *does* that?"

Mark let the question hang there for a moment before answering it himself. "No *terrorist* would show mercy towards the enemy…but a friend wouldn't think twice."

* * * * *

THE END.

Acknowledgements

I wouldn't have been able to finish this book without the help of so many people. First and foremost, I would like to thank Jessica Tate. For about four years now, we've been pushing each other to write via our online writing sessions. I'm not sure what I would do without that push.

Thank you to my fantastic editor, Felicia Sullivan. Wonderful job!

Without my amazing beta readers, this book would have been a complete mess. What I found interesting was that all of them had different strengths. One was great at noticing missing words--and you'd be surprised how often that happens as my mind thinks faster than my hands can type—another caught various plot point issues. Several zeroed in on my many typos, and one was a comma guru. So, in no special order, I'd like to thank, Vicki Boehnlein, Al Kunz, Deb Ivy, Joe Toeben, Lala Price and Allie Brumley.

And last, but not least, a huge thank you to my 'forumily'. You all know who you are. I love that there is a place I can go to get support, feedback, vent, or just get a much needed laugh. You are all awesome!

About the Author

I know a lot of these are written in third person, but that just feels too unnatural for me so I'm going to be a rebel and write this in first person. I'm M.P. McDonald, and I live in a small town in Wisconsin with my family, just a stone's throw from a beautiful lake, and literally spitting distance to a river on the other side. We love the peace and quiet and being able to go down to the beach on a hot summer day for a quick swim. Chicago and Milwaukee are just an hour's drive away in either direction, so we are never far from the excitement of a big city.

As you can tell from my books' setting, I love Chicago. One of my sons used to do commercials and modeling in the 90s, so we spent many an afternoon driving to auditions and look-sees in Chicago. Mark Taylor's studio/loft is based in part on the many cool photography studios we encountered during his years in 'showbiz'. One thing I didn't like was trying to park there, so when possible, we took the train from the northern suburbs, so it was fun incorporating that experience into this book.

When I'm not writing, I work as a respiratory therapist at a small hospital that is part of a large hospital system in eastern Wisconsin. While I mostly love my work, I'm hoping to go part-time in the very near future so I can spend more time writing. That would be the best of both worlds.

I love to hear from readers. No, I mean it. I *love* to hear from readers, even if it's not all good. Without feedback from readers, I might never have undertaken this book. I hadn't planned on writing a series for Mark Taylor, but readers kept asking, so I was happy to deliver.

CONTACT ME

Here are some ways you can reach me, and since I am an internet junkie, I'll probably write back very quickly.

Website: www.mpmcdonald.com

Email: mmcdonald64@gmail.com

Facebook: http://www.facebook.com/pages/MP-McDonald/143902672336564

Twitter: @MarkTaylorBooks

Pinterest: http://pinterist.com/mpmcdonald

Made in the USA
Middletown, DE
20 July 2018